D0336379

THE ENGLISH YEARS

Norbert Gstrein

THE ENGLISH YEARS

Translated from the German by
Anthea Bell

THE HARVILL PRESS
LONDON

First published by Suhrkamp Verlag, Frankfurt am Main, 1999,
with the title *Die englischen Jahre*

This edition first published in 2002 by
The Harvill Press
2 Aztec Row, Berners Road
London N1 0PW

www.harvill.com

1 3 5 7 9 8 6 4 2

© Suhrkamp Verlag, 1999
English translation © Anthea Bell, 2001

Norbert Gstrein asserts the moral right to be
identified as the author of this work

A CIP catalogue record for this title is
available from the British Library

The publisher gratefully acknowledges the financial support of
the Kunstsektion of the Austrian Bundeskanzleramt towards
the publication of this book in English

ISBN 1 86046 946 9

Designed and typeset in Garamond at
Libanus Press, Marlborough, Wiltshire

Printed and bound in Great Britain by
Butler & Tanner Ltd, Frome and London

CONTENTS

I

MARGARET

At first he was a myth to me: Hirschfelder, the literary icon, the great loner, the monolith, as he was described, who stayed on in England after the war, working on his masterpiece. At least, those were the ideas I connected with his name a few months ago and, considering everything I have learnt about him since, I'm surprised to find how readily that image still springs to mind. Until then I'd heard only anecdotes about him, and now, if I run them through my head – remembering that he was said to work on his knees at a special writing desk more like a prie-dieu than anything else, trying to picture him fending off intrusive phone calls by pretending to be the cleaning lady and distorting his bass voice to a squeak, or falling asleep in front of visitors the moment they bored him – well, I tell myself now, all this was pure cliché.

I would rather not have to mention Max, for after all the time we've been apart I'd prefer to leave him out of it, but it was he who drew my attention to Hirschfelder in the first place. Of course that was because he was a writer himself, but it can't have been the only reason, and there wasn't really enough material to justify his enthusiasm: a single book, a book written in the Fifties at that, and when I ask myself what else there was about this man to attract him, any kind of answer seems insufficient. Then I remember our last week together, most of it spent discussing him and, ridiculous as it may seem, I sometimes feel as if it were really he who came between us, as if he was the reason for our separation, although neither of us ever met him and I don't intend to say more about the role of a writer's wife, even if such comments were of any interest.

If I remember correctly, Max was just back from Vienna, where he had been unsuccessfully presenting his tribute to the author, his *Hommage à Hirschfelder*. It met with a poor reception. The reason for that is not important, but it may have had something to do with the title, which I had tried in vain to persuade him to jettison, having disliked the touch of affectation about it all along. I still remember how wounded he was by being accused of simply latching on to a fashion, since there was no other reason why he should take an interest in an exile, particularly when the man was Jewish, whereas he himself knew nothing about it and was told that he ought to have stuck to his tales of village life, instead of persisting in such a doomed venture. At the time, not a day went by without his trying to justify himself, subsequently embarking on monologues explaining what had happened to him and enlarging on his admiration for Hirschfelder. He showed me photographs of various rickety old machines which had seen long service as his typewriters, of worn galoshes that if not exactly his shoes were obviously his footwear, of his false teeth in a glass of water – unless that was simply some kind of diversionary tactic – and I still feel a sense of discomfort when I recall his sarcastic tone in describing himself as a backwoodsman, as if wondering whether he ought not, after all, to agree with his critics that this kind of thing wasn't really in his line.

That was the last time for quite a while that I heard anything about Hirschfelder, and I'm still not sure why I jumped at the first opportunity that came my way to discover more. Perhaps for the very reason that I didn't expect any great revelations, I'm surprised by my own single-minded pursuit of the smallest clues once I began examining them more closely. To say I had a sense of coming upon an old acquaintance with whom I'd lost touch would be going too far, but it may have been something like that, and if I now know the details of his story, then it's the story that Max should have told, turning his cardboard cut-out into a genuine human being.

It was an encounter in London last summer that brought Hirschfelder back into my mind: a chance meeting with his widow, the last of his three wives, who lives in Southend-on-Sea. I met her at the opening of an exhibition at the Austrian Institute in Rutland Gate. I was going to write an account of it, one of the many projects I had planned for those weeks in England, most of which came to nothing – one of my over-tentative attempts to spread my wings before the end of the long holiday I'd prescribed for myself, after which I would take up my new post as junior doctor at the Baumgartnerhöhe hospital in the autumn. The exhibition consisted of photographs of survivors – exiles, according to the press release, who had emigrated from the territories of the former Austro-Hungarian monarchy and had never returned home after the war – and she was among the invited guests because she had contributed a portrait of her late husband aged 18, just before he left Vienna, standing with a suitcase on the ground beside him and a bag with an illegible inscription in one hand, a picture that she later gave me – it now hangs over my desk.

The ambassador sent apologies for his absence, and a man with beads of sweat breaking out on his forehead, presumably the cultural attaché, read a clumsy introduction from notes he was clutching in both hands. At the end, when nobody applauded, he hardly knew where to look. Perhaps it was the lack of any pauses, or his failure to glance at his audience now and then, or perhaps it was his short stature and weedy appearance, or the way he kept shifting from leg to leg as he spoke, shrinking further and further back behind his lectern, the top of his glasses hiding his eyes, but anyway he stood there like a schoolboy publicly reprimanded, unable to sit down until the schoolmaster gave permission, having manoeuvred himself into the position of a defendant, a poor idiot cornered and prepared to confess to anything if he was only allowed to go, to let off steam later at a safe distance. He obviously lacked the assurance that would have helped him through a few moments of indecision and, when he loosened his tie and tried with apparent difficulty to keep his balance, face flushed, leaning slightly forward, arms hanging by his sides, the guests gathered in front of him as if he were about to begin, and in the sudden silence the two secretaries, with whom he'd been exchanging pleasantries earlier, stopped whispering to each other and stared at him.

It was mid-afternoon, and the heat was oppressive even though the curtains were drawn; the spotlights would have fried you in an instant if you missed an opportunity to move a step or so further on, past the photographs on the walls, framed portraits hanging from the ceiling by long silk cords, and when the woman suddenly appeared in the glaring light beside the unfortunate cultural attaché I must have had her in my line of vision for some time. Until then she had kept her distance, inspecting the company with a smile, and it was this smile that I'd noticed earlier, a flashing smile that she tried to suppress, a crinkling of her eyes. With the same smile, she now took the man's hand and led him away, and he followed without protest, head bowed. She didn't seem to be a member of the Institute staff, and what she had said escaped me, for the guests were moving round again, the ladies in their rather old-fashioned summer dresses, the gentlemen in dark suits, all of them older than she was – she appeared to be in her fifties – resuming their conversations and moving across the specially laid heavy carpets, none of them touching the buffet set out on a huge, mother-of-pearl-coloured grand piano in the middle of the room. It was quiet, and the solemnity, even piety with which they regarded one another did not change, but now and then you could hear German spoken, expressions many of them were obviously forcing themselves to use, a mish-mash, standard, but just a little off-target, like a dead language – that was my first impression – a parody of the norm sprinkled with phrases you could imagine only on the printed page, in an encyclopaedia, words with the dull tarnish of silver long unpolished, and I watched her moving quickly from group to group as if it were up to her to play the part of society lady.

We hadn't spoken to each other yet, but I cannot refrain from saying I felt as if I'd met her before, as if much of what she told me about herself, both that afternoon and at our later meetings, simply confirmed what I already knew. When I try to describe her I can't get beyond clichés, details that Max would have mocked, ridiculing me for speaking of her blonde hair streaked with grey, her grey or grey-green eyes, perhaps even mentioning her cheekbones – high, of course, and prominent – as if that really revealed anything about her, for describing her as small, and barely managing to suppress the word "delicate", not to mention coming up with other fashionable anatomical details such as shapely legs and regular features. It isn't really correct to describe her as brimming over with life, or even a good sort, the kind of thing a great many men will say when they can't fit a woman into any other category and won't admit to themselves that their feelings for her are not quite as innocent as they'd like to think. Well, never mind good sorts, she was not a "good sort", and I'd rather stick to the facts: I remember how she came towards

7

husband is supposed to have committed, and I was indeed a total stranger at the time, and remained one even after several more meetings, a complete and utter stranger, while to me she was always Mrs Hirschfelder, whether she liked it or not.

On the other hand, everything she told me about him on that occasion seemed innocent enough, stories she must have repeated a hundred times before, they came out so pat, and it was no wonder she interrupted herself after a few sentences, as if she too felt ill at ease.

"But I don't want to bore you," she said, avoiding my eyes. "You've probably heard more than enough of such things."

I still hadn't mentioned Max and the image he cherished of Hirschfelder, but I clearly remember her quizzical expression when I did broach the subject, her sudden laughter and the way she clapped her hands together.

"Surely you didn't believe any of that?"

I shook my head, and then contradicted myself.

"Why should I doubt it?"

However, this exchange can't have taken place that afternoon at the Institute; I assume it was later, on one of the evenings we spent in Bailey's on the Gloucester Road, and it was probably there that she called me dear child for the first time – oh, my dear child – as she did quite often afterwards, oh, my dear child, surely you didn't believe any of that, and she laughed as you might laugh at fantasies dissolving into thin air.

Nonetheless, her matter-of-fact account of her first meeting with Hirschfelder surprised me, and I remember wondering about the irony with which she summed up that event, as if it had been a business transaction from the first: her lonely hearts ad five years after the death in a ballooning accident of her first husband, the rep for a school textbook publisher.

9

"Don't laugh," she said, as if she felt she had to apologise. "It was the usual kind of nonsense, of course."

But perhaps it was also a way of showing Hirschfelder in a good light – rather an odd way, admittedly – when she told me that at their first meeting he was wearing a shabby old suit and, unlike the other men who had replied to her advertisement, he was not at all spruced up, didn't try to present himself to the best advantage, brought her no flowers or chocolates, paid her no compliments about her age, refused to indulge in double entendres, or continual moaning, or the usual deep and soulful gaze, none of that. In fact, he had been rather brusque: an elderly gentleman who knew exactly what he wanted, and was not about to embark on any kind of foolishness. He'd lost two toes to frostbite, his appendix and tonsils were gone, but that, he said jokingly, need be no impediment, my heart is as strong as a bull's, he added, oh, and he was undoubtedly more of a nightingale than a lark, impossible company until around twelve noon, a social drinker, given to boastfulness only if he was a little tipsy, to be honest about it a connoisseur of beautiful women, and even worse a smoker, also opinionated, inclined to bear a grudge, pernickety about contacting friends, old-fashioned in his opinions, could observe the conventions, but, of course, in case it was a consideration, didn't dance – he talked and talked, she said, he didn't stop until tears of laughter came to her eyes, and by comparison his rivals looked like Sunday school pupils: a prof-essor at University College, a haberdashery manufacturer, a sales rep – pathetic figures with their dreams of a weekend cottage, their promises to take her to the opera, and the visits to the lavatory from which they returned like perfect angels, meek as lambs and polished to a high gloss. She made a particular point of telling me that he had let her pay her own way, and didn't leave a tip in the café where they had arranged to meet; unlike the others, he hadn't tried to help her into her coat amid many elaborate contortions and, last of all, she told me that, as they parted, he called after her that he was Jewish, but she needn't make too much of it, a remark which sounded like an inevitable punchline, a stylised detail in a story she had told again and again.

Three months later they were married. She left her post at the East End school where she had taught since her husband's death and moved in with him in Southend-on-Sea, beginning work again there next autumn. I remember she told me about all this as if seeking some explanation for it in retrospect. It was his sixty-fifth birthday, she had hired a removal van and, as she put it, gone to tea with him taking all her worldly goods, and there she stayed, keeping an eye on the removal men as they carried her furniture up to the attic piece by piece and covered it with dustsheets, and next day she woke up among the books piled high to the ceiling in every room. Later when I visited her she showed them to me, like a museum curator, contrary to her protestations that they meant nothing to her. Although he had invited her, she had never before been to his home. It was in a quiet part of town, a narrow, two-storey terraced house in a steep, hilly street with a view of the sea if you leaned out of one of the bay windows and, if it was true that he had lived there since the war, she ought to have come upon traces of his past at every step, not just the dusty taffeta ball-gown which I saw for myself, or the battered hat-boxes, or the stacked pairs of high-heeled shoes in a broom cupboard. At least he had taken down the pictures, although after a while he put them back in their old places in the bedroom, where they probably still hang to this day, wedding photographs of himself with his two previous wives, mounted on soft cardboard that had buckled in the damp air. I didn't really believe in their existence until I set eyes on them. Apparently she didn't object, he had gone about it as if it were perfectly natural, but I find it hard to believe that she accepted the presence of her predecessors above the bed as other people might accept fox-hunting scenes, landscapes of battlefields after the fighting, or depictions of open-air picnics. I can't think that she never said anything to remind him that she too had been married before, even if it was only the story of the ballooning accident, of which she gave me a detailed account, describing the moment when the envelope caught fire, the fabric appearing to quiver as it suddenly bellied out and the soundless explosion before flames rent the bright summer sky, after which, from where she stood at a safe distance, there was nothing to be seen but matchstick men falling head over heels from the capsizing gondola to the moors below.

Yes, it was in Bailey's on the Gloucester Road, I'm sure of it now, it was there that Margaret told me about her dates with Hirschfelder before their marriage, always on a Saturday, early in the afternoon in a café near London Bridge, a tiny restaurant he had found with just four tables in a room without windows, not necessarily a place to inspire confidence. I listened to her with a sense that what she was saying didn't quite tally with her character, I remember she was wearing a close-fitting dark blue suit, her shoulder-length hair had just been cut and its ends swung at the smallest nod of her head, she sat on the bar stool with her legs crossed, and I tried in vain to imagine him beside her with his bad teeth – he kept them covered when he laughed – the hesitant gestures that the waiter barely noticed when he wanted to order, and the eternal plastic bags full of books on his lap. She mentioned them time and again, whenever she spoke of his constant wanderings round antiquarian and second-hand bookshops, as if they summed up everything there was to say about him. That evening I couldn't picture them together – her perfume and the familiar cheap, shabby place which you entered through the back door. I don't know when he first took the room, but it seems likely that in his early days there he would have encountered the last of the regular guests in the corridors: white-collar workers who wanted, for once in their lives, to sleep with their wives in a bed which, half a century earlier, a banker had considered suitable for himself and his mistress, the celebrity of the season in a West End theatre – flashy people, these late-comers, who ordered cheap meals from harassed waiters in the dining room, eating from the china used in the past by a baron and baroness, for you had only to go back far enough in the visitors' book to see the most illustrious names flung into the air like a handful of confetti. A few ladies and gentlemen of the upper classes probably still looked in now and then, staying the night elsewhere, but taking a nostalgic stroll into their past over the worn carpets, glancing into the empty ballroom as if memory alone were enough to conjure up a ballerina pirouetting to the strains of a string orchestra and, if he wasn't deaf to such echoes, then he must have picked up some of them, or a hint of the ghostly life in the billiard room crammed with tables and chairs, or in the bar with its spotted mirrors showing the faces of the figures who haunted my fantasies, gentlemen in top hats and tails, ladies with feather boas or cigarette holders and hairstyles plastered to their heads, before the time came when whole coach parties of pensioners would descend on the poor maltreated building. Standing on a rise high above the beach, it must sometimes have looked to him by night like a ship run aground, I told myself, whether brightly lit or already dark, a vessel seeming to rock slowly in the autumn wind, an old crate lurching in a leisurely manner, groaning as it deviated from the perpendicular above the milling throng of weekend visitors, and stopping, with a creak, only at twilight. The comings and goings on the esplanade in front of the hotel would have died away, the hooting of horns, the noise from the gaming rooms and, if I try hard, I can still see him standing at his window, its glass smeared as if by the sea spray. I imagine him lingering there, raising his eyes above the struts of the amusement park that reared up grotesquely in the darkness, looking out at the bobbing lights at the mouth of the Thames and the pier – said to be the longest in the world – where the narrow-gauge railway train would set off with a playful rattle in the daytime, as if to carry its passengers on when it reached the end, out over the water and into the sky.

Margaret listened, apparently unimpressed, to the nostalgic fancies into which the mere name of the building had seduced me before I even set eyes on it, and her reaction must have been an attempt to arm herself as best she could against any sentimentality.

"I went on paying the bill for his room," she said in a voice intended to sound steady. "Nothing in it's been changed since he died."

I can't understand now why I took an interest in the subject, but I remember how excited I felt, as if I were on the trail of some sensation, and I tried to imagine what Max would think if he could see me about to discover the meaning of Hirschfelder's game of hide-and-seek, and all the mystery surrounding his masterpiece.

"Then his manuscript must still be there."

I made this remark as if we had been speaking of nothing else the whole time and she would therefore be bound to know what I meant, but I was surprised to see that I hadn't caught her unawares.

"I don't know if that's what I'd call it," she said. "There are several cardboard boxes full of paper, hundreds of pages, maybe thousands, but I'm sure it's not what you're expecting."

Then she told me that for years Hirschfelder had made almost daily notes on his observations of the wind and the weather, headed by the date and time of day, recording the colour of the sea and sky, the changing clouds, the cycle of the seasons, listing the ships as they came into port and put out again, constantly trying to describe the moment of nightfall – and sure enough that was the nature of the manuscript I held in my hands a few days later when I went to see her.

But there was no trace of even a single line of the masterpiece on which he was supposed to have been working, nothing at all, and when I asked her about it, repeating what I'd heard from Max and wondering if there might be a posthumous work hidden away somewhere, she merely made a weary gesture.

"Oh, don't you start too."

Then she looked at me with annoyance, the warmth with which she had welcomed me suddenly gone.

"I've had so many people asking me that since he died," she said. "They all seem to think I'm keeping something from them."

Max had spoken of Hirschfelder's wish to create a panorama of the century, constantly expanding on his original, more modest plan; I still remember the excitement with which he described it: four reunions of the members of a class at a Viennese school who had matriculated directly after the *Anschluss* and, of course, there were to be four fixed dates, as befitted old boys' reunions. Beginning with a weekend which the last three survivors spent in a hotel somewhere in the Alps, and their conversations in which reminiscences of the dead gradually surfaced, the action was to lead back with many meanderings, Max explained, from the present to the past; if I understood him correctly, the other three occasions were to be a cheap coach trip to Paris in the Seventies, an evening at a *Heuriger* inn in the Fifties, and the first anniversary of the matriculation in the spring before war broke out. These were to be the points of intersection of 21 life histories, in which Hirschfelder apparently meant to explore 21 possible ways his own life could have gone, brutally snapped in two as it had been by his exile – 21 studies of what might have happened if he had been able to stay in Vienna. Yet Hirschfelder's true dilemma, Max emphasised, was that he would have had no choice at home, and I remember his saying that this fact alone exposed the contradictions inherent in the whole project, I recollect how simplistic I thought his salvage attempt and how superficial was the claim he then made, to the effect that this was bound to happen with such a subject.

Still, I nodded agreement, without considering whether Hirschfelder might actually not have been working on it at all, as I sometimes think now, because Max had been too insistent in his fears that he might destroy his manuscript before his death to doubt it, and I still can't quite get used to the idea that, apart from the defiant self-justification and outrageous tautology of its title – *The Living Live and the Dead are Dead* – the book may never have existed.

And I couldn't help thinking of this bon mot on the afternoon at the Austrian Institute, when I realised that most of those present were standing in front of their own photographs. They included studio portraits, stiff pictures of young people in their Sunday best looking at the camera with bashful pride, snapshots of laughing faces, groups with an arrow picking out a certain head, pale around the edges now, but with a few exceptions they all seemed to produce the same effect – you felt that the pictures ought to have been moved forwards or back, you needed to glimpse the moment just before or just after they were taken if you were not to get the impression that the most important elements had been erased, everything that might hint at the sitters' subsequent fates, yet I found it surprisingly easy to reconcile them with the people standing there and looking to me like their waxwork replicas. The artificial lighting banished all sense of the time of day, the windows suddenly seemed to me hermetically sealed, so stuffy had the air become, and the whispering of the men and women whose lives, regarded as a whole, covered the globe like a net, as the captions revealed, had something positively other-worldly about it. It was like hearing the characters talking in a silent film. Whenever I glanced at them I felt a sudden urge to draw back the curtains and let in the air and the light, to reassure myself it was still summer outside, a heatwave that had lasted for days, the temperature rising to over 30 degrees and, when it struck me that in many cases I didn't even know where they were born – I would have to look at an atlas to discover exactly where Bukovina was, or the Banat region, or Galicia – I remembered an illustration from a collection of horror stories: a Carpathian landscape buried deep in the snow, a pale moon rising above it.

Hirschfelder's picture was hung beside the sign to the lavatories, which made Margaret laugh when we finally reached it, but I still remember how awkward that laughter sounded. Of course she was being ironic when she said that Hirschfelder was well acquainted with the customs of the country, and probably wouldn't have been in the least surprised to find himself in this of all places, since he was always being rebuffed, and when he came here to the Institute library to read the newspapers on a Friday afternoon, he often found the place locked, or was told by some member of staff that the post hadn't arrived yet, or the self-important porter who sat in his lodge looking like a punch-drunk boxer – a man whose successor I myself never saw awake – would look at the time and say sorry, he'd gone off duty for the weekend 15 minutes ago. She remained remarkably calm, however, and while she kept an eye on the cultural attaché, who had obviously got a grip on himself and was making his way past us with a tray of glasses, nodding busily, accompanied by the two secretaries, I tried to imagine how Hirschfelder had reacted to this snub, how he might have rummaged indecisively for a while in the bookshelves – shelves I later searched in vain for his own book – and finally, perhaps, crept away without a word.

Margaret could not be induced to do more than shake her head when she spoke of it, but all the time I realised how much it cost her not to condemn him for his meekness.

"I can't see why he didn't stand up for himself," she said at last. "But when I asked why he let such boors insult him he told me, well, they're my people, and unfortunately I can't choose them."

This sounded paradoxical enough, but the subject became even more complicated, and I began to understand the comment she several times let slip, that living with him sometimes wasn't easy.

"When he went to Austria he always made out he was English, otherwise he couldn't have stood it," she went on. "The contradiction in that didn't seem to occur to him."

I thought he had been back to his country only once since the war, and was surprised by her abrupt reply.

"No, that's nonsense."

Naturally it was Max again who had put this idea into my head, but before I could explain what I meant she interrupted me so firmly that I fell silent.

"Of course there was the official visit too," she said, as if she didn't like to be reminded of it. "It was just the one, but it was once too often."

She was referring to the award of the State Prize to Hirschfelder, but she wouldn't talk about it, or about the other monstrosities, as she called them: the invitations to anniversary celebrations for former Austrians still living in exile, signed by the Mayor of Vienna, the Purim, Passover and Chanukkah greetings cards that he had thrown into the wastepaper basket with mingled guilt and disgust, or the unsolicited circulars to members of the Jewish community which continued to arrive in the post from time to time until a good six months after his death.

"It got completely out of hand," she said. "He didn't even know what Purim was, and he couldn't care less about Passover or Chanukkah."

Clearly Hirschfelder was nobody's fool, but all the same I was surprised when Margaret told me how he used to go to the Salzkammergut on his own summer after summer, although he would protest for the whole year beforehand that he was never going away again, it was too much trouble, and in any case he didn't feel the area was anything to do with him, even if his father had been born there. He usually began to get restless soon after Easter, she told me, there was something over-strained about his assurances, and on one of the first warm days of spring at the latest he would come out with it – what would she say if he went once more, for the very last time? – but of course it had all been arranged long ago, he had told them at the library, and a few weeks later she would be taking him to catch the ferry at Harwich. He had landed there with just ten marks in his pocket before the war, and perhaps that was why, although he usually looked a real ragbag, as she affectionately put it, and thought little of his outward appearance, he took great care to dress well on these occasions. Apparently he kept a suit specially for them, made of fine cloth, the kind of thing that would certainly be thought very English on the Continent, and he was groomed from head to foot, something I couldn't imagine when I looked at the refugee in the photograph, the young man standing with his legs planted apart and his wide-set eyes looking almost lashless in the play of light and shadow.

"He always called himself Smith when he went away," she said.

"That was the name he used in the war to hide his origins."

She went on to tell me that he had dropped it later, using it exclusively for his visits home, and I didn't know what to make of it when she asked me, in the same breath, not to misunderstand her.

"Because to me he was always the man he was."

I found this too cryptic, and asked what she meant.

"I first knew him under his real name," she replied. "But back then it would obviously have been like a rubber stamp marking him out."

She laid great stress on it, as if she were not talking about one and the same person, and this impression was reinforced by the meaningless remarks she made directly afterwards, just as if Hirschfelder had been like any other tourist, an elderly man who was no longer quite at his best, even a little eccentric, off for a summer holiday. She wouldn't allow herself to say any more; he had probably set the tone with his downbeat manner of discussing the subject, and I listened as she told me about the postcards he used to send her with their recurrent themes of sunsets, lakeside landscapes, and the paddle-wheel steamers he loved, always with the same message handwritten at the bottom, to the effect that he was fine, a brittle structure left standing as if in defiance of itself. I couldn't picture it, I could conjure up no idea of how he might have spent his days, for if her assurances were correct he never once tried to make contact with anyone, and I wondered whether I might not be reading too much into it when I told myself, as I sometimes did, that the photograph I saw later in her house, after all, was enough in itself. It showed him in a basket chair on a hotel terrace, legs crossed, back straight, very much the English gentleman in a pale linen suit, with two-tone shoes and a hat, a poseur, as it seemed, with a great gulf fixed between him and the heavyweight men with the bodies of ageing wrestlers who sat at neighbouring tables in the sun.

This was the picture in which he looked most like the visitors to the exhibition, he seemed to emanate the same reserve and, although I didn't yet know it, I had doubted from the first whether Margaret was right in claiming that he had not, like so many refugees, spent his entire life fleeing from something, but on the contrary had settled down once and for all, as she put it, when he decided to make his home in Britain directly after the war.

"It may sound odd, but that was the one way he could recover his freedom of movement," she said. "It was only by staying put that he felt he could have left."

We had walked from the Austrian Institute to the Hyde Park Hotel, escaping the sphere of the cultural attaché, who was still chasing up and down with his secretaries when we left, as if anxious not to be buttonholed by any of the people watching his every movement like dogs expecting to be tossed a bone, and Margaret had been asking me questions about myself under the watchful eye of the barman, an affected character who seemed unsure whether he might not have done better to refuse us entry. I recollect feeling surprised by my own answers, particularly the way I said more about Max than myself and kept referring to him as my husband, although it was some time since he had been that, and it would never have occurred to me to describe him thus while we were married. In any case, she wasted no words that afternoon, and I kept off the subject myself, as if it were suddenly taboo to mention it, while on the contrary the whale stranded somewhere on the coast the day before, the wedding of a model and a bow-legged jockey, the curiously changeable weather or whatever other issues she brought up seemed matters of vital importance, and the two businessmen standing at the bar beside us fell silent and listened open-mouthed as if their own fate were under discussion. We stayed only an hour, but before we left she asked me to meet her there again in less formal circumstances, and a few days later there we sat in front of the panoramic windows, in the middle of a group of tourists, watching a mounted troop of men in green military capes make their way past the ghostly trees of the park, their torsos moving up and down like pistons in lethargic slow motion, a very surreal effect, as the steaming horses stalked through the sand with their heads bowed. I wasn't sure what she wanted to show me, but I do remember staring out as if expecting the Four Horsemen of the Apocalypse to emerge from thin air, shadowy figures galloping over the ground baked hard by weeks of drought, and making straight for us.

Margaret had phoned me the morning after our encounter at the Austrian Institute and suggested we might get to know each other better and, although I hesitated at first, this was the beginning of a whole series of meetings. I still don't know if she meant them as a prelude, a way of getting me into the right frame of mind to hear the secret she finally told me in her own house: the possibility that Hirschfelder had killed a man more than 50 years ago. I sometimes think there was little to suggest that she was preparing the ground, and when I wonder why she wanted to confide in me of all people I can find no answer, so I assume that the hours we spent together were as innocent as perhaps they really were. I hear her saying, my dear child – oh, my dear child, and I recollect that we could sit opposite each other in a café on Sloane Square, making plans for the day, or end it in Bailey's on the Gloucester Road without mentioning him once, as if he were not the person who had brought us together. When we went to Richmond, or sat on the banks of the Thames and watched the pleasure cruisers, it seemed nothing to do with him, and if, nonetheless, I can establish a connection, it's mainly through the collection of curiosities she showed me as we trudged round the museums in South Kensington, past the miraculous birthing stools decorated with intarsia work showing pictures of saints, devices on which generations of penitent women had borne their babies in the position of canons at prayer, terrifying nineteenth-century obstetric forceps looking like the metallic arms of giant lobsters spread wide, straitjackets of canvas and leather with bits to fit over the mouth, and the heavy, corroded iron cages placed over wooden coffins in the dark days of the grave robbers and resurrection men who stole corpses for anatomists – relics of the history of medicine which left me unmoved at the time, but in retrospect look to me like a hidden menace, a prophecy, some urgent clue she was providing, although at the time its meaning must have escaped me.

It was a Sunday, and clear weather, when I visited her in Southend-on-Sea. I had bought newspapers at Piccadilly Circus and expected to spend a couple of idle hours by the sea, walking in the fresh air, perhaps on the promenade, with children squealing like piglets, tugging their suburban parents from one tacky stall to the next, a scene that Hirschfelder must have observed time and again. I was touched to find her standing by herself on the station platform in her red-and-white polka-dot dress to meet me, and I felt that for some reason or other she was reluctant to take me to the library where he had worked until his retirement, a brick box of a building on a main road, brooding in the bright sunlight with a faint humming sound, but when it turned out to be closed she seemed sorry that she couldn't show me the place. A little later I was walking beside her, following his daily route along the High Street, which looked as dead as a small town in a Western after a bandit raid: a cat curled up in a doorway, a drunk peeing in a flower-bed, and bits of paper blown against the iron gratings over the shop fronts although the air was perfectly still. On the domed roof of a dilapidated building I saw the word *Kursaal*, in German, and there stood the hotel, unwavering on its height above the beach, with the burden of thousands of pointless, wasted afternoons weighing down on it, and part of its façade covered.

His room was empty except for a desk, a chair, and a couch where his curious notes were laid out, and I leafed through them while Margaret looked over my shoulder. The pages were covered with typescript from margin to margin, all the entries obsessively made to fit the identical length, and when I saw at first glance how the same clichés kept coming up again and again I tried not to go on reading, not even his handwritten notes, but just listened to her holding her breath. Then I sat down, and she came round from behind me and opened the window, and the cry of seagulls immediately reached us from outside, and I asked how many years he had been coming here.

I remember that she hesitated before answering, as if afraid of revealing something better kept to herself.

"Oh, one can't put it in terms of years," she said at last, her voice suddenly weary. "It must have been half a lifetime."

These words were still running through my head as I followed her round her house, a house haunted by his two former wives, for something of them remained in the dust on the mantelpiece, the curtains drawn in all the rooms, the porcelain figures among the piles of books in the living room, the model of a sailing ship, the work-basket left open on the floor of the closet as if it had been there for ever. The place smelled of damp laundry, tinned dog food and eau de cologne, and the smile with which she opened door after door, as if he might be hiding behind one of them, faded as the corners of her mouth slowly turned down. I reacted with the sense of discomfort I usually feel when first meeting people on their home territory, where all possibilities have shrunk to the impossible 80, 100 or 120 square metres in which they walk about on stockinged feet, answer the call of nature with the lavatory door open, or fall asleep with their feet up in front of the television, and I tried to imagine him in his rocking chair, leafing through an illustrated book and sometimes stopping for a moment with one finger between the pages, while she sat opposite him as a storm brewed outside and the children next door flew their kites. The striking of the clock on the hour seemed to announce unwanted visitors; he cast her a glance, sat up straight to listen, and sank back against the cushions in relief if there was no one there, and the little creaking sound of their silence resumed, like breaking eggshells, a splintering noise that suggested to me images of a clock face rearing up and then elongating itself until the hands were turning around in empty air.

Margaret seemed a different person, so uncertainly did she move around her own house. The chignon in which she wore her hair that day was perched on her head like a giant spider as she went from room to room, looking round repeatedly to see if I was following her or if I had lost my way among the stacks of books. And it was with that kind of assumed forgetfulness which the elderly sometimes affect that she would stop, apparently to say something important, and then come out with mere trivialities, until finally, without even raising her voice, she told me about the murder.

Of course I didn't believe her at first, and I only laughed when she asked what I would do if my husband took my hand one day and confided that he had killed a man.

"Would you cover up for him?"

I instinctively shook my head.

"It would depend on the circumstances."

"Well, what would you do?"

I shrugged.

"I mean, would you cover up for him or would you go to the police?"

"I don't know," I said, still hesitating. "The right course of action would probably be so obvious that I wouldn't have to decide."

The guided tour was over, and I was sitting opposite her in her kitchen while she cut a second slice of the apple strudel she had proudly produced, Hirschfelder's favourite, made specially for me. Taking no notice of my gesture of refusal, she pushed the plate over to me again, swept the crumbs off the table and brushed down her dress. Then she took off her glasses, smoothed the hair over her ears, placed her hands on her temples, propped her elbows on the table, and looked at me. There were little beads of perspiration on the tip of her nose, and I could not mistake the urgency of her glance.

Apparently it was a few days before his death that Hirschfelder had begun talking about it, and when she told me the details there was no doubt she took the matter seriously. She dwelt on the fact that he had called to her again and again, and whenever she went into his dark, airless bedroom he threw off the sheets and immediately began speaking of it once more. The way she described his gleaming pupils in which his life seemed to be burning up, her assurances that there was something begging and pleading in his manner, her wish to believe him, all this convinced me. She could not have put on such an emotional show even if she had tried, and I listened with mingled curiosity and revulsion, trying to imagine her sitting by his side, talking to him calmly, dispelling his fears that she might think him mad or suppose he had simply imagined the whole thing.

"It was pneumonia," she said, as if the harmless sound of the word surprised her. "People don't die of that any more."

I knew better, but I didn't contradict her.

"He went swimming in the sea early in April, just the same as every year, and a month later he was dead," she added. "During that time I saw what the illness had done to him."

27

I wondered what had happened in the water then, and was going to ask, but she got in ahead of me again.

"I couldn't bear his self-accusations any more."

The bitterness was plain in her voice, and I remembered how she had mentioned, several times, that he could be insufferable over some silly little thing, and how she always stopped herself at that point, as if it were blasphemy to cast the slightest doubt on his sacred authority. But if she was to be believed, there had been exhausting tirades whenever she forgot to put a book back in its proper place, it amounted to a full-blown tragedy for her to feed the dog next door or to ask the neighbours' children into the house for a glass of lemonade, and on the few occasions they went out to visit friends – a couple of sculptors, man and wife, who lived in the same street, or one of his colleagues at the library – he always had some fault to find with her afterwards. It rang true when she said that from the first day he began running a high temperature he had refused to go to hospital, always pointing out that he had survived worse things, and stubbornly forbidding her to let a doctor near him, and I felt it was logical enough that she had not been alarmed at first, it was only a chill, she told herself, quite normal at this time of year, although there had been a mild wind blowing off the sea all day carrying desert sand with it, a wind on which the gulls soared over the heads of walkers on the promenade without beating their wings.

Then she told me how she had seen the first deck-chairs on the beach, and the magnolia was in blossom much too early, and she had just asked him to take her with him when he went away that summer, and I remember how absurd I thought the connection, when she brought herself back from her reveries by saying that he died on the fiftieth anniversary of the end of the war.

"And then a few weeks later part of the pier burned down, which seemed like a bad joke at his expense," she added, as if this were a crucial detail. "I mean, whenever the sight of it annoyed him he used to say someone ought to set fire to it."

After that she looked at me in silence for a while and, when she spoke again, the note of complaint in her voice was unmistakable as she mentioned the name Hirschfelder had uttered over and over again in his last days, although he had avoided answering any of her questions about it.

"First he assures me that there's no such person, and then suddenly it's supposed to be someone he killed."

Apparently the name in question had also been mentioned whenever the two men whom Hirschfelder had known since the war came to see him, his friends from Vienna, the pale man and the man with the scar, as he called them. They visited every two or three years, surprise visits, and I remember that she told me how he and they took over the living-room and they made themselves at home in the armchairs, ostentatiously smoking cigars as if they were the hosts, while he sat there rigid, strange, as if half frozen beside them, a couple of provocative apparitions clearly bent on showing that they had done well in life. Sometimes the strained laughter with which he reacted to their forced cheerfulness could be heard all over the house, and I have only to look at his photograph above my desk to remember how she imitated it, a bleating laugh, and I tried to imagine them falling silent at least momentarily when the three syllables emerged in conversation, lowering their voices and looking now at him, now at her, the lady of the house, not that she understood a word of their German anyway.

"It was the same Harrasser that he kept mentioning before he died," she said. "That's all I really understood."

Then she told me that Hirschfelder always claimed she must have misheard when she asked who this man was, and it had been clear to her that the way in which he received his two visitors from time to time, with a jovial demeanour that merely concealed his reserve, must have something to do with it, just like his habit of drinking with them late into the night, which was quite unlike him, dragging them off down the promenade and along the pier the next day, only to speak in the most disparaging terms about them when they left, calling them riffraff, bastards, Jews, as if he weren't Jewish himself, and pouring the wine they had brought with them down the sink.

It was a strange story and, once again, like it or not, I couldn't help wondering what Max would think of it, and would have liked to tell her not to distress herself about it, but the tale intrigued me too much

"It sounds as if he was still indulging in a little joke with you even on his deathbed," I said at last, with difficulty. "You must have some idea what to make of it."

I had moved my chair closer to the table, and looked at her hands, which lay in her lap palms upwards, but said nothing. She wore matching wedding rings on her ring finger and middle finger, and as I was wondering whether they were from her first marriage or from her second, to Hirschfelder, I suddenly had the impression that her voice was reaching me with a time-lag, and I looked at her lips as if to read what she was saying. I was afraid she might think I hadn't been listening, although there was nothing to indicate this, and I waited a moment before I ventured to lower my eyes again.

"He was in a camp for over a year in the war," she said. "He shared a room there with that man and the two from Vienna."

A car drove up outside and, as I was thinking how ridiculous it was that after all this time I still wondered, in certain situations, what Max would make of them – a nervous habit, an evasive reaction when I felt at a loss – I saw it disappear again through the window behind her. Then the street, which ran down to the sea in a wide curve, was empty again, a quivering succession of images that were always the same but flickered at the edges, as if taken by a handheld camera and unreeled at speed, and I had to keep myself from suddenly grabbing her by the shoulders as though she were a sleepwalker. My glance moved from the blue of the sky to her shoes, ranged side by side in pairs in the hall, and at the thought of her going alone from room to room in the evening, putting out the lights and standing behind the curtains for a moment or so in the dark, my throat constricted.

Meanwhile she had been looking out of the window in silence, and when she spoke again her voice was so quiet as to be almost inaudible.

"It was on the Isle of Man."

I had heard of the internment camps there, although I didn't see how a man like Hirschfelder could have been in one, and I stumbled over my words.

"But wasn't he a refugee?"

She raised her hands in a helpless gesture.

"Then I don't see what he was doing on the Isle of Man," I said. "No one went there voluntarily."

There was another silence.

"It's no good asking me about the background," she replied at last. "I only know he kept talking about the Isle of Man before he died."

That was all I learned from her that day, but now my curiosity had been thoroughly aroused, and I decided that instead of writing about the exhibition at the Austrian Institute I would spend the rest of my time in London investigating this story, although to my surprise she said no more about it all afternoon. When I left, darkness was already falling, and she came with me to the station, saying scarcely a word all the way, just walking beside me and finally taking my arm. I was shocked to feel the pressure of her grip and, from the train, I watched her standing there, waving. I felt torn between relief at being away from her and an irrational wish to get out at the next station, go back and kiss her on the cheek.

The following day I called my mother in Styria and asked her to send me a copy of Hirschfelder's book, if it was in print. I'd requested it at the Goethe Institute in Exhibition Road, but without success and, according to Margaret, there had never been an English translation. I didn't manage to get in touch directly with his first wife, a retired legal secretary who lived with her husband in Islington, but I overcame my dislike of answering machines and left a message on the tape saying I would very much like to meet her. As I didn't know his second wife's home address, I wrote to the Viennese newspaper of which she was an editor and, when I had made another appointment to see my new friend next weekend, that was all three of his wives contacted. I even thought of trying to track down the two visitors whom she had mentioned, thinking I might find out something from those mysterious figures who seemed to have appeared from time to time like messengers of doom, but she didn't even know their names, so I had no idea how to find them.

I was not sure what I expected to come of these approaches, but when, after a walk by the Thames, I found myself back at the Tate Gallery, I guessed I'd gone there just to look at the picture that Margaret had described as Hirschfelder's favourite, Turner's *Snow Storm*, with its unusually long subtitle: *Steam-Boat off a Harbour's Mouth Making Signals in Shallow Water and Going by the Lead* – and there was yet more: *The Author was in this Storm on the Night the* Ariel *left Harwich* and, as if I expected it to provide me with an answer, I stared at the steamer working its way laboriously through the middle of the storm, its prow ploughing into the waves while a light burned at its rounded stern, and the paddle-wheel which seemed to be setting off the whirling of the elements looked as if it were illuminated from within; it was a maelstrom, a circular movement of monstrous power beneath which the fragile-looking boat was almost foundering.

I think now it must have been there that Hirschfelder took permanent root in my mind, and I don't know why, but when I tried to picture him after that I always thought first of the night before he was taken away to the Isle of Man, the night he had spent locked up in a London school with the pale man and the man with the scar, a night of which Margaret had spoken only briefly. I thought of that night, and what might have been passing through his head. Instantly, from the little she had told me of him, the most concrete scenes appeared before me, and I'm still surprised to find how easily my imagination bridged the gaps that remain in the story, in spite of all I discovered about him later. My certainty that it must have happened as I saw it, in that way and no other, was shaken again and again the further I pursued my researches, until I could no longer be sure that it had really been like that, but I was still certain that at least it might have been so.

2

LONDON

17 MAY 1940

It was after midnight when the last of the men finally lay down on the bare wooden floor of the classroom. The smoke from the stove they had lit, although the days were warm now, still seemed to hover motionless in the room, so they had ignored the ban and pushed up both windows. The guards patrolling back and forth outside failed to notice; their footsteps approached and died away again, crunching on the gravel like the sound of waves breaking in the distance, their belts creaked, there was a grating, grinding sound as they switched their rifles from one shoulder to another, and their shadowy figures appeared framed by the windows for a moment, one on the left, the other on the right,

–All okay?

and back came the answer like an echo,

–All okay.

The moon was half veiled by cloud, casting only a faint light on the figures in the room, most of whom had been locked up together since the morning, but in spite of the open windows the air was stuffy, and the place smelled like a men's hostel, a sweetish odour of medicaments and decay, mingled with the smoke and the smell of the children who had been evacuated to a safe place outside the city, the familiar school smell which aroused memories in you of a time that seemed centuries ago. The voices around you had long ago sunk to a whisper, and sometimes it was completely still for a few moments, except for a man coughing over by the blackboard, next to which the desks had been moved, coughing and then apparently expectorating, another man hissed something, and after an eternity during which not even the sound of the guards pacing up and down was to be heard there came a further muffled coughing fit, and you lay jammed in between your two country-men, as they had described themselves, the pale man and the man with the scar, who probably thought you were asleep by now and were quietly conversing over your head. You had closed your eyes and were thinking of those never-ending lessons in winter, when the teachers' voices seemed to come from far away, a soporific mumbling amid which even the worst horror stories merely deepened your lethargy, hours of innocence when the pupils' clothes dried off, rustling, while a venomous yellow sky could be seen through the frost-flowers on the window-panes, penetrated by the roofs of the nearby buildings, hours gone for ever when you were finally brought abruptly out of your daydreams. It had been the headmaster himself who shook you awake, and now you couldn't relax among all these snoring, groaning men, none of whom you had known that morning, and you wondered what you ought to have replied to him, that bewhiskered old gent who had taken his watch on its silver chain out of his waistcoat pocket and said something about the present times without looking you in the eye, he was very sorry, he told you, but he must ask you not to come to school in future, he'd recommend you to get out while you still could, and then he made his way rapidly down the corridor to carry out his duties as a philatelist and amateur ornithologist or some other such trifling matter.

   –That can't be true, you heard the man with the scar complain yet again, I mean, where are they going to take us?

and the pale man was quick to reply,

−How many more times do I have to tell you?

to which the man with the scar answered,

−Away from London?

and the pale man said,

−I've already told you. The Isle of Man. They can send us to hell if they like.

−Vienna's not what it was, said your father, you have to get out of the country fast, and you sat there opposite him in a bar on the Gürtel, that rainy autumn day when he'd been waiting for you outside the building in Margaretenstrasse, you heard what he kept telling you but you didn't listen, didn't want to listen, and you watched him eat without swallowing a morsel yourself. Believe me, you can't stay here, he assured you, it's all been arranged, and your mother and her husband, whose surname you bore, had hardly been dead for a week, suffocated by the exhaust gases they had channelled into their car on a woodland path just outside the city, you had their farewell letter in your jacket, a sheet of paper asking you to forgive them, and you'd been taking it out absent-mindedly from time to time, crumpled up like a handkerchief as it was now, and he wouldn't, he just would not stop talking. A few tables away sat some uniformed men who greeted him like an old acquaintance, and he lowered his voice, you're going to my secretary's cousin in London, and meanwhile you stared out at the drizzle which had set in again and the fog that was rising, bright, white fog like a living thing, car headlights struggled with it in vain, their beams sweeping it once and then trembling gently to a halt. You slumped further into your seat as he spoke, wishing he would say it was all just a bad dream, would take your hand and go out with you, and the banners would all be gone, banners heavy with moisture, hanging from the buildings and snapping as they waved back and forth, with a loud crack when the wind caught them, wishing the eternal marching would be over, and the bands of men singing and brawling as they went through the streets would be broken up, and then you wouldn't wake in the middle of the night any more to hear the stamp of feet coming up the staircase, the knock on the door, the silence that followed it and must suddenly have enveloped the whole world, and you wished he would take you to the Prater again, or play football with you, or walk down the Hauptallee on one of the first days of spring, raising his hat every few paces and nodding to the women sashaying proudly past, you wished he would finally keep his promise and take you to the mountains, show you the glaciers, the metallic gleam of their icy armour in the evening light, a sight you knew only from photographs, would take you home to the Salzkammergut with him and not keep putting it off till next year when he'd have more time, you wished he'd stop talking, stop calling you Gabriel as if you were a child, and stop repeating: you'll like it in England, I'm sure you'll like it in England.

You waited for the clock to strike in the next room, and suddenly, as the uniformed men burst into laughter for some reason, you whispered,

–I don't want to go to England,

and you called him Father for the very first time,

–Please, Father, let me stay here,

and he said, pretending to be calm,

–Father?

with his glance flickering uneasily back and forth,

–What on earth do you mean, Gabriel?

–No point in worrying about it, said the pale man, we'll be lucky to get out of here in a hurry, and you saw him sitting up beside you,

–Did you hear that?

to which the man with the scar said,

–Hear what?

and the pale man repeated,

–Don't you hear it?

and the man with the scar replied,

–What, damn it?

and you were quite calm, listening to one man weeping in his sleep, another muttering to himself as if in prayer, although the pet name which kept surfacing from his litany was not one to suit a saint,

–Can't you hear it?

and you caught a suppressed snigger, heard the man whose objections had already attracted your attention that afternoon – I protest, over and over again, I protest, uttered in a pathetic bleat – you heard him deliver a diatribe about the hard floor and the chilly temperature, complaining that no one would listen to him, and you saw him in your mind's eye walking up and down the school playground and grumbling to everyone, looking weirdly out of place here in his double-breasted suit, with a city hat and a dust-coat draped over his arm, you saw him resist, pushing and kicking, when he had to hand over his passport, his penknife and table cutlery, the case containing his books and the portable typewriter with which he'd been picked up in his hide-out in Regent's Park that morning, you heard him say he was going to complain of this treatment in the highest quarters, he'd been a professor in Berlin and was in correspondence with Oxford and Cambridge scholars, you saw the guards laughing, smoking his cigarettes and making fun of him: yes, sure, Professor, with all due respect, Professor, with all due respect,

−Can't you hear it?

The voice that suddenly came on the line was unexpected, but you knew it was female, a voice that seemed to you familiar but was distorted by the telephone, constantly calling at the most impossible hours, so that you always hung up without a word, putting the receiver back on the cradle, and then it would ring again,

−The night of the long knives isn't far off now,

and your mother would ask,

−Who's that?

and so would her husband at almost the same moment,

−Who was that?

The man with the scar did not answer, and the pale man gave up urging him and lay down again, and suddenly you heard the distant sound of a dogfight, heard the hum of engines, very softly, a sound which you had dismissed as imagination, a tale invented to scare children, but now you heard it clearly, a droning noise coming from the Channel coast, you could hear the grass growing, as you yourself ironically said, and you saw the sluggish moon emerge from the clouds, looking through the low windows you saw the wall around the school playground, the sandbags stacked at its foot and the shapes of the buildings towering behind it, like a frightened herd of primeval animals seeming to lean against the direction of the wind.

−I don't think I heard you correctly, said your father, as he pushed his plate away and tried, with difficulty, to smile, a smile which froze on his lips, what was that you called me?

Your mother cried, Gabriel, please, Gabriel, and although she was alone at home with you she glanced round as if someone might be eavesdropping, no, really, he isn't your father, and here her voice failed her, oh, what a thing to say, and she hastily lit a cigarette and began smoking it, she turned away from you, drawing so hard on its unfiltered end that it made her cough and left her breathless for a moment or so.

—My secretary's cousin is married to a judge over there, said your father before you could answer, you just wait, after a few weeks you won't even want to come back here, thus brushing aside his own question as if he'd changed his mind about it, and he waved to the waiter, asked for the bill, and told him to give the uniformed men a round of beer on him and bring the two of you the speciality of the house to conclude your meal, a schnapps distilled on the premises, no, better make that a double each.

You tried to refuse,

—I don't drink alcohol,

but he merely reacted in his own way,

—Oh, don't make a fool of yourself,

and you toasted each other and drained your glasses, keeping an eye on the uniformed men whose voices had suddenly dropped to a whisper, went out past them into the open air, and no more was said about the fact that you'd called him Father.

Your mother seemed quite beside herself, and you saw that there were tears in her eyes and her lipstick was smudged when she turned back to you again, still smoking, your mother as pale as you imagined the consumptives of past centuries, a transparent apparition who had eaten almost nothing for months, and when she did cram herself with food in ravenous hunger could barely keep anything down,

—Gabriel, please, Gabriel,

and you said,

—I'm sorry, Mother,

and she said,

—I don't know if he put that idea into your head, but he'll be dead to me if it turns out he did, and you said,

–Mother,

and she said,

–Do you want to be the death of me?

and because you were afraid she might hit you, you said no more, you just looked into her huge eyes and thought you must have known for a long time anyway, because he'd always been around, an uncle when you needed something, you thought there must be some reason why he came to collect you once a month and took you for a drive in his car, letting you choose where to go, there must be some reason why she looked straight past him when he stood in the doorway, why she wouldn't so much as shake hands with the succession of women at his side, you thought his secretary could have spared herself the trouble of telling you he was your father, and saying how much he did for you, she didn't need to inform you about the threats, the friends pretending to be concerned and advising him to stop vacillating and stay away from you, she needn't have put pressure on you by pointing out that it wasn't his fault if you were a Jewish bastard.

–You'll be fine there, said your father, as you walked down Schönbrunner Strasse with him, they'll want you to teach the judge's children German and take out the grandmother of the family, that's all you'll have to do, and if everything I hear about my secretary's cousin is right then you're greatly to be envied.

Your mother said nothing, she breathed out the smoke through her nose and threw the cigarette butt on the floor, and you stood there wondering whether to try to reassure her, tell her she didn't need to worry, he might be your father but she was herself, for the first time you noticed the strands of grey in her black hair and thought how beautiful she still was, and how much you'd like to tell her so, you made up your mind to buy her some flowers, and at that moment you saw his secretary in your mind's eye, always putting her arm round his shoulders in the car just as a man might do, crossing her legs to show a glimpse of thigh flashing under her skirt, rubbing her stockings together with a rustling sound – his secretary, who looked at you mockingly as if she knew you dreamed of her, you couldn't sleep when she had laughed at you, and you imagined how it would be to go away with her, his secretary, his latest conquest.

–It'll be like a holiday, said your father, still a couple of metres ahead, looking round at you from time to time as if you might vanish in the fog. If I were your age I'd jump at the chance, he added, as if imitating some sententious character in a melodrama, get over that terrible tragedy and the world's your oyster, and he pretended not to be aware of the broken shop windows you were passing, the gaping holes in the buildings, the devastated offices where anything portable had been taken away and only a jumble of worthless junk lay in the pools of water on the floor, he acted as if he hadn't noticed the words scrawled on the walls, as if the emblem on the flags meant nothing to him. The cars approaching from behind seemed to drive along beside you at walking pace for a moment or so before they got up speed, engines roaring, and you saw that he kept stopping and listening as the sound died away, and then he spoke to you again, and finally even took your hand saying, don't worry, Gabriel, I'll help you as long as I can.

–Yes, you heard right, said your mother, as if she wasn't sure of it herself, and I don't think it was just talk,

and her husband said,

–Help you?

and she said,

–Yes,

and he said,

45

–We don't need any help from that shark,

and you, sitting on your bed in the room next door, heard him pulling your father to pieces yet again, saying he'd denied his former boss access to the sales department once he took over as acting director of the textiles company, a firm which had been in Jewish hands for over 100 years, had threatened him with arrest if something didn't suit him, you heard him tell her not to keep defending that bastard just because he had a sentimental side, just because she'd known him so long, because she had no idea what he was capable of, you heard him saying yes, he'd undoubtedly been a Party member from the first, he hadn't just spread fear and despondency throughout the firm, but had also, of course, helped himself to its takings as if it were the most natural thing in the world.

–That ghastly flashy car, the suits he thinks are bound to make a great impression, as if he were the ultimate pimp, those week-ends of his in Berlin, he said, how else could the man afford all those things?

but she just said,

–Stop it,

and he said,

–So where do you suppose the money he gives you comes from, if he isn't dipping his hand in the till?

and she said, again,

–Stop it,

and he asked,

–And how do you think he keeps his tarts?

and she screamed,

–Stop it, please stop it,

and you knew the sudden silence was a sign that she was crying. You dared not move, you waited for her footsteps, for the creaking

46

of the floorboards when she rose from the living-room sofa and went into the bathroom, the force of expression that noise seemed to convey made his constant marching back and forth a mere nervous posing, you stared into the dark, looking at the faint light coming in from the street, and you didn't want to believe what he said about your father. It couldn't be true, he couldn't be talking about the man whose hand you had held as a child, as if you already knew who he really was, in defiance of your mother and her assurances that you had no father, her lame explanation that your father had simply made off before you were born, no, this couldn't be your father, the person whose friendship you always thought everyone envied you when you sat in a coffee-house with him, everyone could see what a gentleman he was, and when the accusations began again you pulled the bedclothes over your head so as not to hear them, not another word.

–Are you asleep? asked the pale man,

but there was no answer, and after a while he said,

–I asked if you were asleep yet,

and the man with the scar said,

–No,

and for some time, apart from the coughing which began again, the snoring, and the upheaval when someone rose to his feet and made his way over the sleeping bodies to the door, where a soldier met him and escorted him with fixed bayonet to the lavatory, there was no sound but a faint whistling in the air, and you didn't know where it came from, once again you heard the stamping footsteps, their noise approaching upstairs, the knocking on the door and the silence that followed it, a silence in which it would not have surprised you if all the clocks in the building had stopped at once.

You heard the order again, an order with a cajoling softness about it in spite of the menace it held, as if uttered by a child unused to such things, there was a wavering in the voice, a croak that has stuck in your memory,

−Open up,

and your mother, who had been expecting it, said,

−Who's there?

but there was no reply to that, just another,

−Open up,

and she said,

−I want to know who's there,

and all restraint was over now,

−Don't keep us waiting any longer, you silly cow, open up that door or we'll bloody kick it in and show you who's here.

The telephone rang, and the expression on your mother's face told you that she was thinking of the mysterious woman who had kept calling this number over the last few weeks, always with the same prophecy of doom and, when it wasn't answered and it stopped ringing, the knocking on the door came again, a pounding that echoed through the whole building, and you couldn't rid yourself of the idea that it might have been someone else, why not an angel coming to the rescue?

You saw the two guards sitting on one of the window-sills, their shapes close together, you looked at their broad backs turned guilelessly to the sleeping men, and you heard them talking, often with long pauses between question and answer, pauses in which they drew on their cigarettes, shielding the lighted tips so that you saw the palms of their hands in a red glow and the lower parts of their faces in semi-profile, improbable images that might have been carved from stone. Still keeping your eyes on them you lay down, persuading yourself that they, in themselves, were a guarantee that none of you would be sent back, turned out of the country and abandoned to your fate, as some of the men had been suggesting only that afternoon, voicing their worst fears, or exchanged for English prisoners of war, no, you told yourself, these were mere rumours, nothing could happen to you in the care of these soldiers, they'd protect you from intruders, would leap to their feet without a sound, a finger to their lips, and when they told you not to worry that would be enough. It had grown colder now, although glowing embers still showed through the ventilation slots of the stove, and only when they fell silent for a while, and you had reconciled yourself to seeing them set off on their rounds again, did you notice that the sky had cleared and the moon seemed to be rocking gently up and down, while the stars splashed over the firmament above the darkened city were sending out unmistakable signals, although you couldn't decipher them, and bathing the school playground in a pale, lifeless light.

Your mother opened the door and said, show me your ID, but she was struck in the face, and you saw the four of them bursting in, the men who'd been strolling around the building only a couple of days ago with their hands in their pockets, looking as if they were waiting for their girlfriends, and a man wearing gloves appeared behind them, glancing around as if this was not the first time he had been here. At a gesture from him they went from room to room, and you heard the bang of cupboard doors, drawers being pulled out and dropped on the floor together with their contents, the crash of china smashing in the kitchen, you heard them marching up and down the bedroom, overturning the chest of drawers with the framed photographs on it, breaking the wall mirror which had been your grandmother's, you heard the ripping sound as they slit the quilts and shook out the feathers, you heard their curses, their laughter, the way they egged each other on, while she repeated: get out of this apartment this minute if you can't show your identification, standing with her arms outstretched in front of her husband, who had just emerged from the bathroom naked to the waist.

For a moment or so you expected him to say something, but he merely stood there with his braces dangling, and then the phone rang again, and as if she hadn't understood what was going on your mother threatened,

–I'll call the police,

and the gentleman in gloves, smiling, encouraged her,

–Go ahead,

and the four men came back into the hall with her jewellery box and a few banknotes, as smooth as if they'd been ironed, and looked at him,

–That's all,

and you thought what a fool you were to have gone on thinking none of it would affect your family: those notices up in the entrances of buildings saying which apartments were to be cleared, the cyclist who'd smashed a ground-floor window in passing, the rumours of people being singled out beside the Danube Canal and in the parks of the Second District just for having the wrong sort of nose, and made to perform the most ridiculous military exercises to the derision of the public at large, marching up and down, standing in rank and file, putting out their hands for the bastinado inflicted with a cudgel or the flat of the hand.

You heard the two guards laughing, heard them adjusting their rifles, playing about with them, the deep, oily sound as they engaged their magazines, the faint click of the locks, but no bang, you heard the pale man mutter something you couldn't make out, and the man with the scar still said nothing, you heard the wind in the trees beyond the outer wall, the rustle of the leaves and the silence of the night, in which no cars had passed for some time, and all of a sudden it was the same comfortable warmth as the kind that had lulled you to sleep as a child in a tent at camp, with the certainty that you wouldn't have to get up again, you could just lie there, and the ghost stories you told each other before going to sleep were nothing to be frightened of, until, driven into the open by the smoke of the fire, you were standing in the dark in the middle of the forest, watching a mist that felt sticky on the skin rising from the ground.

–Get that Jewish swine out of here, said the gentleman, still smiling, in a business-like tone which seemed to imply, after every word he spoke, an echo, well, don't just stand there, do something,

and your mother, as the four men surrounded her husband and seized his arms, although he didn't resist, cried out,

–No, please don't,

and the gentleman, with an almost casual glance at his watch, said,

–Shut up,

and she tore the gold chain from her neck, stripped the ring from her finger, took off her earrings and held them out to him,

–Take these, please take them,

but he took no notice, in a tense kind of way he was quite calm, as if he wasn't going to talk to her, he was just reciting a text learnt by heart,

–I said shut up,

and she clung to his arm,

–Please, sir, please,

and he said,

–Shut up, will you?

and you saw him shake her off, push her away, brush down his suit as if her mere touch had soiled it, saw him take off his gloves and slap her face, first right and then left in a practised routine, saw him step towards her, break off the movement abruptly, and slowly, very, very slowly trace her face from her mouth down to the curve of her chin with his outstretched forefinger, saw him watching her as he did it, and she had lowered her eyes, did not utter a sound, stood before him in silence and unflinching.

Your mother began clearing up as soon as they had left, went around on her knees collecting the scattered things, with your help she stood the chest of drawers up again, she mended the quilts and took the photographs out of their ruined frames, and she did not leave the building until her husband came back three days later, three days in which, of course, she was only pretending to be optimistic, saying she thought it must be a misunderstanding, telling you her plans for the future, three days passed before he stood there at the door, and although it was not locked he rang the bell and waited for someone to answer it instead of simply coming in as usual, and after that they had less than three days to live.

One of the two guards had turned, was standing in the window-frame with his arms outstretched, like a man crucified, looking at the sleepers as if he could see something in the darkness, and while the other man was peeing against the outside wall of the building, his voice came from quite close,

−Well, I dunno, this lot don't look like criminals, d'you think it was wrong to pull 'em in?

and the response was not in fact an answer,

−How d'you mean?

and that was all until, after a while and barely audible,

−The thing is, most of 'em are Jews,

and you remembered how first of all your mother had lost her job as a midwife because the gynaecologist who employed her had to close his practice, and then she sat at home day after day doing needlework for hotels at starvation wages, until that work dried up too, you remembered how a few weeks later the car firm sacked her husband after he ran into a checkpoint when he was taking a woman customer for a test drive in the gathering dusk, and however much she protested, acting the society lady and threatening that her fiancé's influence was quite enough to get them all transferred to the most remote provinces, there could be no doubt of his intentions towards her, he was clearly one of those filthy bastards who weren't ashamed of their origins and made use of every opportunity to dishonour an innocent creature.

You remembered how, one day when you were 13 or 14, your mother had been sitting in the living-room after work and told her husband how a third woman that week had wanted the doctor to tell her if it was true that once you'd slept with a Jew you could never have a proper baby, you remembered how agitated she had said they were, at first embarking on long stories about how they were either menstruating or not menstruating, sitting with their legs pressed together and their hats still on, looking down at the floor and finally coming out with that question – respectable married women, all of them – and when they looked up there was fear in their eyes, fear of infection with an incurable disease, they were begging for reassurance, wanting the doctor to give them absolution, you heard her voice telling this tale, the rough edge to it, the tiny interruptions, and suddenly you lay there motionless as you did every evening when she looked in on you in your room to see if you were asleep.

–You don't have to go letting everyone know you're Jewish straight away, your father advised you, saying goodbye as you waited to leave on the train from the Westbahnhof, standing outside the station entrance with him because he didn't want to go in with you, ready for departure with your case in one hand and a bag with the essentials you'd need for your journey in the other, just after you'd been pushed this way and that by the photographer he had hired to take your picture. You didn't know how to spend those last few minutes, you felt like walking off, getting away from him, running and running until you were out of breath and then coming to a halt somewhere in the open, or alternatively slinking on to the platform like a stranger to the place. It was early morning, icy cold, the weather had seemed to threaten snow for days, but the snow refused to fall, the sky seemed to withdraw itself from your gaze, your head was clear, far too clear, weightless, and he changed tack, don't get me wrong, he said, it's nothing to be ashamed of, he talked and talked until every sentence had been turned into its opposite, and by now you were listening only to the bright pain with which the air filled your lungs. I'm sorry, he went on, but you'll probably come across people who have a problem with it, and the train which was going to take you away was ready now, you had never been more than a day's journey from Vienna before, only to Semmering years ago, and a little way into Styria, to the Wachau area, to Budapest with your grandmother to visit her sister, and suddenly all the noises died away, you saw the cars passing without a sound, the pedestrians moving like a well-rehearsed entity in an established cycle of progress back and forth, while he called you Gabriel again and began looking at his watch at ever more frequent intervals.

You knew you would be able to remember all this in detail later, and you would know what to say, it would be your own business then, you thought, all you needed was time, you had to keep telling yourself so as not to laugh out loud, and you looked at him,

–I understand,

and he said,

–Well, the judge's wife won't bite,

and it struck you that for some reason or another he had stopped calling her his secretary's cousin, all of a sudden he was unsure of himself and his flow of words had dried up, he seemed to be waiting to see if you were going to speak of anything else, and he probably took your silence as condemnation.

The guards had sat down again, and once more you had a view of their backs, you saw one of them turning and pointing to the sleeping men, you heard him say, well, okay, but they can't just be left running around on the loose, you heard a mutter from his companion, which needn't mean anything, and you thought that of course the judge's wife would be asleep by now. We're supposed to do the dirty work while they sit and watch, said the voice in the dark, oh, sure, that would suit them fine, lounging about making eyes at our women while we do everything for them, and again the only reaction was a sound of indeterminate origin, and you saw clearly how far away you were, far from the family in Smithfield where the judge's wife was probably lying in bed between the two children in their room at this very moment, ready to be beside them at the first sign of danger, how infinitely far away although there was a mere couple of miles between you, far away from the last year and a half since you said goodbye to your father and set off into the unknown. When all was quiet you looked over the heads in the window and out at the sky, and suddenly you felt homesick, homesick for the darkness you had escaped, homesick for the silence of the house where the family lived, a short walk would take you back to it and its secluded position in the middle of the city, to your room in the attic, outside which you had been arrested only that morning, you felt homesick even for the dark, musty smell which lingered permanently in the high-ceilinged rooms, for the mildewed light on days of bad weather, for the autumn afternoons when the judge's wife asked you to light the fire in the sitting-room, rang for the housemaid,

55

and then reclined for hours on the chaise-longue, half-dazed by the tea she drank laced with alcohol, immersing herself in detective stories, complaining of her migraine and listening to every creaking sound, as if the invasion she had been expecting for so long would announce its advent in the rafters.

And you heard her pleading voice again,

–Virgil,

then there was a pause, and you thought you were wrong, you thought you hadn't heard anything, but there it came once more, there it was, no doubt about it, louder, more urgent, yet as if it would fall silent again on encountering the slightest resistance,

–Virgil,

and at last,

–Yes, Elvira, what is it?

and she burst out with it,

–Virgil, I'm frightened.

The judge was sitting in his easy chair, it was mid-day on Sunday, the day war was declared, and it was hard to say if he was even listening to her, he sat there with the wireless on, and he hadn't really paid her any attention since the Prime Minister made his speech, he had smiled as if he were glad that the moment had finally come, he had not let her agitation affect him when the air-raid siren broke into the crackling of the radio set, or her chatter as she pointlessly searched around in the case containing essential items for the shelter in the garden, and she must have been shaking him the whole time, trying to get him to come with her, and she was still tugging at his shirt when the wailing stopped and next minute the all-clear sounded.

–Can't be too careful, came a voice from where the two guards stood, could be spies among 'em, better safe than sorry,

and it was answered at first only by another muttering of,

—Come off it, they aren't spies,

and a reiterated,

—Look, if this bunch are spies then I'm a spy too,

rejected quietly, in a whisper,

—But didn't you 'ear about the parachutists – seems they've landed on the coast.

—Calm down, said the judge, and you saw him take his wife's hand and pat it, saw him looking into her eyes over the top of his glasses, calm down, there's nothing to be afraid of, Elvira,

and she pulled away from him, walked up and down as if she had to keep in motion or she would freeze rigid and never move again, constantly repeating,

—Virgil, oh, Virgil.

You stood there and looked at him, watched him pour himself a glass of water from a carafe on the occasional table beside him, waited for him to tell you to go out into the street and see what was happening, or walk up the Mile End Road to the children's grandmother, who lived there with her husband, he was sure to be out, or take the next train to the children in Bath, where they had been evacuated to a foster family yet again. But he only smiled, he kept smiling, and his smile reminded you of the hysteria that had reigned in the city for months, flaring up in the pubs, sometimes ending in weeping and wringing of hands, you didn't take your eyes off him, and you thought of the drunks who stumbled out into the night singing or stood in line to urinate against a wall, the clownish, melancholy waddle of people dancing, thumbs in their waistcoat pockets, desperately pawing themselves and bending at the knees, you thought of the soldiers being loaded into trains at Victoria Station these last few days, their jokes, the laughter that suddenly stopped short, and you watched him calmly begin to set out the chessmen on the board in front of him, as if

57

that were the only sensible thing to do in the circumstances. His way of reacting to trouble was to ignore it, and you suddenly realised that in all the months since you had come to the house he had never once spoken to you directly, as a rule he had communicated through requests formulated as if you could refuse to comply with them at any time, as if, in case of doubt, he would do it all himself and it was only on a whim that he asked you to take his briefcase to the office, bring coal up from the cellar or clean the car, and you told yourself that you'd been well off, you couldn't complain, but all that was over now.

–Looks like good flying weather, one of the guards began, after they had been silent for a while, river's running low, it'll be full moon in a couple of days,

the and the other replied,

–You don't really think they'll come, d'you?

and there was a fit of coughing that wouldn't stop, answered by a curse somewhere in the room, a clearing of the throat, a sarcastic laugh,

–You've only got to keep your ears open,

and for a while there was nothing to be heard but the wind making an irregular plunking noise as it caught the pipes on the front of the building, a sound like something scratching, scraping and knocking underground, before the answer drowned it out,

–Better not tempt Providence,

and now the pale man spoke up,

–Did you hear those two idiots?

to which the man with the scar replied,

–I'm not deaf,

and once again you heard the voice that had kept phoning for so long before your flight, calling in the middle of the night, until your mother would be there in the living-room at the first ring, shivering, clutching her dressing-gown together over her breasts with one hand, asking her husband to go and make sure the door was locked, and suddenly you realised it must have been the neighbour who always gave you such a friendly greeting when you passed on the stairs, the widow next door, whom your father would surprise with some little gift or other when he came to collect you, as if seriously paying court to her.

The judge abstractedly made a couple of moves, put the chessmen back in their original positions, and with slow, steady movements, as if he had to counter some kind of resistance, swept them off the board and into their little wooden box, and turned to his wife,

–But this is what you've been waiting for all the time,

and she interrupted her pacing up and down, looking at him as if he had accused her of being positively glad to hear the bad news,

–I hope you know what you're saying,

and he took a cigar from his jacket pocket, bit off the end, spat it into the hollow of his hand, and then, still absent-mindedly, put it down again,

–I shan't believe we're in any danger until I see one of those Krauts here with my own eyes.

You knew he didn't take her fears seriously, you knew he smiled at her when she went to see a friend in Kensington, helping to fill sandbags as if it were a parlour game, just the thing for a couple of snapshots to add to the family album, or when she sent the children off in a sudden panic with bag and baggage, and tickets with their names hung round their necks, only to fetch them back again next day because attitudes had changed overnight and evacuation wasn't the done thing any more, when she put on their gas masks in the living-room to get them used to it, and crawled about with them on the floor for whole afternoons on end among the furniture, and of course she had ordered a coat and skirt in coarse uniform-type fabric, and at the first blackout rehearsal she wore the white gloves which looked phosphorescent and were the latest fashion. He would have nothing to do with her agitation, he was not going to play at war before the war had even begun, he found it distasteful to watch the loudly applauded appearances of volunteers, the parades of ramrod-straight veterans exercising with half-rusted muzzle-loaders from some junk room, and you based the most ridiculous optimism on his refusal to follow the crowd, you thought yourself far enough away from it all, on another star, and admired his self-assurance in telling her again and again that he was not about to have his peace and calm disturbed by a horde of bloodthirsty barbarians. It was true that you'd seen trenches being dug in the parks, barricades going up all over the city, but it was not until the day when the shelter was delivered that you wondered whether you could go on pretending that corrugated iron hut in the garden was only a mirage. It stood there after that like a forgotten but ominous memorial, cemented into the ground, its roof covered with turf and planted up, while the judge, unimpressed, stuck to his usual routine of withdrawing to his study after supper every evening, and however great seemed the astonishment with which his wife gazed at him, it was often sufficient to set your fears at rest to see the line of light under the door and think of him sitting there over his legal books.

—Bet you they won't stop at the Channel, said the voice of the first guard again, without any mockery this time, sounding anxious, adding after a brief hesitation, in more determined tone, well, let 'em come, that's what I say, and we'll send 'em back to their forests with their tails between their legs,

and doubtfully, with apparent amusement, came the other man's,

—Best o' luck to you, mate,

and the nettled reply,

—What d'you mean by that?

and again there was a long pause, while another fit of coughing erupted into the darkness, and a couple of the sleeping men started up as if roused by a command, their restless murmurs dying down and merging with the regular breathing of the others,

—Take our officers, now. Mummy's boys, the whole lot of 'em, spineless, weak as water, no idea what a real man's like. Lads packed off to the army to stop 'em from being pansies or writing poetry,

then a laugh,

—Oh, go on, that's just talk,

to which came the prompt reply,

—Well, you can't win a war these days with a set of clapped-out toffs, can you? Times are gone when a few dressed-up dandies would throw 'emselves into battle like they'd get good marks for it. Give 'em a round of machine-gun fire and they're flat on their faces in the mud, them and their fancy ways, wondering why no one at those posh schools of theirs taught 'em to keep their 'eads down,

and the pale man asked,

—Did you hear that?

and the man with the scar replied,

—What?

and the pale man said,

—Those idiots?

and you lay there listening, wondering whether the droning noise would begin again, that apparently harmless rattle in the distance, with pauses when the wind changed direction, the misfiring, its white silence spreading in waves, then shrinking back into a single point.

—Seems like they're withdrawing from the Continent, one of

them went on, if that's right then they'll already have begun evacuating troops,

and again a vague mutter, a clearing of the throat, a couple of mumbled remarks, ending in disagreement,

–Rubbish,

and once more you were looking at the two backs in the window, seeing the barrels of the rifles erect against the sky, gleaming with a dull glow like a mirage when they moved, saw the ridiculous tin helmets perched on the guards' heads as if they had only just put them on, you smelled the smoke of the cigarettes they had lit again, you seemed to be breathing the air you had always drunk in greedily in your father's car until his secretary, disgusted, wound down the window, it was his odour, the odour that could presage one of his good-humoured announcements, to which she reacted with the scorn of a woman who had allowed him into her bed for too long, the odour that, when you caught it at home in the kitchen, told you it would be wise to keep out of your mother's way, and later, a hundred years later, a thousand years later, as you lay smoking in your attic room, you believed that each time you inhaled you must breathe in everything around you to fill the void within, inhaling as deeply as you could, breathing out again only when it seemed you would be torn apart, you felt you must breathe in the whole city, its strangeness, the criss-cross pattern of the streets with their lighting, which seemed to go on for ever and then, when the blackout came, collapsed in the glow that rose and fell before your eyes, as if the tiniest breath would set off a huge blaze.

The judge said nothing, the telephone kept ringing all afternoon, and his wife went to pick it up, always the same questions and the same answers, and in the end, after all, you did go to see how the grandmother in the Mile End Road was doing. When you came back they might never have changed their positions at all: he was sitting in his easy chair, hands on its upholstered arms, his only movement the tapping of his fingers, and she was pacing restlessly up and down in front of him. Although it was still daylight outside they had already blacked out the living-room, pulling the heavy curtains and letting down the blinds, and the maid, scurrying about among the furniture like a giant bat in her black dress with its little white lace apron, looked at you with her dark eyes and laid the table, and you were still thinking of the old lady, you were back in her tiny room with the crumbling slice of cake she had put into your hand, reading aloud to her from the paper until she fell asleep in her wheelchair, and for a while there was no sound except a rattling noise, for the windows shook badly as cars outside approached and then receded into the distance. You still had the smell of her room in your nostrils, yesterday's dinner, the smell of urine, the herbal extract she had herself rubbed with, the smell of alcohol and of her husband, who must be some kind of phantom or ghost, for he was never mentioned except as an absent figure, you never got to see him, he had always just gone out when you came to fetch her and wheel her through Victoria Park, and as soon as you were back in the Smithfield house you guessed that the couple there had been quarrelling. The light in the hall was like the light just before it begins to snow, an ominous, dirty, porous light in which the two of them looked to you as they would in photographs showing no contrasts, all sounds might have been muffled under a layer of snow a metre thick, and through the open bedroom door you saw that while you were out the chests of drawers had been pushed against the windows, any remaining cracks covered with mattresses, and the cat was lying on the bed, a shapeless grey patch on the grey bedspread which it had just been kneading with its claws.

–I must have a word with you, said the judge, and he seemed

uncomfortable, he wiped his mouth with his hand a couple of times, looked at his wife, who nodded, and directed his gaze at some invisible point over your shoulder, it's nothing personal, and of course you can stay, but we'd rather you didn't teach the children any more,

and when he hesitated, his wife said,

–Virgil,

and he turned, evasively,

–Oh, and we must ask you not to speak German to Clara, if possible, not until we know what's going to happen,

and you said nothing, you saw the maid standing in the middle of the room as if caught in the act of something, not scurrying about now, and for some ridiculous reason you couldn't get the game you had always played with the two little girls out of your head, your constant teasing of the younger one, while her elder sister looked at you as if you could only be a stranger against whom she must protect herself, a wicked magician, the wolf in the fairy-tale,

–I'm Nadia,

and the little one said,

–No, I am,

and you said,

–I'm Nadia,

and she said,

–That's me,

and you said,

–Oh, but I'm Nadia,

and you thought of the way she looked at you, as if she were on the point of discovering the ultimate secret, shaking her head, waving her little arms in the air like a doll, always marking the beginning and end in the same way with the question,

–Who am I, then?

The fire in the stove had gone out, and fresh gusts of wind were buffeting the house, plucking and tearing at it, and when they died down there was a sound like a whole army of mice on the march, like the tripping of little feet along the walls, the trickle of sand, and the sleeping men moved in their dreams, drifting like algae under water. The moon had sunk beneath the level of the window-panes, leaving a translucent trail in the ragged grey of the sky, and suddenly there was a smell of spring, of salt and seaweed, of damp and musty earth, and the buildings beyond the wall round the school playground were like a pontoon of fishing boats lashed together, rocking up and down in the troughs of the tide. Further away, where the open sea must lie, a sluggish green light seemed to seep slowly out of the darkness, and nearby the outlines had become blurred, softer, as if a fine mist had settled on them, its moisture suspended in the air in tiny, feverishly quivering droplets.

–I reckon we could lie down for a bit, said the guard who had last spoken, yawning noisily, I guess none o' these poor souls is gonna run for it,

and the other one agreed,

–Where would they go?

and the pale man spoke again, you heard his whisper, his persistent urging, as if he had no greater repertory of comments at his disposal,

–Did you hear that?

and the man with the scar imitated him, repeating his words,

and when all fell silent again apart from the grunts of the sleeping men, the coughing that punctuated them and the incessant wind, it was the footsteps you listened for, footsteps on the staircase, very quiet, hesitant, there was no noise, just the creaking of the floorboards, the opening and closing of the door of your attic room, the click of the catch, and you thought once again, just as you had thought then, that you heard breathing, you thought you heard someone there, and remembered the maid suddenly standing in front of you, holding a candle, its light casting a tawny glow on her night-dress, falling on her bare feet and dancing restlessly up and down the floor.

You put out your cigarette on the window-sill as if caught in the act of something, cupped your hand around the end of it, which was still hot, and spoke her name,

–Clara,

and the first thing she said was,

–Can I sleep with you?

and you repeated, as if to reassure yourself that she wasn't a ghost, without hearing your own whisper,

–Clara,

and your mother's laughter came into your mind, you saw her before you sitting with her hair wet at the kitchen table, assiduously plucking her eyebrows in front of a hand mirror, it must have been the summer when she finally persuaded her husband to go away with her, she'd been back only a few days, and a woman friend had told her you'd been seen at the *Dianabad* with one of the girls from your school, and she wouldn't stop teasing you about it.

–I expect you kissed her, said your father, who always knew everything, and he punched you playfully in the stomach as you walked beside him along the banks of the Danube, here, he continued, laughing, and he brought out a few folded banknotes and tucked them in your pocket as you strolled along, as if committing you by this action to follow his advice, have a nice time with her but don't lose your head, and suddenly he laid a hand on your shoulder: forgive me for asking, Gabriel, and you heard the sound of your footsteps in time with his on the road, but she isn't Jewish, is she?

66

The maid walked past you to the window, pulled back the curtain, and looked out at the dark city where you could only guess at the dome of St Paul's and the jumble of buildings beyond, no horizon in sight, and above it all, disposed according to a secret plan, hovered the barrage balloons, tugging at their ropes in the wind, great whales lost in the sky, their metallic glints flashing in the beam of the searchlights like relics of some long-forgotten nightmare. With trembling fingers you lit another cigarette, gave her one, and you stood side by side smoking, you felt her warmth through the fabric of her night-dress, felt how, at the slightest touch, she waited a moment before retreating, found the crucifix she wore on a chain around her neck as camouflage if she needed it, and you told yourself again that the darkness must surely extend as far as your imagination would reach, it was impossible to think it could be day anywhere, and it was out of the dark they would come, out of the dark that the planes would emerge, you heard her swallow, and thought that it didn't matter, you were ready, nothing could shake you now, you told yourself your waiting was over whether they came or not, your eternal staring out into the night, your dream, now grounded, of going home, just a few more weeks and it would all be back to normal, your mother would be alive, she'd put you to bed and sit beside you until your temperature had gone down, and you became more and more agitated, and without the light of the candle, which had gone out, you saw only a vague figure beside you. Wordlessly, you drew her to you, laid your head on her shoulder and fought back your tears, holding your breath until your lungs ran out of air, and suddenly you realised that you had been avoiding her all this time, you knew it could be only your cowardice, your stupid fear of seeing yourself in her, in the submissive way she reacted when the judge or his wife spoke to her, in her bowed shoulders as she backed away, her lowered eyes, attracted from all sides he couldn't calm down,

–Never mind what they say, I don't imagine they'll get off scot free themselves, do you?

and you heard the guards telling him for heaven's sake to be quiet, somewhere in the room you heard a man speaking in a language you did not know, heard the long pauses between his words, as if he wasn't sure what to say next, and you remembered how the maid had come to your room every night in the weeks and months after that first visit, all through the autumn and the winter, how she could lie motionless beside you, never stirring until it grew warm under the bedclothes when you had no coins for the heating, and the wind came in through every crack in the ceiling of your attic room, you thought of the way she slowly began to rub against you, again and again, approaches that seemed to go even beyond their aim and end in a barely perceptible trembling, you thought of her slowly moving up and down, you knew how quiet she was, and then, as she pressed close to you, there were a thousand questions you had to ask her, and she hesitated over the story of her flight, lay there running her fingernails down your back as she told you how her parents were stranded in Hamburg without any prospect of getting out, and your father came to your mind standing outside the Westbahnhof waving, a tiny figure under that dreadful sky, not a trace of snow in it, he'd said, and there was no rain either until later, on the train journey, rain on the crossing from Oostende to Harwich, a hesitant drizzle, and you had a fantasy of the ferry crashing at full speed into the landing stage, and the ships in the straits coming up like submarines, swaying wildly back and forth with the pressure that had sent them shooting to the surface.

You heard the anxious question she kept asking you, without really expecting any answer to it,

–How much longer can it be?

and you saw her gaze move from the bed to the window where day was breaking, an icy light, reddish, a light to which you always thought no one should be exposed, people shouldn't stay awake long enough to have to watch as lifeless shapes emerged from the darkness, they should spare themselves the realm of shadows at a time when most others were still asleep, and the few passers-by walking over the bridges turned away their faces so that no one would be afraid of the restless gleam in their eyes, and you heard your voice replying,

—Difficult to say,

and after a pause,

—Perhaps they won't come at all,

and sure enough, weeks went by and they didn't come, and you observed her as she rose and looked at the impartial sky, at the unkind streaks of the dawning day, watching as she stretched in the dim light, wearing underclothes belonging to the judge's wife and which she had borrowed for the night, as if by doing so she could free herself from the woman's control, and she had danced up and down on tiptoe in front of you with a light ease which did not suit the tangle of hooks and eyes and seams and all the dangling ribbons, or she might somehow have managed to get hold of a bottle of wine, although food and drink were already rationed, and you were sometimes sent halfway round the city in search of an extra pat of butter bought near Brick Lane on the black market, or a couple of eggs for the children, or sweets so that they could go out without appearing deprived and abandoned.

This was after the tribunals were held to which refugees all over the country had to report, and you had expected to be kicked out again when the chairman, a former colonial officer, briefly interrogated you and then graded you as a risk. For a long time after that you could hear him asking why you had fled, pressing you to tell street with gas masks to get them checked in the testing vehicle, or going all round the house to make sure the windows were properly closed, as if she feared common or garden burglars, but then she would collapse in the sitting-room again, surrounded by cushions, like a bird with a broken wing, lounging there suggestively like the eternal seductress of fiction, with dance music coming from the gramophone and a book lying open on the floor. Or she would read by candlelight, for there were candelabras on all the walls, with the curtains drawn and the ceiling lights switched off, the place smelled like a cathedral, and when she summoned you, you didn't know whether to enter the room or make your escape unseen if possible, hoping she would forget whatever she wanted and you could avoid sitting around at her feet, ready to obey any extravagant command that occurred to her, such as going to King's Cross or St Pancras to find out the times of the most improbable trains, or looking to see if the display windows of the shops in Savile Row were still boarded up, or whether there were any crabs on sale at Billingsgate, or just to fetch the latest editions of the papers. Perhaps it was a change in the weather, or the sweetish smell sometimes carried on the wind from the nearby meat market, mingling with the stink of the delivery truck engines running outside the halls, that cast her into this half-elegiac, half-despairing mood, in which she listened to the silence as if the bell in the tower of the old prison chapel which was visible from the kitchen window might sound at any moment, and the hanged men of past centuries would be led to the gallows all over again as it tolled. Often she didn't have to say anything at all: a glance at her pale face was enough for you, the bright lipstick on her mouth gave her away, or the way she had plastered her hair down on her head, loose strands falling as if casually at her temples, her upper lip shining damply, and it was obvious that she was indisposed. She would then either forget your presence or require you as an audience, and you were prepared for anything after the day when, before your very eyes, she applied food colouring to her legs on the advice of a friend who had recommended her to save her silk stockings, because they'd soon be in short supply, and use gravy browning instead, and she had let her dressing-gown fall open, bared her thighs, which had a pale and greenish gleam, and you watched her paint them slowly up and down with a broad, soft-bristled brush, you looked, you looked away, and you guessed that whatever you did your reaction would be wrong. In the end you were glad of an afternoon off at the pictures, and even the most unforeseeable phone calls from the Mile End Road were welcome if it meant you could manage to get away from her. You pushed the grandmother around in her wheelchair as if it was all you had ever wanted to do, let her point the way ahead with her stick, walked until you could walk no further, and were infected by the old lady's childish pleasure and her excitement when she saw a ship being unloaded at the docks, well, things can't be as bad as all that, she said confidently, although the noise of the cranes swallowed up her voice and her comments hung unfinished in the air.

Outside, it seemed to be mistier than ever, sheet lightning flickered over the sky, its pattern cut short by the window-frame, and one of the two guards gestured at the sleeping men and said,

–Well, it weren't my decision to take 'em like sheep to the slaughter, and I'd sooner be right out of it,

and the other interrupted him,

–Oh, come off it,

and you remembered how the judge's wife was always pestering her husband, going on at him, you thought perhaps you ought to have humoured her more, not that it would have been any use, and once again you heard her voice coming through the half-open dining-room door into the passage where you were waiting.

73

–They ought to deal with these people once and for all, she said crossly, yet also tentatively, as if repeating a comment made to her by someone else, I mean, why bother to check up on them in the first place if they aren't going to do anything about it?

and he, sitting opposite her over lunch, with the two children beside them listening open-mouthed, replied,

–Nonsense, Elvira, what are you talking about?

but she insisted,

–I'm only saying what's in the papers,

and he repeated,

–Absolute nonsense,

and she still pressed on,

–They ought to be locked up,

and he laid down his knife and fork, put on his glasses, which he had left lying beside his plate, and looked at her as if he had to accustom himself to the focus,

–You have no idea what you're talking about.

Only a week ago you had been walking up and down the Mall with the maid on one of the first warm days of early spring, a Saturday, with people strolling in the streets dressed in their best, as if it were peacetime, looking as if they would ignore any air-raid warning, or at least preserve their composure as they made for the shelters, and she was afraid you might both lose your jobs, she became quite upset and wouldn't stop badgering you about it. Apart from the number of men in uniform there seemed nothing unusual about the scene, people had become used to the barrage balloons sprinkled over the sky and the way most buildings had strips of paper stuck over their windows as a precaution, to keep the glass from turning into lethal projectiles if it splintered, there might have been sandbags around since the world began, and never mind the fact that some of the statues on their plinths had been boarded up and some removed entirely, it was a day for landscape painters, and you had no time to spare for her fears. They seemed to you excessive, impossible, they couldn't be true, in spite of these difficult weeks in the judge's house, tribunals were tribunals, yes, but in the last resort no one was going to believe such things, and you walked along beside her like one of the fantasists at present indulging in casual discussion of the new military fashion, or a public appearance by the two little princesses, or simply the pleasant air, never known anything like it before, and if all cars were eventually scrapped as a result of petrol rationing, well, look on the bright side, at least we could all breathe freely again.

–You're hardly ever home in the daytime, you've no idea what it's like, said the judge's wife, well, you can let your own servants wring your neck if you like,

and her husband looked at the little girls, who hadn't touched their meal and were exchanging glances across the table, and he put his forefinger to his lips,

–Elvira, please, Elvira,

and she repeated,

–Virgil,

and he said, again,

–Elvira.

The guards had risen to their feet, and you saw the stocks of their rifles collide with an unexpectedly hollow sound, then their footsteps could be heard on the gravel again just for a few minutes, as if they were not moving very far away, and suddenly all was quiet, the two windows were gaping holes with a view of a void. At last your immediate neighbours seemed to be asleep too, you heard them breathing, felt their backs beside you and, when the wind, which had died down for a while, began to blow again, it covered up the sounds the others made, the constant groaning and coughing, and you smelled the sweat even more strongly, an acrid odour rising to your nostrils like that of some animal into whose clutches you had fallen, a monster reaching out for you in the darkness and pulling you down with it into the depths, down to the bottom of an endless swamp with thousands and thousands of bubbles on its surface, gurgling as it let off poisonous gases from far below. You were surprised only to find how easily you gave way to the pull exerted on you, how little you resisted as you sank, how you could watch yourself go, unmoved, and over the last few weeks, in fact, the feeling you thought you had perceived in moments of calm had grown ever stronger within you, a sense of being driven out of yourself, so that the life left to you was not your own, until a few hours ago you became part of a mass, part of the present company, incorporated into a body steaming in the increasing humidity, with its several dozen mouths gasping for air.

You remembered how the judge took his family to the seaside for the last time at Easter, along with a whole caravan of other people still enjoying the adventure, using up their stocks of petrol and overrunning the resorts with great enthusiasm, as if to make up for lost time while they still could. He wore check plus-fours, a short check jacket and a sports cap beneath which the moustache he had recently grown looked as if it were waxed, and his wife wore a pleated dress in a girlishly innocent pale blue, with her tiny hat tilted at such an angle that you couldn't hide your laughter when she inspected you, giving her orders with pursed lips, both hands elegantly raised, thumbs and forefingers placed together, and the little girls wore sailor suits as they stood hand in hand at the front door or sat on the well-scrubbed doorstep, as if to have a photograph taken, while you were busy packing things in the boot, a heavy picnic basket on top, tennis rackets, and an assortment of hat-boxes in various different colours. It was the picture of the loaded car beginning to move that stuck in your mind, red and shiny as it drove away, hooting loudly, as if in spite of the noise of the engine it might collapse without a sound at any moment, or perhaps, drawn by six barely visible winged horses – white, of course – might make a couple of awkward jumps like a turn-of-the-century aeroplane and then, after rearing up once more, would fall apart, applauded by the maid, who had been standing in the street with you waving goodbye.

After that it wasn't long before, by public demand, the deckchairs that had been taken away to give access to the trenches were being put out again in Hyde Park and, in the days that followed, the newspapers carried the most contradictory reports of the latest fighting on the Continent, and the unexpected quiet of the winter months turned out to have been deceptive. The first gas-powered buses appeared in the streets, there seemed to be more barrage balloons in the sky every night, and the barrels of the anti-aircraft guns suddenly pointing into the air in the most surprising places remained directed at the cloudbanks looming unavoidably on the horizon. When the sirens began to scream not a soul would be left in sight, despite the increasing incidence of false alarms, and the dogs tied up outside the air-raid shelters howled as loud as they could until the noise died down again. Once more a great many people wanted to get out of the city as fast as possible, even if they had only just returned from their country refuges, and again, all of a sudden, there was another dimension to the waiting.

The judge's wife sent the children away and brought them back home several times over the next four weeks, she would spend half the afternoon telephoning various women friends, reporting in the evening on rumours that the king was going to Canada, and Pen Ponds in Richmond had been drained to prevent sea-planes from landing there, and other such nonsense. No tale was too improbable for her to relay it, and when her husband dismissed such notions, she did not hesitate to seek an ally in the maid, who shared her fears, and she would claim that there wasn't the least doubt of it, corpses disfigured beyond recognition had been washed up on the Isle of Wight, great piles of them, the city parks had been dug up for reasons other than those officially given, the digging was really for mass graves, and a paper factory in Birmingham had begun manufacturing cheap cardboard coffins ages ago. Scarcely a day went by without her coming up with further prophecies of doom, but even her incessant talk didn't seem to calm her, and her favourite idea seemed to be that if Britain were invaded the Strait of Dover could be set alight with a vast pool of oil, a shield of fire behind which the country would be safe.

–This is it, she kept saying, as if she might banish the threat by insisting upon it, believe me, Virgil, they're coming,

and he no longer reacted, but either hid behind his disapproval of her ideas or suddenly, resignedly, would agree with her,

–Yes, I know,

and she would say,

–You don't know anything,

and he smiled, as if he thought they were discussing family members who had announced an unwelcome visit, and this was simply the inevitable marital quarrel before they arrived,

–Please, Elvira, please,

and she stood before him, hands on her hips, face flushed, did not answer, burst into tears or fell into a confused stammering.

With the first light of morning the blackboard loomed in the dim classroom, covered with indistinct scribbling written on it the evening before, and you lay awake, thinking how quickly they had appeared off the Channel coast, and the whole city had strained its ears to see if the wind really did carry the sound of droning engines inland. It had not happened without warning, and you could only blame yourself later for being so blind that you didn't notice anything, although there had been talk of arrests weeks before, for believing it must be a mistake when the police came to the house, telling you to pack a few essentials, and there was no doubt about it, you ought to have followed the maid's advice when she begged you to run away with her while there was still time. The judge and his wife had been standing on the stairs, he still in pyjamas, she dressed and with her face made up, in spite of the early hour, as if she were about to go out, and you had felt his glance resting on your shoulders as he wished you luck, you had watched her talking to one of the policemen while the other took your elbow and led you away, and her laughter still rang in your ears, you remembered stepping out between the two officers into the street where their black car stood, vapour rising from it, and a new day was breaking.

Twenty-four hours had passed since the maid pushed you and your case out of your room, so that she wouldn't be found there with you, but it might have been the same day as you looked at the mist rising outside, hearing the guards' footsteps suddenly multiplied as if a whole company were on the march, and their calls as they communicated with each other reached your ear as though across a wide river. Nothing remained of the curious apathy with which you had initially reacted, the numbness which, in those first hours, had allowed you to perceive everything as if muted, soundless, in slow motion, the transports arriving from all over the city, the constant comings and goings, luggage this way, luggage that way, mealtimes, until you felt it could not be yourself being sent from the wall of the school playground to the building and then back, over and over again, joining different groups from early morning to roll-call for the benefit of the clerks hurrying about,

79

calling out your name or reading your number from the strip of flimsy paper to which your identity had suddenly shrunk. You might as well simply have been hearing someone describe these processes to you, and you were puzzled by the mixture of politeness and firmness with which you were all treated – as prisoners, of course, no doubt about that, but at the same time the orders sounded more like requests, the guards actually spoke to you civilly, and the commanding officer who turned up to say that none of you had anything to fear as long as you observed the rules had looked remarkably hangdog and pitiful himself, despite his similarity to the immigration official in Harwich who, as you would believe to your dying day, would have liked to hound you back on board the boat himself, and it seemed to have been only because of some oversight on his part, or some whim or inexplicable coincidence, that you didn't end up back in Vienna.

It gradually grew lighter, a faint pallor dispelling the darkness still lurking in the corners, and the first men had already risen, unshaven figures looking worn for lack of sleep, blankets slung over their shoulders as they stood in a line outside the door from which they were emerging one by one, a crack that opened for a moment and immediately closed behind them, and you couldn't see the guard who took charge of them in the passage, you could only see all the shoes, standing neatly ranged by the wall as if for ever and ever. Scarcely anyone spoke, only a few words were exchanged, then came the eternal wheezing of the man with the cough, who must have been lying awake all night, just like you, and now could not control himself and coughed unrestrainedly, while it seemed to you as if the wall round the school playground was alternately approaching and receding, and the line of buildings beyond it vanished in the mist. The cold of daybreak made you shiver, and when your two neighbours sat up they might have been strangers to you, sitting and turning their heads as far as they would go, as if to assure themselves they were in the right place, and the memory of their arrival drew a smile from you, their stilted and elaborate manner as, like a couple of old ladies, they went round calling on everyone in turn after they had come in late in the afternoon, the last to arrive, apparently thinking they had to introduce themselves all round, con men, the pair of them, and they finally latched on to you, claiming to know your father, an intrusive assumption which soon turned out to be false.

—It doesn't look too bad, said the pale man, casting a glance out of the window, they'll never be able to fly in this mist, and we'll be gone before it clears,

and the man with the scar seemed to be listening to the silence again, you saw him put his hands to his temples and stare ahead of him, saying nothing,

and the pale man said,

—The North Pole or South Pole, that's the place I'd pick to spend the next few years if I had the choice, St Helena or the North or South Pole,

and the man with the scar said,

—St Helena?

and the pale man said,

—St Helena would be Paradise,

and all at once they began encouraging each other with mutual assurances that they'd be free within a few days, or so they hoped, they'd done nothing wrong, as if that mattered, and it seemed to you as if they wanted to win you over, as if their inertia in itself proved them innocent, though innocence was as worthless now as a good conduct mark at school, and you cursed them for their complaints, which reminded you how right they were, and brought home the fact that being right was a useless luxury.

–Aren't you going to ask me if I don't hear something, said the man with the scar at last, oh, go on, I can't wait for you to start on about that again,

and the pale man humoured him,

–Right, then, don't you hear it?

and the man with the scar enjoyed his triumph, he let a couple of moments pass and then said, deliberately, picking his words,

–I don't mind not hearing anything, but when I hear something that isn't there, well, that really drives me crazy,

and the pale man asked,

–You mean the droning sound?

and the man with the scar said,

–No, but since we've been here I've had a ringing in my ears, and I'd really like to know where it comes from.

Then, apparently at the same time as you heard the sound of their engines, the buses arrived to take you all to the railway station, driving up one by one, manoeuvring for a while and finally coming to a halt side by side in front of the building, and you saw everyone crowding to the two windows and staring open-mouthed at those huge lime-green vehicles, which were still juddering slightly. Before their lights were switched off the beams just reached the ground, and the black vapour rising from their exhausts dispersed with maddening slowness into the white of the mist, the wind had dropped to nothing, while the drivers jumped down from their cabs, took up a position close to the front wheels, and before your eyes a race began, all of a sudden there were dozens of guards, and a troop selected for the job the previous day began stowing the luggage before you had even moved from the spot. The shouting had probably been audible for a while as you became aware of the voice coming through the megaphone, giving you all instructions to come out one by one, and when your own turn came you walked over the wet tarmac of the school playground as if you had cast off all burdens, and perhaps, now, you really were the man your father said you must be if you wanted to be more than a mere onlooker in life.

3

CATHERINE

the squares with houses surrounding them as if drawn up in a corral – to this day I don't know which of those buildings are Georgian and which Victorian, and to be truthful I don't mind – he would have pointed out the wrought-iron railings round the tiny gardens as if we were moving into the neighbourhood ourselves on the first of the month, and the steps up to the front doors and the basement flats where the light has to be kept on in the middle of the day, and whatever objections I might have raised, perhaps indicating the shabby rented apartment blocks a little further on, he would have regarded me as nothing but a wet blanket.

Catherine came out of her house to meet me, as if intent on doing the correct thing. I saw her in the street from a distance, and that was the image I always connected with her and could not shake off, even later, the way she stood there with arms folded over her breasts, as if she felt cold in her lightweight dress, and I don't know why, but it struck me that this is not the way you greet a chance-arrival, this is how you look when you have already been waiting too long. I can imagine her sometimes inducing a certain uneasiness in others, a discomfort which, lacking any better excuse for it, they might try to explain away as regret that they had not known her earlier, although I don't think that's the cause of the disquiet. It is not her past, whatever one may make of it, but her present, the aura emanating from her, mystical as that may sound, and I remember how she preceded me indoors and I had time to look at her, impressed by her carriage and the ease with which, despite her age, she climbed the steps. Considering that I met her only once, it's surprising how clearly I can visualise her, a small woman, with slender joints over which the skin shifted like a reptile's at the slightest movement, while the collar-bones stood out at the neck of her dress as if she had drawn a deep breath and would hold it for ever, and it was curious to see how slowly the expression on her face could change, but how long it then remained the same as she sat opposite me in her living-room, an inflexible figure.

Her second husband, if I'm not mistaken, had been an accountant, but in any case I didn't see him; he had suffered a stroke and was bedridden, his presence in the next room, to which the door stood ajar, manifested itself through his laboured breathing and, when he spoke, unseen beyond the wall, to request a glass of water or to ask the time, I felt as though a drowning man were forcing out his last words, and I wished I could shut my ears to that retching sound, waiting a long time in vain for her to answer, until at last he was quiet. I never saw the daughter she had by him either, but I do remember her handing me a photograph, perhaps only to fill the silence that had fallen, a picture from the Seventies at the earliest, showing a young woman in a bathing suit, with an alert gaze in spite of her back-combed hairstyle, a gaze into which you could read anything or nothing, and it would not have meant much to me but for the connection with Hirschfelder and Catherine's comment that he had loved the girl like his own child. Once again I felt expectant, as if I were on the trail of some sensational revelation, and it still makes me uncomfortable to remember that I instantly wondered whether he might not really be her father, and what Max would say about it, as if my enquiries were justified only if they unearthed tabloid-headline material, for without such ingredients the visits to the zoo, the Sunday afternoons he spent at the movies with her, the invitations to his home when she was older would produce nothing but over-exposed memories for an album of totally innocuous items.

Catherine had met Hirschfelder a few days before his internment, and from what she told me it was a strange encounter. Apparently he had run into her in St Martin's Lane one night during the black-out, although he ought not to have been out and about because of the curfew imposed on him, nor did she, as a young woman, have any business to be in the streets, but she insisted that on getting over the initial shock they had walked beside the river, and however incredulously I looked at her she stuck to this story. It must have been his voice which won her over, despite the broken English in which he stammered an apology and, if she was not deliberately misleading me then their accidental if propitious collision ended with their making a date to meet some weekend soon. But he never turned up again, and she didn't hear from him until he wrote to her from the Isle of Man and she finally learned his name, more than two months later it was, in midsummer, and she still had the letter. She took a folded sheet of paper out of the file she had prepared for me, and I looked as if through a magnifying glass at the 24 lines in neat handwriting which were all the censor would allow him, turning the envelope this way and that; it bore nothing but her first name and the address of the Savoy Hotel, London, where she had worked as a chambermaid for the first two years of the war.

In his book, Hirschfelder turned this encounter into a fantastic tale in which a man and a woman are walking in a ghostly city, and their progress through it is all the stranger because it is so dark that they can see nothing, but are wandering and groping around in an underworld smelling of cheap doughnut fat, gas from leaky mains, vapours rising from the sewers, making their way through a great confusion of voices, the enticements of prostitutes leaning invisibly against lamp-posts, the vociferous tones of black marketeers, the shouting of air-raid wardens if a door opened and let a strip of light fall on the road. The narrative is a jigsaw puzzle containing certain set pieces from his own life, a method also conspicuous in the other stories in the volume, whether he is describing a night of bombing over London, or the voyage, resembling the Descent into Hell, of a ship of deportees to Australia: they are all haunted by the same undead and shadowy figures with his own features, photo-sensitive forms dwelling in damp cellars or vegetating, crowded close together, down in steerage in the sultry heat. The shock suffered by a blind man returning from exile is obviously the shock he himself already anticipated; he writes of being torn in two directions, sitting alone in a hotel room in Vienna and listening to his voice on the radio answering an interviewer, his empty triumph in hearing himself speak, he describes his melancholy, his sense that he should simultaneously crawl into hiding and step out into the sun with his unseeing eyes. But close as he is to his characters, it would be too simplistic to identify Hirschfelder with the first-person narrator who tells his readers, unemotionally, how he killed a fellow prisoner interned on the Isle of Man, and yet again the difficulty lies in discovering exactly where the line runs separating fact from fiction.

Catherine laughed when I asked her.

"Oh, it was all made up."

I told her what I had learnt from Margaret and, as if the mere mention of the name startled her, she leaned forward on the sofa where she sat, rubbing her arms.

"That sounds like her," she said, her face illuminated by the last light of the sun, which still stood just above the rooftops of the houses on the other side of the street. "Well, it may be interesting, but what one makes of it is something else."

This was an unsatisfactory explanation and, if it had been in a novel, I would have stopped reading at once, finding a murder case suddenly becoming mere invention, but as matters stood I wondered what she had against her, for in the next breath she accused her of undervaluing both Hirschfelder and his work, claiming that she had seen it as only an outlandish way of killing time, and I remember she went so far as to say it was possible that, out of sheer incomprehension, she might have thrown away the manuscript that was nowhere to be found although everyone spoke of it; in her housewifely obsession she might have treated it as rubbish, thus killing him a second time after his death. I am still not sure why she abandoned her reserve as soon as the conversation turned to her, why she could speak of her with nothing but obvious disapproval, expecting me to take sides, but it must have been something to do with the fact that she had seen herself to the last as Hirschfelder's confidante, and perhaps it can be explained by his regular visits to her, his habit of coming to lunch on the first Sunday of the month through all those years, or so one concluded by the tone in which, waxing nostalgic, she spoke of these things, and I tried to imagine her sitting having lunch with him, with her daughter sometimes present too, bringing out the best china that was usually kept in a cupboard, serving the finest dishes, while her husband walked round town somewhere or, after his stroke, lay in bed in the room next door brooding on fate. Perhaps that was it, or perhaps it was something even more banal, the explanation might be that after his death Hirschfelder belonged equally to all of his three wives again, herself, Margaret, and the other woman who had written from Vienna telling me I ought to let the dead rest in peace – it could be that each of them had her own images, all of them equally valid when the passage of time was suddenly cancelled out, all equally past and present, fragments that had replaced him, and the years in between were no longer of any significance.

It was difficult to talk to Catherine about her two successors, yet the obvious questions had to be asked.

"Have you met Margaret?"

She answered with a shake of her head, adding next minute that she knew nothing about her except what she had been told by Hirschfelder, who sometimes unburdened himself when he came to see her.

"As a matter of fact he always wanted us to meet, but I refused," she said. "From all I've heard of her I don't think I'd have liked her."

"What about the other one?"

I asked as casually as possible.

"Madeleine?"

Her laughter surprised me.

"I felt she was terribly young."

That was something, at least, but when I persisted, trying to find out more, she immediately withdrew into vagueness again.

"I must have met her with him once outside the Café Royal," she said evasively. "But that's almost 30 years ago, and I really can't remember whether I talked to her or not."

Three wives, and she was the first of them, his love for her utterly improbable – a single meeting and then only his letters for a year once he began writing them, the permitted number of lines every other week, telling her how glad he would be to see her again. Whether she answered or not, he wrote, she could be sure he wouldn't forget her, and he kept referring to their first night, turning it into an event of almost mystical significance, repeating over and over again that they were meant for each other and, in a weak moment, calling her darling, but never a word about Clara, as if she didn't exist. Her replies were cool, she told me she felt impelled to answer only out of a sense of duty, anything else would have seemed mean-minded and, once, in the autumn, when she went so far as to send him a parcel containing a pot of jam, a scarf she had knitted herself and a few books – he had complained of boredom, as if the bombardment of London day and night at the time meant nothing to him – well, it was only because that was what one did, other women were sending off parcels as well, to a brother in North Africa, which in her mind could hardly be further away than the Isle of Man, to a husband stationed on Malta, parcels for the refugee camps, for children evacuated to the country, or for the good of their own souls. She was making a sacrifice not to him, she said, but to unknown gods of some kind, and as soon as she had been to the post office she had done her bit and thought no more about it. The memory of that nocturnal walk with him faded, and it was a stranger who suddenly presented himself in the hotel lobby late the following summer, someone she did not know, even though he kept saying he would have liked to come the whole way on foot erecting a monument to her wherever he had stopped for the night, like that king she had told him about, on his wedding journey of several days to meet his wife, or perhaps he was getting things mixed up and it had really been a funeral procession.

"He was carrying a bunch of flowers," she said disapprovingly, and it was some time before she smiled. "Can you imagine it?"

"Flowers?"

I saw nothing unusual in the idea, but I put the question automatically, and was not surprised when she returned to the subject.

"Well, he'd have been more welcome bringing me a pound of meat, but for some reason or other there he was with flowers, right in the middle of the war."

Nevertheless, I was surprised to hear her say she still didn't know why she hadn't told him it was all a misunderstanding, why she didn't send him away – was it pity, or had her courage failed her because he was so sure that, with her, he had found the place where he belonged? I tried to imagine him in his borrowed suit, which made him look like a man who had been up all night at a party that ended years ago, his shirt collar threadbare, standing there under the hotel porter's suspicious eye, and as far as she could tell from that one encounter in the past, he had aged visibly. I could visualize the cheap pub where she took him for half an hour, or maybe it was a tea-room in a basement with the window at street level, barricaded by sandbags, the footsteps of the passers-by muffled, a naked light

94

group of regulars, withdrawn, for his English was still bad, he would switch to a clipped German when he became agitated, and she had the impression that he liked, even relished the resultant misunderstandings, or perhaps they were exactly what he wanted after his arrest; all his life, in fact, he was less able to reconcile himself to that than to his expulsion from Vienna and, according to her, he lost no opportunity of saying that he would have expected better of civilised people. It was not clear to her why he went with them at all after the first time, but he didn't seem to mind teasing, or at least he didn't show it: whenever he mentioned his internment people would tell him he'd had a year's holiday, a year of sea and sun and tender loving care, and then he had to listen to the usual tales of heroism, let them tell him repeatedly all that had been going on while he was away, he had to keep quiet when the more assertive accused him of cowardice, of emerging only when the worst was over. For they had all been bombed, or else the building next door had taken a direct hit, none of them had been able to sleep for nights on end, they had huddled in the shelters, or lay in bed wearing earplugs, and months later they could still hear the drone of the bomber squadrons, the whistling in the air, the sound of explosions, the clatter of incendiaries falling on the tarmac, all of a sudden everyone had a friend who had been buried beneath the rubble, or shot down over the Channel coast, or reported missing over the Atlantic, and she knew it was her fault that they went on at him like that, as if there were anything he could do about it. Her attitude changed, and she suddenly felt sorry, she wanted to stand up for him, but often the best she could do was warn him to keep his mouth shut, or at least not let it slip that he was Jewish, for even here there were still a few prejudiced souls who thought they knew who was behind everything, who occupied the abandoned buildings in the best squares in Belgravia and around Grosvenor Square, who demanded full rent for dilapidated premises, who were profiteering on the black market and weren't ashamed to boast of their wealth either.

This was not the Hirschfelder of whom Max had spoken as if he were a monument carved in stone. It was not the inviolable figure he must have imagined, making him out to be a cosmopolitan, although in fact he spent most of his life immured in his seaside refuge, and I wondered whether he would repudiate Catherine's account of him, particularly since I was having some difficulty in believing her myself. From all he had told me about him, and from the picture Margaret presented of a loner not to be diverted from his purpose, it didn't sound like his habit to impose his company on others, deferential, unaware when he wasn't wanted, a pathetic character who had relied on attracting sympathy, a pitiful creature without any pride.

The sun had set, and although it was not yet really dark Catherine switched the light on and apologised for not having offered me any refreshments. Her husband could be heard in the next room again, but I strained my ears in vain to hear what he was trying to say while she was busy in the kitchen; he made a kind of regular humming noise, a mumbling that had suddenly lost any element of menace, so that I was quite alarmed when it stopped, and felt like getting up and going in to him, but she came back just then. As if there were a moment between day and night that I must not miss, I watched the sunset glow fade slowly in the section of sky visible from my vantage point, while she poured the long overdue tea, and when she had seated herself again she said nothing, but only stirred her cup for a while and sipped hesitantly.

"There isn't much more I can tell you," she continued at last. "I began seeing more of him only when he was transferred to London."

This reaction seemed to anticipate my reservations before I had

97

expressed them, and I tried not to let her see that I thought this was an evasion.

"He couldn't have been in the city during the last big air-raids in the spring," she said, laughing as if at something which had often amused her. "We always made a joke of that, pointing out how seldom we heard the siren once he was back."

In the next room her husband spoke her name quite clearly, repeating it a couple of times as if rehearsing the correct tone of voice, and when his heavy breathing was heard in the silence again it seemed to be breaking through a thin film of ice, but she was not discomposed.

"He'd certainly seen plenty of the effects of the war by then," she said, when at last it was quiet again. "He'd been with a clearing and demolition squad, and that must have opened his eyes."

I had seen the pictures myself: whole streets lying in ruins, houses no longer recognisable as such, piles of debris and, further along, roofless buildings with the sky showing through their empty windows, walls ripped away to reveal a view, as if on stage, of separate rooms apparently frozen in the middle of the performance, the props strewn everywhere you looked, tottering and crooked structures held in crazy equilibrium, as if all the bricks were pushed together at random, so that the faintest breath of air would be enough to make the whole thing collapse, and I don't know why I had difficulty in imagining him, a tiny figure with a shovel or pick in his hands, wandering about with a few other men as if they were the only survivors far and wide. Anecdotes may be validated after the event, and if it was true that he had once been persuaded to retrieve a ball from a cordoned-off area in Hyde Park that contained an unexploded bomb, into which a group of teenagers had kicked it, well, perhaps it was mere thoughtlessness, perhaps it really was what is called heroism, or perhaps it was simply stupidity, but I can't help it, all I saw was the ladies sitting in deckchairs near the rope of the cordon, applauding, nor did it bring me any closer to him to hear that he always had tears in his eyes in the cinema when the organist played "The White Cliffs of Dover", or when, at the end of the performance, everyone stood up, held hands and sang the national anthem, looking at the likeness on screen of the king and queen and the two little princesses. It was like those children's drawing books where you have to join the dots, and I always had to keep beginning again, hoping that I would get a better idea of him some time, and the final picture would not be an angular clown with a potato nose, a duck laboriously waddling away, or a horse galloping at full stretch.

Apart from Catherine he had hardly anyone in the world at this time, and once, when she did ask him about other women, and he mentioned Clara much as if he were an old man looking back on a youthful love affair half a lifetime ago, she was satisfied to hear him say he had lost contact with her, and asked no more questions. He could hardly be said to have had any friends, and he avoided organised meetings with other refugees just as he did before the war, disliking those conversations, always the same, devoted solely to the superiority of everything at home, although two or three times he had been to such a dinner, dragged there by that pair of fellow countrymen whom he had met during his internment, and once, early on, she had accompanied him at his request. It was at a house in Marylebone where all the guests behaved in a conspirator-ial and patriotic manner, evinced a liking for spiritualism, and the party ended after midnight with table-tilting while he sat smiling beside her, his astonished gaze fixed on the speakers who followed one another in rapid succession, rising to their feet, clanging spoons against their glasses, and thrusting out their stomachs whenever they drank to each other as good companions all, or to the renaissance of their native land, while he played footsie with her under the table and stared as if hypnotised at the décolleté of their hostess, a lady of good family from Vienna who had married and come to England in the late Twenties. He was clearly amused, there was not a trace of the brooding gloom that often came over him in company, and she told me how later she had heard him say ironically that it was a very fine sight when a whole group of people suddenly discovered its Russian soul – something extremely fashionable once the fighting had moved to the eastern front – when they fell into each other's arms sobbing at the slightest inducement, indulging in lachrymose fraternisation, downright nostalgia, and an entirely anachronistic belief in the basic goodness of the world, but he would have nothing to do with it, and he dismissed the subject when she pointed out that he himself had let a wasp-waisted lady persuade him to perform a Cossack dance, she was a sharp little woman in a long silk dress, playing the provocative *demi-vierge* and of course speaking French, no, he was disinclined to remember how he had thrown his empty glass over his shoulder, and was still lying flat on the floor in front of an open fire in the small hours of the morning, either expressing his opinions on everything in the world or just staring gloomily into the flames.

There was no doubt that this subject amused her, and whenever she had to pause because she was laughing so hard it struck me that she could hardly believe she had ever seen him in a really relaxed mood, and was simply trying to assure herself of the fact.

"That must have been when he said his family came from a village on the old Austro-Russian border," she said. "I've forgotten exactly where it was supposed to be, but he did mention relatives in Berditchev, and that's in Ukraine."

I hardly knew what to say, and examined her as inconspicuously as I could. The light cast shadows on her face, making her eyes retreat as if they were veiled, and I waited while she patted her hair, which lay close to her head and was wound into a knot at the nape of her neck. I hadn't noticed the rings she wore on all her fingers before, and I stared at them now as if each of them concealed a riddle on the point of solution.

"It was really only his mother's husband who came from the east, but in company he made out it was his real father," she said. "People could never hear too many stories like that, and of course he laid it on with a trowel."

Out in the street I heard shouting, immediately cut short again, as she began to leaf through her file without looking that way, avoiding my eyes. Suddenly the rectangular section of sky I could see was blue-black, heavy, and I longed for the rain that was still reluctant to fall, realising that it was her mouth which reminded me of the scorched grass in the parks, now growing only in tufts here and there, surrounded by sand or dried, cracked earth, so that you expected to come upon a skeleton at every step you took. When she continued, I could not rid myself of the feeling that she was inspecting me, and this was one of those moments when I regretted having given up cigarettes and therefore being unable to hide behind a melancholic cloud of smoke or a swift and agitated puffing.

"Well, I'm sure you don't want me to go into detail," she said. "I don't know if you see what I mean, but the way he used to brag about it made me feel really strange."

She added that he depicted the village and its poverty in glowing terms, without having the faintest notion what it was like, and I remembered the picture which must also have been in the Austrian Institute exhibition, a black and white photograph of an unpaved road somewhere in Galicia, with an ox team stuck knee-deep in mud after a thunderstorm, while she did not conceal her distaste.

"It was as picturesque as anyone could wish."

I looked at her thin, translucent earlobes and, when she said plaintively that this wasn't all of it either, she seemed to me as vulnerable as a little girl.

"By the time his two friends interrupted him he'd dragged in a rabbi too, allegedly one of his ancestors," she said, and there was a raw edge to her voice as if two strands that had run parallel for too long were being wrenched apart. "Forgive me for speaking so frankly, but the show he was putting on was a folksy stereotype."

I took my time before I asked about the two mysterious men of whom Margaret had spoken as if they were not real, but mere figments of the imagination or fictional executioners from some novel who might, nonetheless, drag Hirschfelder off to a gravel pit one day, but she came out with their names at once.

"Lomnitz and Ossovsky."

I had no chance to respond, because she suddenly gave a start, struck her forehead as she sank back on the sofa, and then looked at me as if this in itself were a daring revelation.

"I always thought they weren't genuine," she said eagerly. "I mean, only secret agents in some kind of book have names like that."

Her subsequent laughter was hollow, and I saw her shaking her head at herself before she started giving me the description I knew already.

"One of them must have been unusually pale, while the other man had a scar on his forehead which he tried to hide by plastering a lock of hair over it, and they were obviously inseparable."

For a long time these two men were the only link to Hirschfelder's past known to Catherine. However, it was not the fact that he scarcely mentioned it which she found disconcerting, it was not that all he ever told her about his mother was how she and her husband met with their sad end, or the contradictory expected anecdotes of the rough lot who frequented the pubs around the meat market, the nurses whom you sometimes saw standing in groups in the sun outside St Bartholomew's at mid-day, as if they had mistaken the witching hour, or recounting stories of dark deeds from the sinister archives of the Old Bailey. It was usually a particular place that reminded him of something, for instance an unwelcome meeting with a man who had been at school with him and who had also escaped from Vienna, or a girl he had followed down a few streets, or a story connected with Soho Square, Blackfriars Bridge, even Electric Avenue in Brixton, and once when they were out for a walk and came to the Mile End Road he pointed to a bomb crater and said that was where it had stood, just where there was a gaping hole between two blind brick walls, the house where the old lady lived and where he came to look after her, but when he actually got around to making some enquiries locally no one knew anything about her, an old lady, oh no, there hadn't been any old lady living there, he must be wrong, and he looked subdued and gave it up when people started asking what her name was, did he belong to her family, where did he come from?

It was just before the end of the war when a letter reached him from the Isle of Man, a letter which turned out to have been on its way to him for four and a half years almost to the day, a letter from the housemaid in Smithfield, and he never answered that letter, he ignored it as if he did not want to be reminded of the distant past. She had sent it care of the Jewish Aid organisation in Bloomsbury House, but he received it only after it had been hither and thither in a long series of peregrinations which couldn't be retraced now, it was ironical that it had taken so long, because she had posted it at Port Erin or Port St Mary in the south of the island when he himself was still in the capital of Douglas, hardly an hour's bus ride distant, but now her news of being taken away two weeks after him, first to prison in London and then transferred to the Isle of Man from Blackpool, came too late, and far too late was her declaration that she would love him wherever he was, she wanted to live with him and have his children, she would wait for him. All he could say was that she was daydreaming, and he showed no sign of brooding on the absurdity of the situation, of feeling at all upset, reflecting that back then he had only to run away, as other internees had done on one of their outings on the moors or along the coast, and a brief day's walking would have brought him to her, he could have bribed the guards on the gate of the women's camp, or one of the locals who could get in and out of the place with an entrance permit, or he could have pretended to be a member of her family, and when meetings between the men and women were organised later he could have met her in the darkest corner of the storage shed, an ideal place for the purpose, or in some empty hotel ballroom, he could have placed a surreptitious hand on her breast and whispered sweet nothings in her ear, or perhaps said not much at all in his emotion. No, the fact was that he did not seem to be thinking much of what might have been, if only he had guessed she was so close in all those months, he didn't seem to be regretting missed opportunities, he accepted it with resignation bordering on indifference, and never mentioned her again except once, when he was asked what he would call a daughter and he spoke her name, saying Clara, and repeating that Clara was pretty, he'd like a girl to be called Clara.

The picture I had of Hirschfelder seemed to be getting less and less clear the more Catherine told me about him, as blurred as the photograph she had taken casually out of her file, which showed him in a uniform made of cotton drill in front of some unrecognisable background, and I remember looking at it and seeing no similarity with my own picture of him, the one which now hangs over my desk. His rigidity was striking; he held himself very erect, it looked as if a whole company on parade had been airbrushed out to right and left of him, and I still wonder how he could have made such an impression on her, a penniless man with a distant manner, a half-starved former internee with the foreign accent that marked him out, and all this time, if she was to be believed, there wasn't a touch or a kiss between them, nothing except in the tension of that first night when he held her hand in the darkness, and on another occasion when an air-raid warning near Aldwych took them by surprise, and he drew her close to him in the Tube station, that musty, fly-infested vault where a preacher was warning a close-packed, anxious crowd that the Lord was nigh. Otherwise he was just there, whether she asked for his company or not and, when I try to imagine him, I see him standing a few paces behind her like a shadow, or perhaps her guardian angel, ever ready, always around at the time when the attacks were no longer being taken quite so seriously before they flared up again next winter, the time when a few aircraft would appear above the buildings once or twice a week, dropping their bombs and turning their guns on a couple of streets apparently out of pure boredom, or as if by some previous agreement made years ago, he was there when the miracle weapons, for so long the subject of the most extravagant speculation, struck like a biblical plague and you could still perish suddenly even at this late stage, and he was still there when the war ended, and he asked her to marry him as the bells pealed again for the first time in over six years, the whole city was out and about, with searchlights flickering across an impenetrable night sky from which the traces of gunfire had disappeared, he asked her quietly amid all the noise and she did not say no, she said yes, yes, Gabriel, she said, I will, and that was it.

"I think anyone could have asked me to marry him that day

and I'd have fallen for him on the spot," was her own explanation, which she obviously did not doubt. "At least, I felt that now it was impossible not to be happy any more."

I looked at her in silence.

"Do you see what I mean?"

I nodded.

"Ah, but you don't know what it's like when the sound of a rocket stops just above you and you're waiting for it to hit," she said, and her voice dropped to a whisper. "I can tell you, you die in that sudden silence, however much noise there is all around."

When I saw the corners of her mouth trembling I wanted to comfort her, but I couldn't think of anything to say except the usual commonplaces.

"It must have been terrible."

"That's not the right word," she replied, without looking at me. "You die, believe me, you die, even if it doesn't get you in the end after all."

Then she put her hands together and looked at them, as if noticing for the first time how well they matched, she spread them until only the fingertips were touching and raised them to her face, and I don't know why it made me think of a priest presenting the Host to his congregation, since she wasn't holding anything, but she gazed fixedly into the distance as though she might see something there, and spoke as if to herself.

"Then, suddenly, it's all over and you're alive."

She was expressing her relief, but also the paradoxical feelings she must have entertained at the time and, whenever I remember how she said she had been mistaken in Hirschfelder, she thought he could only go forward now and the way back was barred to him, he had burned his bridges and must have a future because now he had no past, I know it was something to do with the whole situation. The way she spoke of her plans suggests the expectations she had of him, and so does the store she set on letting me know she had thought of studying, she even contemplated going to Austria with him, ready as she was to start all over again, he only had to say the word, but he ignored the subject so persistently that she felt all the more convinced it was a good idea and, in the first instance, she would have liked to spend a few days by the Adriatic, whether or not it would have been possible that post-war summer. I can see that he would have had to be a magician to satisfy her, to be able to prove that the end is followed by a new beginning and things would not just go on as before, except that now you knew in the morning that you'd probably still be alive that night, no, it couldn't have worked unless he denied reality, and I remember how anxious I suddenly felt that she might ask herself, in front of me, just when she had made the one mistake which ruins a whole life, might speak of the opportunities she could have had if she'd never met him, I was in the grip of the horror that always comes over me when the elderly dissect their youth, attempting to pinpoint that single mistake, as if it were the only one, and if only they had done the right thing they would have been spared old age and death.

However, the reality was Southend-on-Sea because rents were lower there, and her father knew a senior civil servant in the local civic government who got her fiancé his job in the library, and it was also her father who later advanced him the money for the house, for in his line of business – buying and selling anything and everything that wasn't brand new – he had done very well out of the Americans since they turned up, everyone's idea of GIs, taking over the dives around Leicester Square, looking like over-fed children in their tight-fitting uniforms, chewing gum, their mouths crowded with too many teeth.

"It was a real dump," she said. "The idea of living there still takes my breath away."

"Well, at least it's by the sea."

"I can do without that sewer at the mouth of the Thames, thank you."

The laugh she attempted trailed miserably away, and I stopped trying to talk her into a happier frame of mind when she gave me a black look and let me know how she disliked even thinking of it.

"I hadn't been waiting years for that."

But it was still some time before she realised that for Hirschfelder, it was not a temporary solution but exactly what he wanted, before she discovered that he was beginning to settle in, never tired of pointing out the advantages of the place when, in those first few weeks, they walked along the Marine Parade in front of the pier in the evening like an old married couple, looking out at the dark water as the ebbing tide imperceptibly drew the ground away from underfoot. Only gradually did she notice that he was acting as if the war were still on, he still had and sometimes wore his Pioneer Corps uniform although he had been demobilised long ago, and he still exhibited a ridiculous leaning to parsimony which preyed on his mind and made him keep saving as if he must deny himself the slightest wish, these were the habits of an anxious old man, and he wasn't 30 yet, but he seemed to her like someone with his back to the wall. He appeared not to see the shabbiness surrounding him, or if he did he didn't mind it, the whole town was full of bomb damage but he was blind to that too, blind to the wretched efforts of the fun-fair when it started up again in the amusement park, you pressed a button and the tinny music of a brass band played out of tune as it used to before, drowning out the squeaking of the struts and the clatter and rattle of the merry-go-round machinery, lights blinked their unchanging signals into the innocent night, and he suddenly looked at it like a child expecting to leap up and be carried away by a whirlwind until sight and hearing failed him.

The stages were marked out in advance, I just don't know whether I have them in the wrong chronological order, whether he took his study in the Palace Hotel before or after she moved out, her first job with a transport company was nearby, in Gravesend, I think, but she soon had a new position in a solicitor's office in Chancery Lane, commuting daily to start with but then coming back to Southend-on-Sea only at weekends. Anyway, he must have settled in by then, and after all her efforts to persuade him to go to Vienna, she went by herself – she couldn't make him change his mind, he had always told her he had no one left there and, after his visit to the Salzkammergut, a journey hastily undertaken in the first months of peace, apparently to find out if his father was still alive, after that, in all the time she was with him, he never went further away than an occasional trip to London, a week in Cornwall once and a week in Wales, but I don't want to ascribe too much importance to her visit to Vienna, although she herself says that he never forgave her, he regarded her trip to Vienna as such an affront that it finally broke up their marriage. True or not, in the end she had another husband and he another wife, always the same old story, as she was sure I knew, and it was more than ten years after the war that her daughter was born, an event of which he knew nothing at first, his book had just been published without attracting the slightest attention at the time, she had her own life and he had his, as the saying goes.

Catherine was tired, and there were gaps in her story; I was disconcerted by the way she could brush aside whole years in a single sentence, then linger over some small detail, circling round it again and again before making her approach, or suddenly seizing on it, then losing interest and letting it drop. Her pauses grew longer and, when she went on, she now sounded unwilling to give me any information. Often I couldn't tell what she was looking at – a glance at the clock, and then she would stare straight ahead again. At her request I opened the window, and cool air flowed in, bringing with it the smell of freshly baked bread coming from I didn't know where, voices out in the pub garden I had noticed further up the street, and I was about to take my leave, but she kept me back.

"However, that's all over long ago," she said, putting a hand on my shoulder. "Why are you bothering with it now?"

This question was bound to be asked, but I had no answer, while I merely sensed that my research had more to do with Max and his enthusiasm for Hirschfelder than I cared to admit, and my own explanation took me by surprise.

"I'd like to know what happened on the Isle of Man."

In fact I had almost forgotten the tale of the murder, and it disturbed me to find it forcing itself to the front of my mind, since I didn't really believe that was my reason, but having mentioned it again, to Catherine, I knew there was no point in correcting myself.

"Oh, then you'd better ask the men who were in the camp with him," she said defensively. "You're far more likely to find out something about it from them."

Lomnitz and Ossovsky were thus rendered anonymous again, but just as I was wondering whether it might be an idea to look for them after all she mentioned Harrasser, calling him the third in the league, she knew about him only from hearsay, and I was prepared for just about anything except what came next.

"I don't know if he's still alive," she said. "But he was deported to Canada during the war, and as far as I know he stayed there."

This was rather too much to take: one and the same man who in one account didn't exist, in another was said to have been murdered, and now this – all I needed was to have her make him out a knight in shining armour who had achieved wealth and distinction in the New World, in the classic manner, and no longer wanted to have anything to do with the events of the past.

I saw her close her eyes and blink as if a glaring light were shining into them, and I tried to imagine her looking at Hirschfelder like that, with the same mixture of abstraction and amazement, the same flickering glance suddenly coming to rest, I pictured her face assuming the dramatic expression it wore now, only to lapse gradually into gentle lethargy when he began boring her with tales of his time in the internment camp.

I told her what Margaret had said to me about Harrasser, but she insisted that he must have left on the first ship from the Isle of Man, and laughed when she remembered the name of the vessel.

"It sounds so artificial," she repeated several times, as if unable to believe it. "But it really was called the *Duchess of York.*"

Then she said that one man had been shot by a guard when panic broke out on the crossing, and I didn't know what she was getting at: was this some reference I didn't understand, or had she added it simply for the sake of her story and would be happy for me to enquire into it no further?

I remembered how Margaret too had told me that many of the prisoners on the Isle of Man were deported overseas and, during the first weeks of his internment, Hirschfelder had been afraid he might be one of them, might be picked out at roll-call, ordered to pack his bags and present himself at the camp gates at daybreak next morning, and then, in the faint light of dawn, with no one about except an early riser walking his dog on the beach, in an unobserved moment, a moment outside time, he would be taken away with a few other poor devils all marching in step along the promenade, with the funnels of the ferry already belching vapour.

By now Catherine was quite carried away, one thing leading to another, and I listened as she suddenly told me that Clara might still be living on the Isle of Man, she had married a hotel proprietor there directly after the war and Hirschfelder received a notice of the wedding, Catherine even knew the name of the place in Port St Mary. She spoke of her as if she were an acquaintance of hers rather than her husband's former mistress, I heard her say it was strange where life could cast someone up, a young woman so far from home, no news of her parents' fate, just the certainty that they had been killed, and I didn't ask myself how she knew all this. In fact she could have said anything that came into her mind and I wouldn't have interrupted, nor did I see any reason to do so when she went on to say that all his life Hirschfelder had never known where he belonged either, or he wouldn't have ended up in Southend-on-Sea, he'd have found some other career, he would never have wanted to be a librarian, and surely he wouldn't have embarked on writing, oh, I ask you, she cried, as I still remember, a man with the use of his hands just sitting behind piles of books all day, I mean, really, I ask you, and I thought of Max and how glad I had always been to hear the clatter of his typewriter, how safe I felt, as if he would take care of me, when he lay in bed beside me reading until late into the night and time stretched endlessly ahead, I thought how calm he was then, and I could only look at her, feeling baffled. She made it sound so simple and, when she showed me more photographs of Hirschfelder, I was disappointed, although I don't know whether that was because of their commonplace nature, there wasn't one in which he was not smiling broadly, or because there were pictures of him in existence at all, but I had to pretend interest, I picked them up one by one and took care not to put them down again too quickly, and I fear that I looked in just the same way at the manuscript she finally produced from her folder, that package of yellow-grey sheets of paper with an unpleasant

"Why should I?"

"Well, he was," she said. "I can assure you he was, but it was for medical and not religious reasons."

I saw her lower her head, and I couldn't help smiling. Although she was obviously waiting for me to help her fill the silence, I did not let her induce me to speak, and just stared at her. She might almost have been blushing, but when she looked up again I was relieved to see her smile.

"However, if you ask me about his bar mitzvah I'll have to tell you he didn't have one," she began again. "He wasn't Orthodox."

I tried to interrupt her.

"That made no difference at the time."

"He seems to have thought the kosher principle odd," she said, undeterred by my remark. "But he did like chopped liver and carp in aspic."

I didn't know what she was getting at, and when she mentioned a dish called Polish hotchpotch which his mother apparently used to make, I pretended to know what it was and let her go on.

"Don't be afraid to ask me any questions," she said, and it looked as if she was about to launch into narrative vein again. "I mean, if I don't know, who does?"

This assertive style did not suit her, and only when I was leaving did I remember that she had spoken of Margaret in the same way, with a grim and opinionated determination which I did not notice in her otherwise, perhaps because she was really unsure of herself. As she showed me to the door I listened in vain for her husband, who must have dropped off to sleep in the next room, and I said goodbye, shook hands with her, and left without saying any more, certain that she was watching me leave, although I did not turn to look back. I could hardly believe it; I had spent only a couple of hours with her, but the streets were empty, although it was not yet fully dark, and the restaurants I passed were crowded. As far as I was concerned extra-terrestrials might have landed while I was at her house, so strange did the people there look to me, and I told myself the old man I had seen a day or so earlier, wading into the Round Pond in Kensington Gardens after his model boat in fisherman's boots and with a pipe in his mouth, must have been a scout sounding out the ground for them, using his remote control to send coded messages which he kept muttering to himself so as not to forget them.

I had made up my mind to go to the Isle of Man, and I needed no justification now, let alone the murder story, which took me back to the Austrian Institute next day to search the library for whatever I might be able find about the internment camps. But I ought to have known there wouldn't be anything, of course not, and I felt a sense of instant discouragement facing that jumble again: editions of the classics that hadn't seen the light of day for a long time, authors whose names were unknown even at home, but whose books were dispatched by the parcel-load to cultural institutes all over the world, where they stood in serried ranks awaiting the Last Judgement. A wrinkled, elderly lady sat knitting in a wing chair, supervising the place, and at first glance looked like part of the furniture. In fact I noticed her only because she had a quiet coughing fit that lasted some time, so that I turned round and saw her put her needles through the knot of her hair and stare at me with deep-set eyes, as if I rather than she were the surprising sight.

It took me some time to explain what I wanted, but then she rose to her feet, a ball of wool trailing after her as she walked along the shelves, taking out a book here and there, sometimes leafing through one before putting it back with a shake of her head, and she had quite forgotten me when she finally came to a halt in front of the window and began muttering to herself in an undertone. I could hear the sound of instruments being tuned in the room overhead where cultural events took place and, when I climbed the stairs and glanced at the photographs of the exiles still hanging there, I found the two girls whose concert that evening was announced at the entrance, innocent little chicks who had not yet lost their downy plumage, or so they seemed to me, fluttering and cheeping, no doubt just the thing for the few visitors who would totter in later and sit with their heads nodding as they let the music lull them gently to sleep. I found the new director of the Institute watering her flowers; I had entered her office because the door was open, and she was bending over the plant pots and jumped with surprise when I spoke to her, but then she proved helpful, shifting the watering can from one hand to the other and pushing up her recalcitrant glasses, which immediately slipped down her nose again, pinching her nostrils and giving her voice a note of distinction that she might otherwise have struggled to achieve in order to conform to people's preconceptions.

"I can only recommend you read Katz's autobiography," she said, after listening to me with her chin thrust out. "I know that's not what you're after, but she'll give you an impression of what it was like to be an exile here at the time."

"I know her book already, though I can't say I'm a fan," I replied. "She's such a moaner – and hopelessly conceited too."

I remembered how Max, mockingly, had described her as very much the *grande dame*, and for once there was something in what he said, but I wasn't going to talk about that, I just said how uncomfortable her writing made me feel, how distasteful I found the way she treated that period, how wrong it seemed for her to present herself centre stage against that grim background.

"Reading her book, you sometimes think that in spite of everything it was all one huge party," I said. "There comes a point where you don't want to hear any more about the wonderful people she kept meeting."

The director glanced at me as if I had said something blasphemous, and then looked out at the open space in front of the building, where the trees were swaying in the wind.

"You mustn't forget what a hard time she had."

"Maybe she did, but I still don't see why she feels she has to dilute everything with her clever little anecdotes."

Like Hirschfelder, Katz had never made much of a fuss about her Jewish origins, like him she had fled from Vienna and arrived in London, an up and coming writer who had not gone home until the Fifties, and I had always been surprised that, with such a history behind her, she had so little sense of priorities that she couldn't refrain from babbling away like an enthusiastic schoolgirl in full flow.

"When she gets to her flight from Vienna she tells us the letters written to her by a world-famous tenor were lost, so now, poor dear, she can't prove that he was once at her feet," I said, trying to explain myself again. "I mean, the way she describes it, that seems to have been the worst thing that happened to her during the war."

Once again I merely drew a horrified reaction.

"Oh, but think of her description of her youth in Vienna, the years in Heiligenstadt, her travels in Italy."

The director might have a point there, and on another day perhaps I would have been infected by the melancholy in her voice, but in my present mood I could only laugh.

"The bombs were falling on London, and she sat there in her Notting Hill apartment wondering which of her many invitations to accept."

I gave the director no chance to get a word in, but told her that Katz was just name-dropping, she couldn't refrain from listing everyone who had praised her first book and quoting extensively from assorted reviews, while she scarcely thought it worth mentioning that her father was literally dying of homesickness in London.

I had no real idea why I was getting so worked up, and I tried once more to tell her why I was so interested in Hirschfelder, why I compared his inflexibility with Katz's arrogance. It turned out that she had never heard of him, which annoyed me so much that I told her his story as far as I knew it, as if it were an invention of my own, as if I had the rights to it, and I urged her to read his book, assuring her that she'd see Katz in a different light then. My agitation did not strike me as odd until I had left, when she must have been wondering why I had over-reacted, so self-righteously, and indeed who was I to hold forth on subjects of which I knew hardly anything, who was I to condemn Katz, who was I to champion a dead man's memory in so dubious a manner?

There was a parcel waiting for me at my hotel, sent express by Catherine without any explanation, and turning out to contain Hirschfelder's attempts to describe his period of internment, making a start several times and breaking off after a few pages, some of them were dated, and if the facts were correct then the last time he tackled the subject was in the year before his death. I was on the ferry to the Isle of Man when I looked through these notes more closely and came upon fragments of a diary, entries which often ran to only a few lines with gaps of many days between them, and once he recorded nothing for six weeks, but these were the months in question, from June 1940 to August 1941. It began with the comment *Crossing from Liverpool*, no more, but when I read those words it was enough to know that I was just where he had been at the time, standing on deck looking at the disused docks and trying to imagine how different they had probably appeared to Hirschfelder, who would have had a view of the same tangle of funnels, cranes and huge tanks, but with the machinery now hidden under grey tarpaulins still in working order in his time, steaming and thudding, red-hot to the point of explosion, with pillars of smoke rising vertically and spreading to form an impenetrable, sooty cloud overhead, with people scurrying back and forth on the quays, and large numbers of ships in the river mouth, where whole convoys came in and went out week after week. While the mainland slowly disappeared into the distance I told myself that he must have felt relieved to get away, after those days in the transit camp of which he complained later, I thought he must have had some idea of what awaited him and, if I tried, I could see Hirschfelder himself leaning on the rail, evidently concerned about the zigzag course they were following, I saw him staring at the water and taking no notice of the guards standing behind him with their inevitable fixed bayonets, as if he might jump overboard at any moment.

Although it had looked like rain all day the sky had suddenly cleared, there was a dramatic sprinkling of ragged cloud, and the ferry steered straight towards the setting sun until it sank, leaving only a faint glow above the horizon, and I saw the shape of the island emerge. There was no wind, the sea was flat as a pancake, blue-black in colour, and twilight had rapidly fallen over the illuminated oil rigs which had been visible for a while, to left and right in the distance, so that it was no use my trying to make anything out in the universal grey. Then the first lights began to wink on, isolated specks restlessly dodging back and forth, and when I turned round the evening star was standing motionless in the sky above the surprisingly white triangle of our wake.

4

DOUGLAS
ISLE OF MAN

21 JUNE 1940

had given up shaving, were still in their pyjamas in the middle of the morning, and there was nothing left now of their original relief at getting away from the transit camp on the outskirts of Liverpool, a place you would have liked to erase from your memory. People thought everything would be different now, after those four weeks in the buildings of a recently completed housing estate with makeshift tents put up among them, everything was going to be better once you all reached the Isle of Man, no more standing in line up to the knees in mud when it had been raining, no more queuing outside the field kitchen or waiting your turn to slop out when everyone had diarrhoea, no more straw sacks doing duty as mattresses, no floodlights from the watch-towers by night, lighting the place up as if for target practice, all that would be over and done with, there were even rumours that newspapers would be available, and at last you would get to hear something more than the few scraps thrown your way by the guards, have some definite informa-tion about the progress of the war on the Continent, and now you sat there between the pale man and the man with the scar, and you didn't need to look at the faces surrounding you to know it wasn't bromide in the porridge at breakfast, as some had claimed, it was the same old story, it was boredom and resignation leaving its mark on them, just as it had been wearing you down too. Without actually listening you knew that the complaints were starting up again, complaints about the food, kippers every day, the cold water in the showers, the sudden ban reimposed on mail, you knew there was nothing to be done about it, and remembered what it had been like when you all arrived, what wild hopes most of you had until your whole party was standing on the quayside in the drizzle, as if you had merely been on an excursion, and then, as darkness fell, walked down the promenade lined with curious onlookers, but you were singing all the same, you remembered the angry cries and shouting as you were marched past the rows and rows of hotels and boarding houses, past the washed-out façades of the buildings running round the curve of the bay, their outlines blurred in the last of the daylight, you remembered the barbed wire emerging in the distance and how, as you came closer, you could hear the sound of the raindrops falling on it, saw them sparkling and glittering, saw the first stars in the sky and the soundless sea, a dark glimmer far away, an emptiness which seemed to absorb the noise of footsteps on the tarmac.

The camp was in the exact middle of the bay, four blocks consisting of 34 hotels and boarding houses whose evicted owners had left only the most basic furnishings in the buildings, which had numbers as well as names: the rooms contained no chairs or tables, but there were beds, even if they often had to be shared, and there was at least one lavatory on each floor, a kitchen and bath-room in each house, and a canteen where you could get cigarettes. Bordering on one side was a building resembling a castle, with soldiers going in and out of it during the day and, further down the promenade, beyond a monstrous structure with domes and turrets like something out of a fairy-tale book, formerly a dance hall, two more enclosures surrounded by barbed wire fences could be seen, both of them still empty, while on the other side there was a cinema with a white tiled façade, obviously disused, dwarf palm trees battered by the wind in the gardens in front of it, an octagonal pavilion for orchestral concerts with a colonnade attached to it, and a theatre. The place was less imposing at the back, where a tangle of fire escapes led down to the bare inner courtyards, but anyone who ended up in one of these rooms had compensation, since many of their windows looked out on nearby dwellings and rumours were circulating from the first day, so that the best places were rented out at night and men waited, packed close together, to see if a woman might appear at some time, give them a wave or even call out a word or two, and not draw the curtains at once.

Sometimes whole groups of prisoners stood lined up by the barbed wire, critically inspecting the recruits exercising on the beach, who never came up to their standards, and ignoring the request to speak English if possible so as not to make a bad impression. Someone only had to claim that they'd never have been allowed to get away with that sort of thing at home for everyone to laugh at the joke, and then the older men came out with tales of their own heroic deeds, and the mere mention of some theatre of war where they had fought in their youth reminded you of your mother's husband, wounded in the Kaiser's army. You listened, and you remembered how he always used to mention the fact when you kept asking him why you didn't all just go away, and he would say that nothing bad could happen to you, not to the family of a man who had fought at the front, those were his words, and he stuck to this belief long after he must have known he was deceiving himself. These were the only times he ever spoke of his past and, few as they had been, few of them as you could still recall, the sentimental bragging of a handful of veterans suddenly conjured them up, bringing back his tales of his grandfather's collection of clocks, of a carriage journey over a broad plain covered with snowdrifts, his first childhood memory and at the same time as improbable as something out of a nineteenth-century novel, and then there was his story of the corn bending in the wind somewhere beyond the seven mountains, he compared it to the sea as if such a comparison had never occurred to anyone before, and he spoke of what he called the field of honour.

Then it struck you how quietly he had lived with you, you and your mother, how little you really knew about him, only that he was the older partner in the marriage, but by how many years you afflicted everyone else too, it was the monotonous regularity of the day, knowing that the bugler would blow for reveille at seven, there would be morning roll-call at seven-thirty, and then gymnastics for those few who wanted to exercise, with an instructor who by his own account of it had only just missed out on selection for the Berlin Olympics and always avoided giving a straight answer if anyone asked whether he was Jewish and, after that, there wasn't much to do except cook, wash up or clean, depending on the task allotted to you, until everyone assembled in the street in the afternoon. The barbers among you were back at work, out in the open air with their combs and scissors beside chairs draped with towels that had been provided at their request, and they charged next to nothing, two cobblers and a watchmaker with their own tools joined them a little later, a Viennese café, rather pretentiously, opened in the dining room of one of the buildings for a couple of hours in the evening, and from the very first day there had been lectures on the most unlikely subjects, but that wasn't what you wanted, on the contrary, an arrow on a piece of paper with the clumsily written legend EXIT, or the menu card hung up by some joker offering a five-course festive menu, reminded you all the more forcibly of what was lacking here, and you were merely baffled by other men's ability to settle in as if the constraints of the whole situation were not omnipresent, playing at living a life where there was no life in reality. The only activities in which you did participate from the first were the English lessons given by the professor whom you had first noticed, along with his complaints, at that school in London and who was then with you on the way to Liverpool, he held conversation classes in his room between ten and twelve, although they were cancelled for the time being, because he was in solitary confinement for a week for trying to smuggle letters out of the camp, letters in which, if the rumours were to be believed, he had written to the few members of Parliament known to him by name and even to the king, asking them to put in a good word for him.

All other diversions had left you feeling despondent. The morning swims for which you and your companions were taken down to the beach in groups of 200 at a time – the clear, cold water, the sudden idea that you could head straight out to the sharp line of the horizon until the white bodies on the bright sand had disappeared beyond the waves – or simply the prospect of a walk you were all supposed to be taking some time in the next few days, the opportunity of seeing past the two hills marking the limits of the bay, the unfounded hope that something might lie beyond them other than another section of shoreline empty of humanity and stretching on into the distance, none of this made you feel anything but a wish to be alone, not with strangers all the time, people whose company you had not sought out for yourself, and under observation every moment of the day. You had long ago given up watching a ship put out to sea, that way madness lay, you didn't want to wonder where it might be going, perhaps it might just fall off the edge of the world. When a girl really did come cycling down the promenade and the others all raced to position themselves where they could get a good look at her, you knew it would be better not to let yourself in for that kind of thing, before then imagining a whole parade on the basis of their comments, conjuring up, from their exclamations or the way they stood in silence, a procession of stunning visions that you had only to hold in your mind, instead of lying motionless on your bed and staring straight ahead of you.

At such times you thought of Clara and wished you hadn't told them even what little about her you had let slip. Or at least, you regretted telling them how glad you would have been to stay with the family in London, whether or not the city was bombed, how you had sometimes felt you were very well situated in the Smithfield house during those last months before the war, when you came back from taking the old grandmother somewhere and sat opposite her in the kitchen eating a late supper, with the judge and his wife out for the evening and the children in bed long ago, and the sound of footsteps outside on the pavement suddenly transported you back to the days when night watchmen went their rounds in the city, and gas lamps still had to be lit before darkness fell. You didn't write to her when letter-writing was still allowed, you hadn't wanted to go in for the farce of using school exercise-book paper and the insulting obligation to keep to a certain number of lines on pain of a penalty, so that not so much as a sigh would escape the censors. Smiling, you'd watched the others labouring to string a few credible sentences together, but you refused to answer any of their questions about a girlfriend, and the harder the pale man and the man with the scar in particular pressed you the more brusquely you reacted, as if you feared they might say something derogatory about her, or make fun of you for being soft if you gave away too much about her and yourself.

It was the day you were all to be questioned, the day of the interrogation, and you, the pale man and the man with the scar had scarcely been back in the camp half an hour, led down the promenade by the corporal who had escorted you up it in the morning, the baby-faced lad who took charge of you at the gate and marched officiously along beside you, rifle slung around him – you had been handed over, back in the cage under lock and key again, and already you felt as if none of you had ever been out. As if the order had never come at roll-call to hold yourselves in readiness after standing down and wait for further instructions, for it seemed so long ago and so improbable now: the hotel down by the harbour, a first-floor room sparsely furnished with a table and bed, two chairs and a cupboard, and then there was the major, probably disabled on active service, who summoned you in one by one and who sat there, legs apart, as if showing by his attitude alone that you had been delivered up to his mercy. The other men from your building had gathered around you now, but without asking many questions and, if the newcomer had not rushed up on your return, the man who shared the room with you and the other two and who had not joined you until Liverpool, before the crossing to the island, if he had not come up as if he knew very well that the whole performance had been solely on his account, it could all have been simply an illusion.

Down on the beach a couple of lads were searching for bait, and a boy was walking through shallow water towards the jutting rocks near the pier when the newcomer began going on at the three of you again,

–Come on, where have you been all day?

and the pale man and the man with the scar didn't answer him, just sat there watching the guards who had gathered on the other side of the barbed wire to put down their guns and have a cigarette, and pretended not to hear him, because it was only the previous day he'd shouted at them furiously,

–I'll murder you,

again and again,

–I'll murder you,

and you remembered how they'd filched his photograph of his girlfriend which he took out of his suitcase every evening before going to bed, looking at it the way you yourself, as a child, used to look at the little pictures of saints handed out by the priest taking Religious Instruction in the Bible class to which your mother always sent you, illustrations of the Sacred Heart and the Virgin Mary, and you saw him before you again, watched him follow them downstairs, yelling loud enough to be heard all over the building,

−I'll bloody murder you.

You merely wondered what it was all about, why he was over-reacting like that, what exactly got him so worked up about his girlfriend's photograph, and you were thinking that even though the NCO in charge of your group didn't like the man, he had obviously not reported the trouble, when the newcomer started up again,

−It can't possibly be over that stupid little business,

and the pale man and the man with the scar laughed out loud, but he wasn't giving way, he immediately changed tack and resorted to begging,

−Look, just forget the whole thing, do,

and that was all, except for their fixed expressions as they looked out into the distance, and the wind rising in the evening as it had ever since you arrived, blowing down from the western hills in great gusts, surrounding the town, falling upon it until you felt you were hanging weightless in the air and couldn't take so much as a couple of steps without losing your balance, and a strange sense of lightness came over you, a state of intoxication in which the whole island seemed to be turning constantly round and round.

You saw that the newcomer never took his eyes off the pair of them, and you thought of the previous night when you stood at the window hearing their breathing in the room behind you, the deep breathing of the pale man, the lighter sound made by the man with the scar, which reminded you of a woman's breath, while he made no sound at all, as if he weren't sleeping but merely pretending to sleep, and was as wide awake in the dark as if it were broad daylight. It gave you a strange, eerie feeling to turn around and find yourself unable to see him, although you couldn't help imagining him sitting there upright, watching you, and you thought of speaking to him but refrained, for fear he couldn't answer, for fear he might just sit there staring at you, eyes fixed on your silhouette against the night sky, while the others turned in their sleep, unaware of anything, and you credited them with a sensitivity not perceptible when you saw them by daylight. You would have liked to wake them, but you were incapable of any movement, you merely guessed at that watchfulness of his, that oppressive presence, all forgotten in the morning when he jumped up and threw his pillow at them, and you felt the draught behind you, heard the creaking of the building which made you feel much further from the ground than you actually were up there on the fourth floor, as if you were about to find yourself on a platform swaying in isolation above the sea, while the other blacked-out buildings along the bay might have been obliterated as they lay there in a semi-circle, the outlines of the hotels now softening at its two extremities, at first glance always seeming to quiver again before the pale blue background.

When he turned to them once more it was with the same urgency as on the ferry, the same persistence you knew to be typical of him already, given the dogged way he had gone on at you during the crossing, as if it was essential for him to know every detail of your life before the party reached the island, and you heard him once again asking about your father and mother, heard him asking where they came from, and now you were not sure whether in fact you had given him his cue and it was only later that he said he came from the Salzkammergut too, his family had kept an inn for generations on the banks of Lake Traun, he was heir to it now. Anyway, he told you, the outbreak of war had unexpectedly found him in Brighton, and he was arrested before he could leave the country, he had stayed on in London with the money his family sent him from home through the Swiss Embassy, he repeated several times that he was not a refugee, he was only abroad to take a language course, and you thought of the oily gleam of the blue-black water as the boat cast off in the harbour, water that made you feel afraid, the haze

133

that had risen, the windless air, the gulls always soaring over the stern of the vessel and away, over and over again, and the slow zigzag manoeuvring as you made your way out to sea. As soon as you could all move freely on board he had come over to your group on the afterdeck, a strikingly well-groomed figure, as if manners in the transit camp where he had been were more polished, as if he were not a prisoner at all, in a suit that, with its appliqué trim on cuffs and collar, reminded you of the years when one couldn't go anywhere in Vienna without bumping into idiots of some kind in traditional costume, and you could only shake your head when you thought of the way he waved his hands about while he talked, as if giving instructions to the men standing shoulder to shoulder by the rail, not that they took any notice of him; they were on the look-out for mines, and jumped with alarm at the slightest irregularity in the sound of the engines.

For all that, when you were sitting outside the first-floor hotel room next to the pale man and the man with the scar, forbidden to talk while first one of your companions and then the other was called in, and you tried to guess what the expressions on their faces meant as they re-emerged, it never entered your head that this might have something to do with him. Although you three had been acquainted for over a month you didn't really know much about the other two, only that they were students and their flight from the Continent must have been fraught with danger: they had escaped the front line coming hourly closer to the Dutch coast by putting out to sea in a tiny rowing-boat in the middle of the night, and were picked up by an English ship at dawn, and you thought that through the closed door behind which they had vanished in turn you heard the remark with which they usually concluded their story, you thought you heard them protest that they had got away with nothing but their bare lives – there was not a word about him.

All you could deduce from their silence was that you had better be prepared for a serious discussion, and he was in fact the last thing that would have come into your mind there in the stuffy corridor, the walls painted brown like dried blood up to eye level and white above, with the corners rounded as if to prevent anyone from trying to knock his head against them.

There was also the flickering light, a suite of rooms and, at the end of them, a window with a hazy view of the ferry moorings and the terminal building with its clock which seemed to have stopped when the final tourist boat arrived last summer, from time to time you heard the muted clatter of a typewriter as if played by a tape recorder, there was a woman in a red dress who appeared with a stack of files, then vanished again, and the chain-smoking corporal who ground out his cigarette stubs on the floor, nodded off for a few minutes now and then, and grabbed the barrel of his gun when he woke with a start.

It was hours before your turn came, hours during which the light in the corridor did not change, and you kept thinking of the advice the corporal had given you and your companions, better not act all meek and mild, you ought to insist on being treated as POWs, never mind all that nonsense about being under the protection of the Crown and kept in custody for your own safety, and when you finally entered the room it was bright in there, the major looked up from his desk, indicated the chair opposite his, and you sat down, watching him glance at a sheet of paper while the orderly who had brought you in disappeared, and he remarked,

–It says here you're Jewish,

showing the same scepticism as the guards always did when they asked about that, the same surprise, as if you were the only one in the camp, the same bafflement – for why, in that case, would you have been interned at all?

135

–Well, so are you Jewish?

and you interrupted him,

–Is that why I have the honour of making your acquaintance?

and he laughed and said,

–Honour or not, just as you please, but it says here you're Jewish, and I'd like to know from you personally whether that's correct,

and you remembered how the judge's old mother once said a Hun is a Hun, and how you had stopped dead in the street, just letting the wheelchair stand still in the middle of the road, staring down for quite a while at her head gently nodding back and forth, and you let him catch you unawares when he reached over the desk to offer you a cigarette case with gold decoration, you simply accepted and helped yourself, although you knew this was a mistake, that you ought to have refused, that it might make him think you were easy prey.

However, it did surprise you when, without hesitating or waiting for your answer, he continued,

–Are you satisfied with conditions in the camp?

and you looked not at him but at the heavy typewriter on the table, a black colossus with an excessively large roller into which a blank sheet of paper was inserted, at the vase beside it holding a set of unidentifiable dry stems, the stacks of folders and the little pigeon-holes full of pedantically sharpened pencils, their ends pointing at you, you saw the strips of sunlight falling on the flowered bedspread and continuing their way over the floorboards and the rug, and you said,

–Yes,

and he placed his hands together,

–No complaints?

and you said,

–No,

and he reminded you of the priest to whom you had confessed once or twice as a child without being turned away, who listened behind his grating, he reminded you of the questions the priest went on asking until you admitted to lying and stealing and heaven knows what else.

The guards had started on their rounds again and were pacing stiffly up and down by the barbed wire when the newcomer tried again,

–So here we sit on this damn island, caught in a trap, and you lot act all stuck-up, won't condescend to open your mouths,

but the pale man interrupted him,

–Caught in a trap, are we?

and he gave him an unfriendly look,

–Listen, we're caught in a trap whether you like it or not, and when they're actually coming, when it gets to the point, you can be sure we'll be the last to know,

but a laugh followed this,

–Coming, are they? That's just rumour. Oh, sure, they're coming,

and while the click of the bowls could be heard again outside, just the same as on the days before, like the ticking of a giant clock running down in the street where the players, always the same four men, had taken up their positions, you remembered how once, in the transit camp, panic almost set in when the rations were doled out sparingly, nobody knew why, and rumours immediately began circulating – this couldn't be chance, the invasion must have succeeded – and when at the same time they also started giving out gas masks, finding old stocks to supply the prisoners who had none, next morning a man who had hanged himself with a pullover was found in one of the buildings, dangling like a sack from a hook in the ceiling.

The major had taken a cigarette himself, lit it, put his head back, narrowed his eyes to slits, stared abstractedly at the match, which was still burning, and blew it out, his pursed lips suddenly looking ridiculously soft, and as a voice came into the room from somewhere in the street outside he smoked for a while as though lost in thought, and then began again,

–If I may raise another item, I'd be interested to know how you get on with the other men sharing your room,

and you told him,

–They're my friends,

which he repeated, with irony,

–Your friends?

and you said,

–Yes,

and when he rose to go past you to the wash-basin, ceremoniously washing his hands, and then went to the window and looked out as if he were alone in the room, you still weren't thinking of the newcomer, you just stared at his back and wondered if someone might have told him about the drawings which the man with the scar sold in return for some small item from the canteen, or perhaps he'd heard something about that remarkable set of observations which obsessed the pale man, and that was why he reacted so brusquely.

The omission couldn't have been more obvious, the fact that he had not mentioned the newcomer, but it didn't put you on your guard when he returned to the subject,

–So those two waiting outside are your friends?

and you thought of the way they had been going on at you to stick together, even back in the transit camp, and you avoided giving a direct answer,

–We're all from Vienna,

but he wasn't letting it go,

–Those two are your friends?

and you made out you didn't understand him, nodded until your nodding became a shake of the head, and repeated,

–We're all from Vienna,

a remark he dismissed with another comment,

–Clearly the other two are Jewish as well,

and although he seemed to be concentrating entirely on what was going on in the street you feared he might turn round and ask you, and you would have to tell him whether the pale man really expected to get anywhere with his observations, with the list he had compiled giving the daily times of the ebb and flow of the tides, the changing of the guard, and the dates of the new moon, yes, he might turn to you, and you would have to speak of the fact that the man with the scar sat out of doors day after day in front of a kind of easel, a makeshift structure he had cobbled together, he might want to know details, and you would have to say that he had begun his experiments on the very first morning on the island, a spot or so of blackout paint, just a couple of quick scratches with a wooden stick on the window of your room, they could have meant anything at all, you'd have to describe the way he could concoct an oily kind of ink out of pencil leads, margarine and soot, and trace pictures in it on a piece of linoleum or a scrap of paper for anyone who asked, you'd have to explain the whole idea, admit that he had already provided for half the camp and now had the staff for customers too, you'd have to mention the bottle of potato spirit one of the sergeants had traded for a really fine example, a negro woman with breasts like udders hanging down to her navel, and a long splash of something still wet, black and shimmering between her legs.

The major had seated himself again, and said nothing, but of course the tone in which he spoke of the two Jews had not escaped you, or the accusation behind it. It must have been something to do with his contempt for men who were fighting on neither one side nor the other, who in his view were just skiving off, something to do with his rigid notions of army life, upon which the corporal had held forth, and you went to some trouble to hold his gaze steadily. You watched him grind out his cigarette and then remove his boots without letting it provoke you, and suddenly you remembered those conversations in the camp about the guards, some of the prisoners discussing at length whether so-and-so had any experience of service on the front line or not, how you could tell, how the others back in the rear weren't good for much, and the mere idea of how, despite the wound he might be supposed to have sustained, he would fare in their estimation gave you some satisfaction.

The chugging of a marine engine broke the silence, the major waited until it had died down and, when he suddenly spoke of the newcomer, it was clear to you that everything he had said so far had been mere preliminary skirmishing, and you interrupted, sarcastically,

–But he's not Jewish,

to which he said, sounding irritated,

–I know, but surely he's your friend,

and you said,

–If you say so,

and he rejoined,

–So is he your friend, then?

and you repeated,

–If you say so,

and he said,

–Tell me, is he or is he not your friend?

and you saw him slowly pull the typewriter closer to the edge of the table, and before you could wonder what he was about or why, he had all his fingers poised over the keys and was leaning well forward, shoulders raised, arms at an angle, clattering away, and trying to meet your eyes over the sheet of paper, as if he expected you to start dictating to him.

The newcomer had risen to his feet and moved a couple of paces away to smoke a cigarette, and the pale man took this opportunity to remark,

–Seems to think himself someone special,

and the man with the scar agreed,

–First he treats you like dirt, then he acts as if nothing has happened. We never ought to have let him share our room. He really gets me down, the way he keeps telling us they're coming,

and the pale man said,

–Well, he has less to fear than most. No reason for him to get worked up. Even if the worst comes to the worst, I don't suppose much would happen to his sort,

and you sensed the men in front of you and the others and behind you moving closer and listening, anxious to snap up any information which would provide them with a subject of conversation for days, something to give them hope or confirm their fears that they would be interned until the war was over, with many of them you had as yet scarcely exchanged a word, but they seemed like old acquaintances, as if you had spent half a lifetime together behind the barbed wire.

The major shifted his legs restlessly back and forth under the desk, and hesitated for a moment or so before saying, apparently casually,

–There are rumours about him going round the camp,

and you looked at the three buses parked beside the harbour basin, their windows blank as if forgotten for good, you looked at the fire-tower and the circular cistern on the edge of the car park, you let your glance move over the swing bridge where a figure in a raincoat stood, your eyes strayed over the gasworks on the other side, from which a yellowish vapour rose, and the stone quarry beyond with a sprinkling of gulls on its steep slope, and you tried to give another evasive reply,

—You know more than I do, then,

but he interrupted,

—At least I can see which side he's on.

—They placed him in Category One at the tribunals, said the pale man, after some moments of silence, not that it necessarily means anything,

and the man with the scar said,

—No need for you to take his side,

and the pale man shook his head,

—I've had enough bellyaching from those fools who think they have to keep justifying themselves, complaining of being wrongly classified,

and the man with the scar said,

—It's always the same characters you find telling the guards they're Jewish, or they fought in the Spanish Civil War, or they've been refugees ever since that gang was in charge at home,

and the pale man said,

—Fought in the Spanish Civil War?

and the man with the scar repeated,

—That's right, the Spanish Civil War,

and there was laughter,

—And I'm the Emperor of China,

and you thought of the self-congratulatory tales of memorable experiences in those sanctified brigades, stories that were indeed common in the camp, while most of the men sitting around listening to you fell silent and looked away, as if they didn't much care for the tone of your two companions.

142

–It's the people he mixes with that concern me, the major began again, there are several shady characters among them, as far as I can tell,

and without looking at you he read out a list of names, mentioning the London representative of a Bavarian brewery, a doctor from the German Hospital in Hackney, a restaurant proprietor who had lived in Manchester for 15 years but originally came from Alsace, and the crew of a German merchant vessel which had been lying at anchor in the Thames when war broke out, he asked if you were acquainted with any of these people, and added,

–I'm sure you know about the Brown House,

and before you even had time to think how to react he continued, lowering his voice,

–I don't suppose it's any secret that they are accommodated there, and I hardly need to tell you how the place gets its name,

and you could only wonder why he was trying to make it seem as if all this hadn't been settled long ago, as if the malcontents, quartered in the boarding house they immediately requisitioned at the back of the block of buildings, were not dismissed as nutcases remote from reality, people who could do no one any harm if they were safely shut up, why did he make it look as if they'd been taken seriously, as if you hadn't all been amusing yourselves on the crossing from Liverpool at the expense of the seamen who, on being taken prisoner, had failed to sink their ship as honour dictated, laughing at their preservation of group identity and their habit of always looking at their captain, carrying out an order from one of the guards only with his consent, and standing to attention at his slightest gesture, as if they regarded him as lord of life and death.

So that was why you were here, you thought idly, while the major assured you in a quiet voice,

–I trust you believe me when I say I wouldn't be bothering

with them if they were just a bunch of Pathfinder stragglers,

and he added,

–Have you heard what they sing?

to which you replied,

–No,

and he thrust out his chest,

–*Heut' fahren wir gegen Engelland,*

and although you realised he wouldn't take it well, you couldn't help laughing, because his German accent was so appalling, and you repeated the words,

–*Heut' fahren wir gegen Engelland?*

and he nodded,

–That's what they sing, and your friend stands in the front row beating time, bawling it out like a madman,

and you stopped objecting to the term, watched as he took a paper-knife out of the desk drawer and began cleaning his finger-nails with it in front of you, you listened to the silence, for suddenly there was no more noise from outside, not even the scream of the gulls, and the strip of sunlight on the floorboards and the bed-spread had disappeared.

They had certainly struck a discordant note from the first, but you had thought no more of it and, if the newcomer had fallen under suspicion, it must be bad luck rather than because he was really one of them; he had known the majority of these men in his transit camp, after all, hence his contact with them. Making a mountain out of this molehill was ridiculous and, even if it was true, as it seemed to be, that the morning after your arrival a pastor had prayed for a swift victory on the steps outside their house, leaving no doubt whose it was to be, it wasn't much more than a bad joke, for when a little later a cardboard notice appeared in one of their windows saying NO JEWS HERE, a couple of NCOs into their arms. You had never been more clearly aware of the paradox than at the moment when the last note died away and, if only a few of the others had been as carried away too, imagining a December afternoon at home, Saturday after school, time once again moving in the endless cycles of those past days, if you had not been alone with your thoughts of the sense of safety when you came home early in the twilight after walking for hours, if you had not been the only one to remember these things, surely all of you would have made common cause with them. But this was sentimentality, and there was a lie behind it, a lie for them and for the rest of you alike, although for them it was at least a functional lie, since as they saw it their waiting would be over soon, they would only have to obliterate the memory of a dark period and they could go back, could carry on as if nothing had happened, while most of you had nowhere left to go, and if, later, you remembered the way you recoiled when the lid of the piano was closed, then whatever soothing things you told yourself, it was like a seal confirming the necessity of letting no one blur the edges of the truth. The silence that followed troubled you, and you found it distressing to see other men suddenly standing there like disappointed children, men who you had thought in these last few weeks would never be deceived again, not after everything they had been through – men who had held visas for Palestine for years, only to have their long-cherished plans of emigrating changed because of some small detail, men with a ticket for America whose voyage was suddenly cancelled when the war began, men who had already been at sea on their way to Cuba, but whose landing permits were withdrawn when they were lying off Havana, let alone those who had got away from Dachau or Buchenwald and kept quiet when the usual complaints were voiced, or would say only after some time that they had known camps of a different kind, and compared to them you were all in Paradise here.

Although they themselves were not sure where they belonged, you had felt like one of them for the first time, and you did not know what to make of it when one of them, who had been allowed to keep his Iron Cross when he was interned, apparently sold it to the guards, but the incident was a subject of discussion, and not only the most die-hard old soldiers but men who might well have burst into mocking laughter saw it as blasphemy, began speaking of the Fatherland, and could not forgive the scapegoat for betraying it, they said, so thoughtlessly. Many of them were Jews who observed only the three major festivals, or not even that, Jews like you who, back at home, had answered questions about their parents by saying oh yes, my mother and father are Jewish, as if it were some symptom of old age, and who for the most part still felt more German or Austrian than anything else. It was odd, certainly, and to complete the grotesque picture you had only to think of the consular officials in the London embassy, sometimes said to be coming here soon, then it was claimed that they had already arrived and were being held outside the camp, your representatives were actually on the island, but compared to the rest of you the grandees would be living in luxury, with greater freedom of movement, allowed to go out every day and perhaps even visit women, a privilege much discussed, as was the assumption that the commandant, the lieutenant colonel whom the rest of you had not once seen face to face, was going to ask them to dinner some time in the near or more distant future.

The major had long since changed the subject and was talking about spies, but you were scarcely listening, so abstruse did his remarks seem to you, reminiscent of the worst hysteria in the months before your internment, the stories they told in London of their own parachutists being attacked by farmers with pitchforks while out training in the countryside, and when he said,

–Well, keep an eye on your friend,

147

you replied, defensively,

—I'm no informer,

and he leaned forward as if he had not heard what you said, propped his arms on the desk and put his hands together, obviously unaware that his voice had dropped to a whisper,

—I expect you know Paris has fallen,

and it seemed to you unreal, as if nothing of any importance could still exist for you outside the camp, not even the fact that there was a war on, when he repeated,

—Let's not misunderstand each other: I expect you to keep an eye on him and tell me anything odd about him at once.

You hadn't even asked the pale man and the man with the scar if he had put the same request to them, and as the newcomer approached again you just said,

—One can't think he'd do anything bad,

and they laughed,

—Well, you should know,

which surprised you, and you said,

—Me?

and they added,

—You know him best,

and you repeated,

—Me?

and they said,

—Well, you spend all day with him,

and absurd as it was, the idea suddenly came into your head that they might be agents planted to watch you, that you were the subject of their observations, and some time or other you would have to refute whatever obscure accusations they threw at you.

Silence fell when the newcomer sat down again, and the pale man and the man with the scar, indifferent, looked out to sea where a shower was falling over the surface, a constant ripple replicating itself as it went out towards the horizon, which seemed to have come closer. While the two of them moved as far as possible away from him, and he monopolised the space by spreading his hands, the other men around you froze, never taking their eyes off him. He sat there with legs outstretched and, when he coughed, you thought he was going to mention the photograph, explain what it meant to him at last, but he only looked now at one, now at another, and seemed to be waiting for something.

–I'll give you 24 hours to think it over, decide whether you're going to come off your high horse or not, said the major, it's up to you whether or not you want to help me, but don't blame me if you find yourself kicking your heels behind barbed wire for the whole of the war,

and you avoided his eyes again, looking instead at the patch of watery blue sky in the window, at the distant hills where the gorse shone bright yellow,

–I don't think I can help you,

and he shook his head,

–You could be home next week,

and you saw him stand up again, take off his jacket, lean his arms on the back of the chair and look down on you, as if unable to comprehend such obstinacy.

Yet again the pale man and the man with the scar did not reply when the newcomer could no longer restrain himself, and asked with sudden urgency,

–They're not letting you out, are they?

and then he turned to you,

–Are they letting you out?

and before you could reply he added,

–I mean, perhaps the judge has pulled strings for you, or his

149

wife wants you back to be her little lapdog,

and you knew it had been a mistake to tell him anything at all, and kept quiet while he went on repeating the same question like someone possessed,

–They're not letting you out, are they?

louder and louder every time,

–They're not letting you out?

The major had taken another cigarette, but this time he did not offer you one, just lit it, stood there inhaling and then said, with a smile,

–Of course we can send you away on a nice voyage, if you'd prefer that to working with us,

and you couldn't help thinking of all the rumours in circulation from the first, the possibility that you might all end up overseas sooner or later, the threat of settlement in some God-forsaken spot, and you guessed that it was his habit to wait, looking at you, as if he had plenty of time, before he went on,

–I'm afraid I don't know whether you'd prefer the desert or the Arctic Circle, but a few years in Canada or Australia wouldn't hurt you,

and the summer was almost close enough to touch outside the window, it must smell of flowers, of the colours out there, red and yellow, although none of the fragrance reached your nostrils, only the stuffy atmosphere in the room, a smell of sweat, mothballs, and the usual sweet aftershave which still, in spite of the war, seemed to be available in such large quantities that the whole company was redolent of it.

There was no reason for you to wish yourself away from the island, let alone want to be moved and, but for Clara, you would probably have found it difficult to understand those who had relatives in London and feared for their safety. Although you knew the questions being asked – how much longer would it be, how long would internment last, how long would the war go on? – and had heard the answers often enough, ranging from a few weeks to a few years, you could not join in the conversation when they spoke of their wives and children, even if many had no news of them yet. At such times you would think of the letters your father had written to you once or twice a month in his childish handwriting until the beginning of the war, letters so innocuous they could have been the work of a naïve girl leaving the nest for the first time and enthusing over everything she saw, grotesque documents, whether they had been censored or whether he prettified them himself for fear of the censor, letters in which he told you how business was going, described excursions, a day out skiing with his secretary, whom he had finally married, everything unremittingly wonderful, letters arriving in outsize envelopes swamping the single sheets of notepaper, his dutiful exercises, pointless reminders to you to be respectful to the judge and his family, to fit in with what they wanted, and when they finally stopped coming you were not sad about it, you did not feel the emotion that left you breathless the moment you thought of your mother and her husband.

The major had seated himself again and put on his boots, and when he called the orderly and told him to fetch the guard, there stood the corporal in the doorway next moment, and he pointed his index finger at you and said,

–Take him back to the camp with the others,

and the corporal said,

–Yes sir,

and when he did not move at once,

–Well, what are you waiting for?

and you saw him stand to attention, and for a moment indulged in a vision of getting out through the window, you had only to stand up, climb down, and then, once at ground level, just walk away as if it were the most natural thing in the world, you'd have to find out when the next ship sailed and, in a couple of hours at the latest, you'd be off and away.

The newcomer had calmed down again and stopped wondering out loud if anyone was going to be set free, and instead sat rigid like the others, his arms crossed over his chest. All of a sudden he gave the same stubborn impression as on the couple of times he had refused to obey the NCO's order to fetch firewood, and no, what made him think he was going to tidy the window of the room you four shared, what made him think he was going to sweep the floor or empty the rubbish buckets, what made him think he would help in the kitchen, no, no and no again, and you thought of the way he was always suggesting he might do something himself, not just occupy the bathroom for hours, or mislay the key to the lavatories and get annoyed when everyone had to go outside for a piss in the night and then the place stank like a pigsty in the heat, never mind the angry comments made about him. There was no doubt that he would take possession of the bed you shared jointly that evening, he would not bring out the playing cards, his usual companions, in the normal way and suggest a game to decide who slept where and who must pay a forfeit by running round the block clad in his underpants, you would find him there smiling innocently while you had to make do with the floor, or else you'd have to lie side by side with him as the other two did, the pale man and the man with the scar, who started the night one each end of their bed but woke up with their heads together in the morning, and you wondered what you had done to deserve being landed with someone like him.

Outside, the guards had reassembled when a group of schoolgirls stopped at a safe distance to look at the camp, figures standing awkwardly, clamping their straw hats to their heads with one hand

and, from a distance, you noticed the long rope, the barrier keeping back the crowd, with soldiers in front of it, one every few paces, uniformed men with their faces turned away from you. A fine rain had begun to fall and, when the shouting suddenly began, it broke into the grim silence your party preserved and drowned out the sound of the engines and the ship's propeller, which was making a crunching noise as if it were running aground. These were the cat-calls you had all heard before, it was impossible to make out the words, but you could hardly mistake the content. You had expected nothing else, you had never believed those soothing lies saying that the island landlords would be glad of you, dependent as they were on being paid for your accommodation by the government, and they'd been used to foreigners for years, you had never believed it would be different here from the way it was at the port of Liverpool, during your transfer from the transit camp or your transport from London a month ago, the same crowd every-where, at all the railway stations you went through, those nameless places from which the signboards had been removed in anticipation of invasion, each the same as the next, and fists were raised every-where as you passed slowly through at walking pace. No, you were not hurt by the idea of a repeat performance, nor did it even strike you at first that, once again, there were many women in the crowd, but when you did notice their head-scarves, when the gangplanks were out, you felt you'd had enough of being treated like this, as if you and the other internees had planned the whole thing, as if you had taken their menfolk away and it was your fault there was a war on, your wilful malice alone was the reason why they sat in their empty boarding houses not knowing where to turn for credit or how to feed their children, you thought how ridiculous it all was and could not understand how you had been able to remain calm so long, these were women whose ill will was bound to be doubly forceful, whatever devil had got into you, they were women and if they hated you then you were all lost, if they cried out to heaven to condemn you there was no hope left.

At first it was in whispers that the men around you began talking again, but the newcomer remained silent, looking from time to time at the pale man and the man with the scar, while you thought how still it had become, only the steps of the guards who had gone on land could be heard for a little longer, their clattering footsteps on the metal gangplanks were muted, and finally there was merely the gurgle of the water while the ship's side rose and fell lazily just off the wall of the pier, and you felt dizzy when you tried to see to the far end of the bay. A mild wind had been driving the shower inland, a damp mist suddenly cast on your faces, you scarcely felt the droplets, and you had only to remember how the buildings in the distance had disappeared and then emerged into view again for the same feeling to come over you, a sense of being cut off from everything, you sat there unable to understand a word that was spoken, you felt the same soundlessness spreading, the same inertia, as if some semblance of movement were maintained in your field of vision alone. Although no more than a few moments passed in this way you had begun waiting at the time, and you had to be careful not to lapse into the same state again, you were relieved when one of the NCOs appeared, and the others were immediately running hither and thither like sheepdogs rounding up a frightened flock, repeating his orders.

–Get a move on, was the cry up and down the line of houses as you hurried to take your places, step on it, at the double now,

and there was the usual muttering, until the man with the scar hissed,

–Hush,

and the pale man said,

155

–Here they come,

and the warning spread like the wind,

–Here they come. Hush. Here they come,

and of course the two were beside you again, and you had lost sight of the newcomer, you saw that the duty officer with his troop of men had appeared at the gateway, saw him stop briefly, saw the guards saluting him, settling their guns on the ground with a sharp crack, with a sound like breaking bones, as they looked past him into thin air with that glance learnt only in the army, while he simply marched in, sagging slightly at the knees as he walked as if to emphasise the weight of the pistol buckled to his belt, and you noticed that he held the rank of captain.

–You can start, he told the sergeant beside him as he stood to attention in front of the first squad, number them off,

and the sergeant passed the order on in louder tones to one of the corporals, among whom you could not make out the man who had escorted your party to the interrogation,

–Number off,

and the corporal shouted,

–Number off,

and off you went, on the count of one, the first ten men moved a pace forward, on the count of two the same again, and so on to three, ten each time, and as far as you were concerned this could have gone on for ever, need never have stopped, casting you into a trance, spinning you into a cocoon of long lines of men, its increasing size putting you beyond reach, a mummy concealed from all eyes.

5

DOUGLAS
ISLE OF MAN
29 JUNE 1940

It was already getting light when the newcomer put his proposition, after you had been up all night again playing cards, no need now for him to persuade the rest of you; it had become almost routine, after the evening when you first began, for him to start the game as darkness fell, and then you would sit up until the small hours of the morning. This time it was he who contributed the potato spirit for which there was a flourishing black market, a market that would not dry up until the last watch, the last wedding ring, the last item of any value at all had disappeared from the camp. He had brought it along in a matter-of-fact manner, and he now poured what remained into the two glasses standing on your suitcases, which were piled between the beds where you sat. He put down the bottle and waited, looked at the rest of you one by one, and once again he named the sum, while the cry of the gulls grew louder outside and the wind drove their shadows past the windows. The candle had burned down some time ago, but you had drawn back the curtains and, in spite of the blackout on the windows, the light that came in was sufficient for you all to see him gritting his teeth, to notice the long grooves at the corners of his mouth and observe how large his eyes suddenly looked, and there could be no doubt that he meant it seriously, everything

you had staked so far was ridiculous by comparison, the eternal
cigarettes and your efforts to break them in half at the middle, or
use the contents of two in order to roll three increasingly thin
ones, which the pale man and the man with the scar helped each
other to lick, tubes no thicker than a straw, and lighting them called
for some skill if they were not to burn up at once in a tongue of
flame.

–We play up to 15 points, he repeated, turning to you with a
confident air, you and me together, right?

and the pale man and the man with the scar confirmed,

–And the two of us,

and then he explained the rules once more,

–The two losing partners turn up cards until one of them gets
an ace, and the other one packs his things ready to go,

and the pale man interrupted,

–Three hundred pounds?

and the man with the scar whistled through his teeth,

–I suppose that's nothing to you,

and he said, quite casually,

–Three hundred pounds,

and the pale man asked,

–Where on earth are you going to get three hundred pounds?

a question to which he gave no reply, but instead pulled a bundle
of crumpled notes from his pocket, tore off the paper band round
them, and began counting them out on the bed beside him, very
deliberately, as if he would like to linger over every one of them,
dampening his fingers repeatedly, and then he laughed,

–Three hundred pounds – chicken, are you?

and the pale man stammered,

–They won't be worth the paper they're printed on tomorrow,

and the man with the scar agreed,

–Then you'd better make sure you use them in a hurry,

and he just stroked them until they rustled, fanned out one of the three packets he had made, put it together again, took the other two, hesitated for a moment and finally waved them back and forth in front of their noses, so that you could hear a quiet crackling.

This softened them up, and they all looked at you, waiting for your answer, and you repeated,

–The loser goes?

and the pale man picked up one of the two glasses, emptied it in a single draught, and did not scruple to press you for an answer when he put it down again,

–Well, are you playing or not?

and the man with the scar supported him,

–You're not going to back out, are you?

and you realised that you couldn't escape them, either you joined the game or they would be on and on at you until roll-call, and no question of your going to bed first to snatch at least an hour's sleep, they would keep trying to persuade you, accusing you in outspoken terms of letting them down, you clearly saw that unless you agreed you would be treated as a traitor for the next few days, they would egg on the other men in the building to hammer on the table with their spoons when you entered the dining room, they would tell everyone you were a spy, the usual term of denigration, they would think up any number of unpleasant things, and you had to reconcile yourself to it – either you gave in to them or you wouldn't have a moment's peace, and that was why you did not protest,

–The loser goes,

and everyone nodded,

–The loser goes,

and there was no need for you to say anything when the

newcomer began shuffling the cards, as if he had known well in advance that you would never dare stand up to him and the others.

This was at the end of a week when, once your 24 hours' respite was up, you had been waiting daily for your number to be called out in the morning, but still there was no sign of life from the major, you had not yet been told, sarcastically, to be kind enough to keep a couple of hours free, it was at the end of a week when you had first feared and then hoped that your interrogation was a mere misunderstanding, and that in retrospect your attempts to worm something out of the newcomer – something that would at least do you personally some good – your efforts to persuade him to confide in you were as innocent as you wished they had been all along. You had cultivated his company from that first evening, as soon you could contrive to shake off the pale man and the man with the scar you would be sitting with him, so alarmed were you by the threats of deportation, you hadn't moved from his side, but all along you had the impression that the more questions you asked him, the more you were giving yourself away. There had been nothing, absolutely nothing to report, unless it was of any significance that his mother came from Bohemia and had met his father when she was working as a chambermaid in his grandparents' inn, unless it would increase or detract from his interest that he left grammar school early, unless the fact that he learned his trade at the Hotel Imperial in Vienna had any influence on his subsequent career – and indeed, unless that was really the kind of thing they wanted to hear, small details of some kind or other distinguishing him from the rest.

Although you had long since reached agreement with the pale man and the man with the scar about the interrogation inflicted on all three of you, they were not trying to pump him themselves. To all appearances, they had been back on excellent terms with him since the first night spent playing cards, but they confirmed him in the belief that the only trouble had been the photograph incident, of which they now made light, laughing amiably, although instead of calming your fears their casual demeanour troubled you, but you could not have said why. Since they had initially ignored him, the mere fact that they were getting along with him again struck you, perversely, as a betrayal of yourself, and absurd as it was, you could not quite shake off the suspicion that they might all be ganging up on you.

It took the whole week for you to discover that the major had suffered a riding accident on the very afternoon of your interview with him, and was in hospital with concussion and cracked ribs, hence the delay. He would not be back on his feet for several more days at least, which was fine from your point of view, the uncertainty was over now, but it was a nuisance that while any sequel to the interrogation remained an unknown factor, you had no way of finding out whether he had his eye solely on the three of you, or whether he was after other internees as well. You wondered why he hadn't gone straight to the newcomer himself, or why not one of the tough characters who obviously thought they were a cut above the rest and could order the guards about, unless one of the NCOs who did their own deals was really at the bottom of it, one of the house-masters, as they shamelessly called themselves, one of the men whom you might all have done well to cultivate for your own good.

The newcomer had stopped frequenting the Brown House, which strictly speaking had ceased to exist when its occupants were allocated to other buildings without notice, an almost cloak-and-dagger operation carried out so smoothly as to surprise you, there were no objections, although the merchant seamen would not move until they got the official order to comply from their captain, and now hardly any of them were still together. The brewery rep had been sent to your building, and turned out to be far from the uncouth businessman you might have expected, but a rather irritable middle-aged character who avoided awkward subjects, immediately spoke of something else if anyone asked him how he thought the war was going, and pretended not to have heard if you persisted, or else he talked for hours about his six children, and it would never have occurred to you to see anything suspicious in his having a conversation with the newcomer, particularly as you generally joined them anyway, no, that would be ridiculous, and if any proof was needed it came on your excursion out of the camp, the promised walk along the coastal road, when the pair of them stayed in your group like docile schoolboys, rather than joining their former comrades once you were beyond the town and the guards allowed the crocodile to break ranks, merely blocking any access to the letterboxes outside the front gardens as you passed them. You had also finally asked the newcomer straight out why he had flown at the pale man and the man with the scar, overcoming your reserve and your fear of annoying him, and you were convinced by his answer and the fact that he was indeed annoyed, by the question he put in turn, saying surely you weren't stupid enough to believe the rumours that it was something to do with their both being Jewish, when he had wanted to share a room with the three of you all along.

If what he said was true, then the photograph had indeed been the sole reason for his flying off the handle, the picture of his girlfriend, and when he showed it to you next day he had only to speak her name, no more, he had only to say this was Rachel, he didn't even have to stress the fact that she didn't look Jewish for you to be reminded of your father's way of asking if a girl was a Jew, evidently an inevitable question. It disconcerted you to have him nudge you again while you looked at the picture: a young woman with her hair pinned up, impeccably blonde hair, and her pale appearance reminded you of early photographs of your grandmother, standing posed beside her husband with eyes wide open, holding her breath so tensely that she looked likely to fall over in a faint next moment. You had the impression he was waiting for your consent, your approval, your verdict – what did you think of her? – but you saw only her face, and nothing was further from your mind than any stupid decision for or against, you saw how unformed her features still seemed, with only the mouth appearing to have taken its final shape, a double bow with the lips not fully closed, a tiny opening between them, you saw how low her ears were set, their curve like the natural continuation of her chin, you saw her eyes, and you hated the idea that ultimately what seemed to matter was whether a person belonged in a certain category or not.

There had been a letter, a request sent to the authorities by your mother's husband when the rumours back at home refused to die down – rumours that your family was going to lose the apartment and you'd have to move out – it was that letter of his which really opened your eyes, or more precisely its hesitant first words, at which you had glanced as it lay on the kitchen table, the opening formula, Respected Sir, and then: even though I am Jewish, I make so bold as to approach you, and after that you could not pretend to yourself any longer. It still made you uneasy to remember his saying the one good thing about all this was the fact that those high and mighty gentlemen couldn't be on the right side any more, as he had told himself when he heard of the first property requisitions, and it was clear that he meant the converts, respected citizens who went into the professions, attended the Burgtheater and the opera, had entry to the most select circles, some of them more German than the devil himself, the Jews who had been living in Vienna for a long time, to whom he himself in the worst case was a Pole, in the current term of abuse, an unwelcome reminder of a past with which they had cut all their connections, a very distant relation indeed who had emerged from the gutter and might drag them down into the dirt through his mere existence. You felt you had a great handful of loose ends when this occurred to you, remembering how he had gone so far as to say it was lucky that they weren't in fact immune or they'd be right behind the squads of thugs, urging themselves on with orders to scrub the streets just to keep on the right side, being on the right side meant everything, he had the lowest imaginable opinion of them, and later, when you heard that not only the usual gutter press of London but also the *Jewish Chronicle*, of all papers, had backed the internment of people like you, you were no more surprised than you would have been by the opposite, it was merely confirmation that there was still a dividing line between the haves and have-nots as part of the natural order of things, which meant one was living in a free country.

It was odd, but once the newcomer had mentioned Rachel he began talking about her at every opportunity, as if he had nothing else on his mind, and it wasn't long before you had heard the whole story, the tale of the girl who had been to stay at their inn with her father for several weeks every summer since she was twelve, you soon knew that her mother had died at her birth, and he and his sister had brought her up, he was a university lecturer in Vienna who had lost his post in the last peacetime months, at the end of May or the beginning of June just before the war, when he turned up with her again. At first you noticed his agitation, you saw how worked up he was, how he couldn't drop the subject, repeating several times that no one had expected to see them again, since they didn't come the year before, and suddenly there they were, obviously in flight, with what possessions they still had packed in the cases he carried up to their rooms for them, while they climbed the stairs after him without a word and did not reappear that day, although it must still have been quite early. This was before the season began, and it was only with reluctance that his parents had been persuaded to take them in, you could not forget what he had said about their arrival in a pitiable state, wet through, for despite the rain and their luggage, they had walked from the station on foot, a journey of two hours, and it looked to him as if they had spent the night out of doors, the child trembling all over, the man who seemed to have nothing in common with the imposing gentleman he remembered, and who now handed him much too generous a tip, and when he didn't want to take it compressed his lips and insisted.

That was how it began: it was the story of his love for the girl that the newcomer confided to you, and you listened to him as breathlessly as he himself told it, trying to picture him going down to the lake with Rachel day after day, as if those first hours of warm weather merely heralded another summer, as if the time they would have together were not finite from the first as her father waited for the affidavits which would get them to America, waited to hear the news that they might yet get away, that one of the people to whom he had written would stand surety for them, one of his acquaintances, or one of the strangers to whom he had turned, picking them out of some telephone book because they had the same surname and might be prepared to help. Apparently he had just three weeks with her, three weeks in which her father went back and forth between the post office and the inn, three weeks of swimming in icy water, three weeks of the most ridiculous hopes brushing aside the fear that it could all be over any time, sudden moments of exuberance as they lay on wooden loungers in the sun, as if she didn't know perfectly well that everyone around could positively scent the fact that she didn't belong there, and you drank in word after word, wishing he would never stop, would start the story all over again, telling you how he had kissed her, how he stroked back the wet hair from her face and she, laughing, tried to catch the drops with her eyes closed, he would express his wonder at the whiteness of her skin over and over again, sprinkled with freckles over the shoulders as it was, told you her word for them, fly-specks, and repeated that she was no longer a child. You would have liked to ask him not to stop, just go on and on talking, as if nothing was finally lost as long as he talked about her, as long as he remembered her, as if there were a chance that everything would turn out well as long as he withheld the end of the story, in which she was taken away on the very day her father was suddenly summoned to Vienna, as long as there was still a moment left before that time, and you knew why he clung to her photograph, why he hadn't allowed the man with the scar, for instance, to prop it on his easel and use it as a model for his drawings, let alone cracking jokes about it with the pale man, laughing, and perhaps infecting you with his laughter so that you would have joined in.

It was then that you told the newcomer about the housemaid, and you felt sure the whole camp was making its confessions, you had only to think of the professor, now out of solitary confinement again, you had only to remember how he had complained that his fiancée didn't write to him when mail was still allowed, how he had called her an ungrateful creature, living it up in London without a thought for him. There was no one who didn't have his own story, no one who hadn't been imagining what it would be like when he got out, as if his misfortunes began only with internment, and paradise was waiting outside, and you wondered if you were already as bad as the old boys who produced their wallets at every opportunity and handed round photographs of their loved ones, or the prisoners who had been married half a lifetime and were suddenly raving about their wives, grown women, as if they were young girls, with tears in their eyes and saying they weren't used to being alone so long, you wondered whether you were in as bad a way yourself, whether it was obvious how much you longed to spend a few hours away from male company, a few hours with Clara or indeed with any woman to escape the smell of the cage, even with the judge's wife, with her silent company in the darkened drawing-room of her house. The scope offered by the barbed wire enclosure was too restricted even for your daydreams, and while at first you had tried to stay in your room, at least on mild evenings, by now it usually was not long before you felt impelled to go out into the street, finding it impossible to resist joining the others and staring foolishly out to sea like a man in love, for everyone had someone he adored far, far, away, it was as if you were all tormented by the same frustrations as boarding-school boys waiting for the weekend to come so that they could see their girlfriends.

Tedious days followed when it was sunny from morning to night, and then suddenly the street was wet and as if in consequence a shower would fall, and you wished for nothing more than a storm to whip up the waves breaking on the beach, throwing sea spray over the promenade, swallowing the cries of the gulls that echoed through boundless space. The morning after your interrogation, more internees had moved into the camp next to yours, and you and the others had watched the silent column filing past the barbed wire, no singing now, as when you yourselves arrived, only the footsteps and your absurd idea that if all the troops marching on the Continent happened to fall into step at the same moment the world might be thrown out of its orbit, while the elderly gentleman marching in front of the party with his gas mask strapped to him as instructed, wearing corduroy riding breeches and gaiters, reminded you of your school headmaster in Vienna. After that the windows of the buildings were numbered, to make it easier to identify anyone who contravened the blackout regulations, and that same afternoon the first parcels from aid organisations were handed out – children's clothes, books from Brazil in Portuguese, which nobody understood – and then everyone was talking about the escape, the man more than 50 years old who had disappeared overnight was the sole subject of conversation, a Frankfurt banker who had apparently been interned on the island in the last war too, and you wondered where he could go, tried to imagine him wandering about until, after 48 hours of liberty, he finally appeared at the gates in tears, and asked the surprised guards who were about to send him away to let him in.

In the midst of this excitement came the announcement you had been expecting, a call for people who would like to leave the island, and all of three dozen men volunteered at once, even though they were not told where they would be going, men who believed the promises that in any case they would not end up behind barbed wire, would be free and could be joined by their wives, 36 men out of 2,000 swallowed the bait, no more, but that hardly surprised you. It was said that one ship had already left Liverpool with prisoners from England, and others would follow over the next few weeks, but obviously any idea that the camps on the island would be among the first of the bombers' targets, excessive as they had seemed to you, was now forgotten, far greater was fear of the dangers of the sea voyage, of mined waters, the uncertainty of being shipped off to somewhere or other unknown, a place from which there would be no getting away in a hurry, the talk of exile had done its part, and when the request was repeated at roll-call next day no one else at all put up his hand. It was impossible for you even to consider it, and you reacted with the same horror as most of the rest to the news that further choices would be made arbitrarily, some system of selection would be found, or alternatively men would be picked at random to go whether they wanted or not, and the word "quotas" went through your head for hours afterwards.

This was the state of affairs on that last morning, and now here you were, risking being sent away instead of someone else, sitting and watching the newcomer shuffle the cards again, mixing the two halves of the pack when he had dampened his fingers once more, placing them on the suitcases, interleaving them and suddenly letting them drop, you sat there and thought how his name had been read out at roll-call and he was told he had been picked, he would be going next day, and it seemed to you like some kind of farce. At first he was the sole selection, although there were a few more men on the list by evening, and you could only suppose that this was the major's doing, it couldn't be just chance, the major must be behind it, since no one else had been told to get ready to leave, but you felt no sympathy with him, you kept your eye on his hands and didn't stop to wonder whether it was your fault, your clumsiness during the interrogation, your obstinacy that had brought this on him, whether you should blame yourself for the fact that he, or someone else in his place, might be on a ship making for some unknown destination by mid-day at the latest. You wondered where the money came from, why his cash hadn't been taken from him as it was from everyone else, but since the pale man and the man with the scar didn't ask, you accepted his explanation that it was his emergency reserve, and just looked at the three piles of banknotes lying on the bed beside him.

It became even quieter than before when he rose, pushed up the window and then sat down again, with no sound but the footsteps of the guards outside, the cry of gulls reinforcing the silence, the wind over the sea, the sun that must be about to rise at any moment, and then perhaps it would be an hour and a half until reveille, until the noise began in the corridors, the banging of doors as the first men gathered outside the bathroom and the lavatories, and he said,

–Hard to believe there's a war on,

and the man with the scar replied,

–Go on, deal, or we'll still be sitting here tomorrow,

and the pale man, who had reached out for the cards so that his shirt cuffs shot up to his elbows, agreed,

–Yes, go on, deal,

and he repeated yet again,

–I hope the stakes are clear, gentlemen. The loser goes. The others share the three hundred pounds,

and they said together,

–Oh, deal the cards and stop talking,

and he did it, pressed them into your fingers and put his own on his lap, and you knew that this was your last chance to back out if you were going to, because the moment you had looked at your hand then whatever you did, even if you said you felt ill, pleading a headache or something of that sort, they would make you play at least one round.

The newcomer patted his pockets in search of cigarettes and when he had found a battered packet somewhere asked you for a light, and after he had offered it to the other two and they helped themselves, you knew for sure that they would band together against you, and the pale man said,

–I could swear it was the tribunals tipped the scale, decided who was picked and who wasn't,

and the man with the scar immediately took up the theme, not surprisingly because those two had been interned without going through any of the procedure, straight from the ship which fished them out of the water as they tried to escape,

   –Of course it was the tribunals,

   and the pale man didn't have to say whom he meant when he pointed out,

   –Whereas you're in Category One,

   and there was a coughing, a stammering and stuttering,

   –Yes, but by God, there are others in it too, you know, and say what you like no one can rely on the tribunals,

   and you remembered how they had tried to cheer him up, saying he couldn't be the only one to be sent away, there were bound to be some picked ahead of him, the men from the Brown House, or anyone who still had a skeleton in the cupboard from his past life, and sure enough, together with the constantly complaining professor and the poor fellow who had made himself conspicuous by escaping, it was the most dubious characters in the whole camp who were summoned to present themselves with their luggage next morning, among them the brewery rep and the merchant seamen with their captain.

   Of course no one had to tell you how wrong-headed the classification often was, or how the category in which someone found himself frequently depended on minor details. Quite apart from your own experience, you knew men who had come to grief in answering the question of whether they could envisage becoming British citizens, because there really was no right answer to it, while others had been asked what they would do if they were blackmailed with threats to the lives of their parents at home in Germany, with a risk to the safety of their loved ones who hadn't managed to get away, in the circumstances might they not be prepared to betray their new homeland and, however they tried to wriggle out of this dilemma, they were either a danger to the country or cowards ready to disown their origins. The game of postal chess one man had been playing with a friend in Paris was his downfall because it was mistaken for a secret code; another fell foul of the habits of his two-timing girlfriend, a lady of easy virtue on whose ill-gotten gains he was accused of living; while a third had made the mistake of loitering outside the ministries in Whitehall gaping at the windows in the blank façades, and you knew that any rumour of being a Commie was more than sufficient to damn somebody in the eyes of the judges, however persistently he might point out that he was already in the Resistance at a time when no one in London was even aware of the disaster approaching the world.

–They were real witch-hunts, said the newcomer, as if he had to justify himself, and all the top brass wanted was to cast suspicion on as many people as possible, so that no one will object to seeing them locked up,

and the man with the scar replied, dryly,

–According to them we're all spies,

and the pale man agreed,

–Saboteurs and spies, only there's nothing to keep an eye on in this bloody island, nothing worth blowing up except a bunch of dirty sheep,

and you thought of the sudden flashing from the lighthouse the previous night, which you had taken for an attempt at intimidation, the beam of radiance quivering over the water, and then it was dark again, not a light anywhere, not even along the bay, although no one in the town took the blackout too seriously, and you had stood beside the others at the window, all of you interrupting your game to look out, you stood there waiting for the release of their laughter, which was much too loud when it came.

Then of course they had begun talking about the U-boats again, not a morning passed now when someone didn't claim to have spotted one and was asked how many shots of potato spirit he'd drunk, or was he a case for the men in white coats already, and you knew it was because during these two weeks on the island they had become accustomed to relating everything outside the camp to themselves, dismissing any objections of yours with a lofty wave of the hand and ignoring your occasional pitying smile. They thought it was no coincidence when clouds of smoke rose into the sky at the southern end of the bay on two consecutive days, and as soon as an aircraft appeared overhead it was an enemy bomber, despite the absence of any warning, until they could finally see the marks on the wings, when they grabbed your arms, babbling excitedly. A convoy of army trucks driving past the barbed wire was enough to silence them, and you remembered afterwards how their voices had broken, pregnant with foreboding, wondering how many men each could take as its payload, as if you were all going to be taken away. The pale man was still compiling his tidal calendar and had got past the first half of the cycle, from which point on the times would repeat themselves with a shift of a few minutes a day, and the man with the scar claimed that his ridiculous art-work had won him a commission to paint the commandant's daughter, but otherwise they did nothing much, just sat beside you in the sun and cracked jokes about the few determined souls who had set to work again with desperate patience, weaving baskets, carving chessmen or launching model ships in bottles.

You saw the other two arranging their cards and passing each other information about them, winking, exchanging gentle kicks and, just as you were about to come to some agreement with the newcomer, the pale man began again,

−I suppose it's that girl of yours,

and he said,

−No,

and the man with the scar said,

–Come on, it's because of her you don't want to go,

and he repeated,

–No,

and the man with the scar insisted,

–You'd go if you could take her with you,

and he said nothing, just as he never did say anything when they probed him on the subject, he clutched his cards in both hands and sought your gaze, as if their idle talk had nothing to do with him, while you remembered Clara saying she was at the end of her tether, standing by the window in your room in the judge's house, and suddenly suggesting not running away but putting an end to everything when they came, because then there would be nowhere in the world for the two of you to go.

You knew what the newcomer might have told them, it was still ringing in your ears, for he had said it to you at noon that very day,

–I love her,

and he had sat down beside you on the steps outside your building and told you the story of the girl for the hundredth time, as if he had nothing else on his mind the day before he was to be deported from the island to somewhere unknown,

–I love her,

again and again,

–I love her,

and he had started on once more about the morning when she was taken away, her father had set off for the station just half an hour earlier and suddenly two uniformed men came to the door, his mother opened it while he was making breakfast in the kitchen, and there they stood as if with something particular in mind, and he didn't have to repeat it, he'd told you so often before, they were local men, he knew them, and yet there was nothing he could do.

You looked at your hand and heard the pale man bidding the

suit, relished by the man with the scar, who welcomed it with an exaggerated sound of pleasure, you heard the newcomer announcing trumps, his glance no longer on you, and tried to imagine the uniformed men, hesitant at first in front of his mother, then rendered speechless when his father joined them. Without attending to the cards you were playing, you remembered how he had told you, yet again, that the bluff had worked, they had been about to leave when the girl appeared on the stairs, they'd been on the point of going away when Rachel suddenly materialised, standing there with her suitcase as if she had been waiting all this time, had come step by step downstairs in her overcoat, although it looked like being a fine day. Apparently she was wearing a dirndl skirt under the coat, a point he kept emphasising as if it were important to him, and the end of the story still rang in your ears: she had simply embraced him wordlessly in front of them when he tried to stop her, she had pressed her photograph into his hand, and then she went out with them and never once looked round.

Rachel's father had not come back again, and he himself was in England a week later, said the newcomer, and you were sorry you hadn't asked him more questions about that, merely listening when he told you his parents had wanted to get him out of the country. He spoke quietly when he blamed himself once again for agreeing to get away fast and not come back until no one local connected him with the girl any more, and you thought of his assurances that he had heard nothing of her since then, he had no idea what had become of her. Suddenly you felt nauseated by his self-pity, the histrionic manner in which he spoke of her, and you thought of asking him why he didn't go after her, why he hadn't held on to her, why did he leave so meekly if, as he claimed, he couldn't live without her.

Then, for a while, there was just the sound of the cards being put down, until the man with the scar mentioned the girl again, recommending,

–Better forget her,

and the pale man, having relit his cigarette, which had gone out, and blowing smoke rings in an apparently casual manner, said,

–You can't lose your mind over her, you know,

and the man with the scar replied,

–She'll have found someone else long ago by the time you get home,

and repeated,

–Better forget her,

and you didn't know if this was some kind of macabre joke they were having with him, or if he hadn't told them of her fate and they really had no idea what they were doing, and you were glad when they stopped it and concentrated on the game again.

And these two, of all people, hadn't been ashamed to compare the outlines of the island with a woman's body when the first hills came into sight on your arrival, and you suddenly heard their voices again as they slipped into bed at dawn, after the card games you had all been playing over the last few days, you sensed the newcomer on the floor listening as your own breathing grew louder the more you tried not to make any sound, and remembered how the pale man whispered,

–They'll hear us,

and the man with the scar, after a considerable pause during which you had strained your eyes in vain peering in their direction, replied in a hoarse voice,

–They're asleep,

and the pale man said,

–Listen,

and the man with the scar repeated,

–Really, they're asleep,

and the pale man said,

–They'll hear us,

and then there was just the silence, the rustle of their bedclothes, their muffled groaning into their pillows, and you told yourself that from far enough away, all islands looked like recumbent women if you were silly enough to make the comparison, all islands had breasts, prominent pelvic bones, knees crooked at an angle and long legs disappearing into the water in the dim light, with a dull glow lying like a thin film over them, making you want either to reach your journey's end or describe a wide detour around them.

The two of them had begun winding each other up again, accompanying each trick with the phrases you already knew – your turn to play, Jew; your turn now, Jew; wake up, Jew, they kept inciting one another – as you remembered how the newcomer had said his parents owed avoiding arrest to their good connections. At that point it had always seemed as if he wanted to say no more about it, and when you looked at him holding his cards in one hand, and reaching abstractedly out to the empty glasses with the other, what he had told you about the girl was very far away indeed, for he seemed to be moving in a different world. At least you no longer thought of his grief, so emotionally displayed and, when he suddenly started his conjuring tricks again as he shuffled the cards, making one disappear and producing it from his sleeve, he might have been out drinking with his fellow regulars somewhere at home but for the sense of grave concentration about him.

The sun rose, and you and he were losing when you turned and saw it emerge from the haze in the distance, seeming to quiver where it stood in the sky for a few seconds. It cast a pale orange light on the opposite wall, a light that looked as if it would change to blue at any moment, a light that made you tremble, and the tide was at its highest, the sea lay like armour, muttering with tension and rippling as it made for the horizon, where it began to flicker. Although white crests were visible it gave the impression of total immobility, and you sat rigid, nor did the other three seem to move; heavy with fatigue you stayed where you were, listening to the guards calling to each other, and then it was quiet again, with that silence which absorbed all sounds and always made you feel you had gone deaf.

A few moments went by, and none of you so much as coughed, until it was your turn to deal, and you scarcely heard the man with the scar loudly announcing the suit, and the pale man nudged you in the ribs and you had to repeat what trumps were and, although it had not previously troubled you that you knew scarcely anything about the two of them, only the few scraps of information they had let drop on the first day, it now seemed to you very curious. You could say of literally everyone else in the camp with whom you had exchanged only a couple of words where he came from, who his parents were, and you could at least give the names of the places where they had been before they landed here, and you recollected that these two had usually avoided questions about their past by indicating that it didn't matter, their real lives began with their flight across the Channel, what went before was of no importance, you thought of the insistence with which they had dwelt on that, and you played your cards like a child, putting them down unthinkingly on the suitcases, not even looking to see who took the trick. You had always supposed there was some catastrophe behind their silence, you had persuaded yourself they had their reasons for saying nothing, you had remembered your mother and her husband and asked no more questions, and only now did it occur to you that the situation might be completely different, perhaps they had something to hide and acted with such detachment only for their own protection, and you found yourself staring at them, studying their faces, grey in the light of dawn, as if this were the first time you had seen them.

One did not have to be excessively suspicious to wonder about their flight – apparently at the very last moment, as they assured anyone who asked – and of course they couldn't prove what they said. They might just as well have come up with something else, painting a dramatic picture of their fate, and if the fact that they did not had seemed to you particularly convincing, you now told yourself it might be simply a matter of arrogance, a sense of superiority which led them to believe they didn't need to say anything. At least, nothing would have been easier for them than to tell you some tall tale; the stories of other men here must equally often be invented, or the facts adjusted, no one could check on these narratives, but at least they were stories and the people who told them were genuine, not lifeless dummies, as these two suddenly appeared to you.

The major should have taken an interest in them rather than the newcomer, you told yourself as you listened to the guards calling to each other outside again, he ought to have asked you about them, not about this idiot who spilled out everything about himself, he ought not to have dismissed them if he really took the gossip about spies in the camp seriously. You suddenly felt you had been naïve to suppose, even for a moment, that he might have asked them the same questions as he asked you, and it struck you once again that perhaps the nub of the matter was not the newcomer after all, perhaps you had been summoned for interrogation so that you could be misled, and they had really been told to watch you and not him, perhaps they were informers infiltrated at an early stage by the top brass, spies passing information about you to the major. The two of them were playing as if they wanted

181

to get to the end of the card game as soon as possible, and you went cold at the idea that they could have arranged things with the newcomer, far-fetched as the notion might still seem to you, it took your breath away to think that the major hadn't been interested in the story of the photo, whereas he might be involved too, you were the only one left who believed he had no idea of it, and while they were wondering if they should go and wake the NCO who supplied liquor and see if he had another bottle of potato spirit for sale, you never took your eyes off him, you looked at him staring at his cards, then putting them down, wiping his hands on the bedspread, for they were obviously damp with sweat, and constantly casting surreptitious glances at his watch without once looking at you.

The pale man had picked up a cigarette stub from the floor, which the man with the scar lit for him, taking another himself, and it irritated you to watch them smoking, putting down their cards with narrowed eyes, fag ends in their mouths. It reminded you of the way, during afternoon exercise out of doors, they sometimes wore their hats at what you saw as slightly too jaunty an angle, it reminded you of their treatment of others, the lordly air they could assume as if they weren't refugees at all, but absent from home of their own free will, holidaymakers, who had nothing in common with the depressed figures in this place, cast up here merely by chance, and it was clear that you could expect nothing whatsoever of them, that their assurances of friendship were worthless, their repeated assertions that you should all help each other, no, in any doubtful situation you would be right out there on your own. They were not looking at you now either, and all you could do was ignore it when they began cracking jokes again, saying what a lovely day it was for a sea voyage, letting them talk, for you knew that every point you lost removed you further from them, making you a suspicious figure who was better avoided because he attracted bad luck, a man who had an unlucky aura and would never be rid of it whatever he did.

The game went on at an even pace until the first sounds were heard inside the building, but then the newcomer suddenly began bidding, thumping the suitcases with his fist so that the cards lying there jumped up in the air, and almost shouting,

–Three,

and they laughed,

–Did you say three?

and he repeated,

–Three, gentlemen,

and so did they,

–Three?

and he repeated,

–Three, go on, are you chicken?

and you heard, as if from a distance, their voices bidding against each other, pushing up the bids, until finally he picked up the piece of paper recording the score and counted, passing his forefinger over the careless scribbles, and said that was it.

Then there was silence for a moment, and without even looking at the cards in your hand you knew they didn't justify his bluster, and all at once you felt the warmth of the sun on your back and looked at the others one by one. Voices could be heard in the stairway, and you could not get it into your head that this would not be a day like all the rest, a day when they might let you all go down to the water again, you felt it was only a fantasy that you could be taken away for deportation in a few hours' time at the latest. It was the idea of the first people outside the camp already on their way to work which brought home to you the grotesque nature of your situation, the realisation that in spite of the war a perfectly normal life was going on in the town, a soothing repetition of routine procedures, as yet not influenced by the fighting on the Continent, a life gradually getting into the swing of a centuries-old rhythm, and you felt like throwing down the cards and putting a stop to the game, overriding the ridiculous rules that kept you sitting there, the code of conduct fixed as if carved in stone, laying down what a man must and must not do, you would have liked to stand up and walk out, go down for a cheerful chat with the guards, who were glad of any diversion after a night on duty. Obviously the barbed wire really was a magical boundary, and when you suddenly remembered the shots heard yesterday morning, shots in the camp or close by – no one knew why, but by evening there was a well-established rumour to the effect that one of the sergeants had been shooting seagulls, bringing down those creatures on whose wings the merchant seamen were said to have painted swastikas – when you thought of that, it was enough to remind you of the uselessness of believing anything at all.

Then everything happened very quickly, you played card after card, putting them down in the order in which you held them in your hand, and it was over, and the pale man couldn't refrain from saying,

–It was a pleasure,

and the man with the scar passed both hands through his hair, linked them at the back of his neck, and spread his elbows as far back as they would go,

–We might play again another time, gentlemen,

repeating,

–It was a pleasure,

and the pale man laughed,

–Canada or Australia?

to which the man with the scar said,

–There are worse places in the world,

and they fell silent, looking at one another over the suitcases and listening for the sound of footsteps from the corridor, the noise of men going upstairs and downstairs, all of a sudden as loud as if the whole building were up and about.

You were beginning to wonder if you had missed hearing reveille when it suddenly sounded, and you glanced at your watch, but it had stopped, its glass still clouded with the water that must have got into it while you were swimming, and the newcomer pressed the money into their hands without a word, a bundle of notes for each of them, and then turned to you,

–Ready?

and his voice had an uncomfortably familiar sound as he explained about turning up the aces again and repeated, unconcernedly,

–The loser goes,

and he expected no answer,

–Ready?

at which point you struck him in the chest,

–Do you have to say everything a hundred times?

and he restrained his laughter,

–I asked if you were ready,

and you watched him pick up the cards and begin to shuffle them again, fanning the pack out and mixing it, then knocking all four edges against the wooden panelling at the head of the bed, and finally placing it on the suitcases.

Provocatively, he took his time, although he must have made all these movements again and again before and performed them with startling virtuosity, he took his time before he asked you to turn over a card, and you did, trying to look him in the eye, and he did not avoid your gaze any more either, although it still seemed as if he didn't want to see you, as if something else a long way behind you had claimed his attention, and suddenly he was no longer the poor sod who poured out his heart to you, and the idea came into your head that the story of the girl might have been entirely invented to soften you up, he could have been playing on your sentimental feelings to make you agree to the game, and there was no Rachel, or if there was she had been taken away by the two uniformed men and disappeared without trace, while everything he had told you about his relationship with her was pure fantasy. It seemed hard to imagine anyone at all falling in love with him, given the way he sat there obviously just waiting for his moment to con you, and you wished you could have taken her retrospectively under your own wing, you wished you had warned him to be careful if he didn't want to have you to deal with, to keep his hands off her, not exploit her for his own purposes. Sometimes your mother's husband had used a word that suddenly came back to you, although it would never have entered your own head to describe someone as a goy, but he was, he was a goy and had no right to make a saint out of her, he was a goy and he would shame her memory with every word he spoke, it was your duty to defend yourself against him however many aces he turned up, or whatever else he did.

In the corridor outside all was briefly still, but next moment the noise began again, and it was clear to you that you couldn't count on anyone's noticing the switch of identity if you had to step forward in his place at roll-call. The process would certainly not take long, and as soon as they had the right number of men no one but the major would care whether he or you was really the one on his way to the boat and, as he picked up the remaining money and pushed it nearer you, you told yourself it mustn't come to that. You watched him closely, you wished you need not do anything, make any decision, you wished you could just sit there until the day was over, forget that such substitutions had often occurred and had passed unnoticed, wished you still hoped that someone would check carefully, examine every individual's identity closely at the camp gates before he stepped out with the others, particularly since one of the post-bags carrying the documentation relating to the internees had been lost on the crossing to the island, and the records were in a state of great confusion.

–Hanging about won't make it any better, you heard the pale man say, as if he was not talking to you, take a card and get it over with,

and the man with the scar, who had gone to the window and was looking out, did not even turn to you as he said, mockingly,

–Poor fellow, he's shitting himself,

and suddenly you were sure they were only decoys, designed to sweeten the trap for you, and you replied,

–Oh, take a card yourselves and shut up,

and you wondered why it had not occurred to you before, remembering the day back in the London school, that they had never since said another word about whether they really wanted to get away, nothing at all about wanting to sit out the war somewhere at the other end of the world, as they kept telling you at the time.

The two of them said nothing, nor did the newcomer, when there was a knock at the door and you saw the handle being pressed down. For a moment you contemplated speaking up, using the skeleton key the brewery rep had given you and your room-mates for a few cigarettes to let the unknown visitor in, and then the whole farcical performance would be over, but the opportunity passed, and you heard them all simultaneously sighing with relief. If it had not been clear enough already, you would surely have known then at the latest that you were intended to lose, they had probably worked it all out a long time ago and were just waiting until there was no turning back, and suddenly the gulls outside were

6
CLARA

The Imperial Hotel, where I had booked a room for my first two nights when I arrived in Douglas, is on the Central Promenade in the middle of the bay, and although he never mentions it by name there are several indications in Hirschfelder's diary that it must have been part of the camp where he was interned. From his description, it could only be the blocks of buildings here, most of them still hotels and boarding houses, their signboards desperately competing with each other, while Castle Mona, over to one side and vainly trying to keep its distance, was obviously the grandiose complex of which he speaks more than once, while on the other I did indeed find a building faced with white tiles, no longer a cinema but a leisure centre, if that is the word for it, with a ground floor containing the inevitable games machines and a gym upstairs. Beyond it I saw no monstrous dance-hall, to use his own term, but whatever once stood there had undoubtedly given its name to the oblong structure of the Palace: a forbidding construction of the Sixties or Seventies combining the functions of hotel and casino, which emerged fully illuminated from the darkness.

It was almost midnight when I arrived, and I did not see the repairs to the tarmac in front of the hotel until next morning, when the landlady pointed them out to me, darker areas in the otherwise light-coloured surface every few feet where the posts for the barbed wire fence had once stood, small squares still visible after more than 50 years, between the lines for the horse-drawn tram running along the bay. Over breakfast I had told her why I was visiting Douglas, and she showed me where the camp boundaries had been, her arm outstretched as she stood with me at the top of the steps outside pointing up and down the promenade, which was deserted apart from a few people out walking, while the members of a travel group, all of them elderly and the only guests except for me, disappeared behind the condensation on the windows of a coach waiting for them in front of the building. I am not sure what made me say so, but I told her that my father, who in fact was only just born at the time, had been interned on the island, thus at least avoiding the need for lengthy explanations and, feeling that I had won her confidence, I listened to her reminiscences: during her war-time schooldays, she told me that she and her girlfriends would often see how close they could get when the prisoners went down to the beach to swim.

"You've no idea how the sight of them disappointed us," she said, laughing. "We'd expected something quite different."

I was glad she didn't stop to ask more about my father, as I had feared she might, and obliged her by asking what she meant, although her answer was disconcerting.

"Oh, we thought they'd be real monsters."

I was surprised by her irony, and followed her glance out to sea until she turned to me again, eyes wide, as if to make sure I was still there.

"I mean, they were Germans," she went on. "After all we'd been told about them at home we were really surprised to see such ordinary-looking people."

The wind had blown her hair about, and she ran her hands

through it as she told me that many of them came back to visit the island after the war. I wondered if she wasn't exaggerating when she assured me that she had never left it herself except for an occasional day in Liverpool. Some men, she said, turned up almost every year – she obviously couldn't understand why – the last of them this very spring, and they must have been something of a nuisance to her with their requests to see their old rooms again, and the way they tiptoed about as if the floorboards burnt for fuel at the time had not been replaced long ago, and they still had to be careful where they put their feet. I had the impression that she thought this behaviour rather odd. Apparently there was an internment camp on this part of the promenade for just under ten months and, after that, the hotels and boarding houses had troops billeted in them, but she acted as if the smell of the prisoners had clung to the place ever since, revived again and again, and you felt she wanted to blame them for everything that had gone wrong in her life, for the way her seasonal business went from bad to worse, for the frailties of old age, for her husband's early death which left her to face her own inevitable decline alone.

"There was no point in it, that's why I didn't like them visiting," she said, to all appearances unaware of the emotion with which she spoke. "It's not as if anyone can get the past back again."

She had taken a rubber band from her apron pocket and was holding it between her lips, so that only a mumble emerged as her hands continued fiddling with her hair, and she never took her eyes off me.

"Did you say your father was here?"

By now I wasn't expecting the question, and I could only repeat the remark I had made on impulse, although of course I guessed I was only getting myself into further difficulty, so predictable did her reaction seem to me.

"Jewish, was he?"

Before I said no, I knew what that would imply, I had only to look at her gaze – but there were no two ways about it, either he was or he wasn't, and saying no left me little room to manoeuvre.

"Not Jewish?"

"That's right."

"Then I'd like to know what brought him here if he wasn't," she said, her tone noticeably colder now. "I mean, what was he, then?"

This seemed to confirm my own reservations – had I, perhaps, formed an entirely erroneous idea of Hirschfelder's internment? It was not by chance that the night before, when I had found sleeping difficult, I had leafed through his diary, getting out of bed several times and going to the window to look out. As I did so I had asked myself once more what it was about his story that really intrigued me, and yet again I could find no better explanation than Max's enthusiasm; I had stared out into the darkness, up and down the promenade, at the tramlines gleaming in the moonlight, and recoiled from the idea of facing this view daily, as he did, the regular ebb and flow of the tide, the water in the basin of the bay rising and falling lazily, inexorably, like a mighty hourglass, the constant backward and forward movement bearing away time, which only appears to stand still, in sections of a few hours. Once the festoons of lights had been switched off and there were no more cars about I might as well have been on a gigantic aircraft carrier, so empty was the deserted street, with no trees in sight, and when I finally did nod off, to be woken by the scream of the gulls when it grew light, I immediately found myself remembering his description of the sea, how it was sometimes a dazzling white at this time of day, a virginal surface beneath the heights of the sky, making him feel exposed, and it seemed wrong for me to be here, if only because I could leave at any time, which made it presumptuous of me to believe I could even begin to imagine what it was like for him, and in fact one of the first ideas to come into my head was that I should get on the next ferry and leave the island.

What brought me to that point I didn't know, but it was certainly not the sanctimonious attitude of a Viennese historian, allegedly an expert on exiles but in fact an arrogant know-all, whom I met a few weeks later after a lecture about the author Katz and her life in England, it was not the supercilious horror of his reaction when I told him I had been to the Isle of Man and stayed in a hotel that was once part of an internment camp, at which he took positively ludicrous offence, as if my mere presence there was a desecration – no, it was something to do with the magic of the place, or rather with the total absence of it, since a kind of vacuum formed as soon as I stayed still for just a couple of moments.

To this day I find it uncomfortable to remember that scene in an inner city pub where he was well known, when he lowered his voice rather than raising it to reprimand me, although he was still looking at the rest of the company round our table and angling for effect.

"You say you've been to the Isle of Man?"

I simply nodded, and he informed me that he had published several papers about the camps on that island, asking if I had read them, and when I said no he examined me with his head tilted to one side, as if I couldn't mean it.

"I know my way around the place better than my own home," he said, leaning forward, and I could smell his sour breath. "So why do you think I've never been there?"

His reproach lay in the silence following this remark, to which of course I gave no answer, nor was he expecting one, but I was surprised that he didn't expatiate further on my crime, instead merely casting triumphant glances around him.

Since then I have tried to read his papers, but I always gave up after a few pages, so severely is his view obstructed by the close attention he pays to every little scrap and crumb of information gleaned from various archives, and I don't know whether to wish he would visit the place as soon as possible and get at least some idea of what the island is like, or hope that its people are spared his turning up to tell them what they ought or ought not to do, or alternatively reproving them by his silence for being real people with real lives, not just figures he can push about as he likes.

At the time, however, that morning when I made my first visit to the cemetery on the outskirts of the town, which lies above the terraces of houses so that you can look over their rooftops and see the sea, I once again had the vague feeling of something missing, perhaps the firm ground on which one can usually rely and which suddenly was not underfoot, and the memory still makes me uneasy, although it was months ago. There are 18 graves of internees in the Jewish section of the cemetery, a small separate area beside a row of military graves from both World Wars, as well as the tombstones of two ladies who died aged 85, with inscriptions stressing the fact that they were virgins or at least spinsters, and the last resting places of two unknown foundling infants, and I remember looking for additional information on the plain stones bearing the Star of David, but in vain, since with one exception they gave only the name, date of death, and occasionally the dead person's age. You had to piece together the stories behind these few facts for yourself, and I don't know why I wrote them in my notebook, where the ink has smeared, making it difficult to read them now, but whenever I leaf through it they catch my eye, and the gaps in their history sometimes strike me as retrospective justification when I wonder why I ever began investigating Hirschfelder's life.

I did not see the hotel landlady again after our conversation that morning, and it was only when I moved to a boarding house he stood in the doorway pretending to be busy, but really eager to strike up a conversation. He obviously put on this show for the benefit of his wife, who clattered about in the background, casting a glance through the serving hatch now and then, and finally pushed open the swing doors and placed the obligatory plate of scrambled egg and bacon in front of me without a word, but once he had begun to answer my questions he seemed to think he should carry on, letting her outbursts of annoyance wash over him and simply laughing when she sent him out on some errand, either to keep him active or to prevent him from showing off to me.

It was not until after the war that the two of them had come to the island, where they first rented and then bought their boarding house in the late Fifties, early Sixties, at a time when other people might have wondered if it was a wise move, but still, it was the time in which they too lived, and probably, as I realised on my first walks round the town, Douglas was then only just past its prime as a leading holiday resort, popular with the industrial workers of the north of England. Later I never managed to think of them, a couple who seemed as if they had been elderly even when young, without simultaneously remembering the plaster peeling from the façades of buildings all along the front, the empty shops with builders' cranes standing beside them ready to put up new office blocks, the display windows stuck up with brown paper and the empty cartons. When I saw them, husband and wife, he with his thumbs hooked behind the inevitable braces, she always in an apron, reminding me of Max's mother shovelling away the snow in front of her house in her long-dead husband's old anorak and boots, which were much too big for her, I couldn't help reflecting that they were left over from the days when people expected the town to offer bandstand concerts, round trips by boat with wind music accompaniment, a camera obscura and almost daily amphitheatre shows, not to mention daring bathing beauty or beauty queen contests. Their only other lodger was an elderly gentleman, and neither the trill of their morning greetings nor his own stiff Good Morning can have changed much over the years, an expression of hope springing eternal on the slightest incentive, hope that life might go back to what it had once been and, thinking of them, I always remembered the great enthusiasm with which they told me about the high point of the season, the annual motorbike races in May, the famous or perhaps notorious Tourist Trophy, when it seemed there wasn't a bed to be had in the place for two whole weeks, an idea that called to mind images of rowdy drunks still half-clad in their leather gear, grunting and snoring as they fell into a restless sleep in my girlish room with its pink carpet and pink flowered wallpaper.

To me there was something extremely desolate but at the same time attractive about such seaside resorts, all alike steadily declining over the years, and they reminded me of Hirschfelder's Southend-on-Sea with its inhabitants, who might have been sidelined from life, and the carefully hoarded moments of happiness that made them so similar, they all seemed to be lying athwart the current of time, discomposed by the whirlpool thus engendered, and Douglas was no exception. Or anyway it contained the same old ladies sitting idle behind panoramic windows in their little terraced houses, gazing at the waves as if waiting for the dead to come home to tea, the same exotic creatures in their flowered Sunday dresses looking at me as I passed and, if one were to believe the posters, posters faded after only a few days and inviting audiences to attend events in the distant past or perhaps never held at all, *La Bohème* at the Gaiety Theatre and Opera House, and a Viennese Evening, of all things, at the Villa Marina, we could have been back before the war. The idea made me imagine that the façades of the houses had not been colour-washed until later, and I was on the artificial set of a film planned long ago but never made, co-starring my land-lords, a couple who in all seriousness spoke of each other as Mr and Mrs Stewart, he assiduously referring to her thus as if he were her servant, and she to him as if to restore the sense of respect for him which, in her opinion, I must have lost because he was so ready to be at my disposal for hours on end.

"Don't believe everything he tells you," she had said to me directly after our first conversation. "Whatever can he have to talk to you about all the time?"

I don't remember now what I replied, but no doubt it was some-thing evasive, and I was glad she asked no more questions, because I was scarcely sure what to think of him myself, and could only wonder how he knew the camps in such detail when he had not been on the island during the war.

Nor did he really answer when I asked him.

"Oh, you can read all about it, and I have to occupy myself somehow," he said. "Try spending an autumn and winter here, and you'll know what it's like to have time on your hands."

On this occasion I had already told him about Hirschfelder, and I don't know why, but I also mentioned the suspicion of murder which had been the starting point of my search, although I had doubted for quite some time whether there was anything in it, so I was surprised to hear him say that it wasn't such an outlandish notion, there had often been brawling among the prisoners and once a man was killed, although it was at a camp in Ramsey, a few kilometres further to the north of the island.

"A Finn, if I remember rightly, but later in the war," he said. "They found him with a knife in his chest and blamed it on one of his countrymen."

It was not this which sent me straight to the cemetery, but once there I did find myself looking for the name of Harrasser and, although it had nothing to do with Hirschfelder, I pricked up my ears when Mr Stewart added that this was the only such case of murder known to him and, so far as he was aware, all the internees buried in the town had either died a natural death or committed suicide.

"And as for that affair, I don't know if anyone was ever tried for it, but it must have been one of the usual disputes between those who sympathised with the Nazis and those who didn't."

This came out so suddenly that I did not succeed in hiding my amazement from him, and he looked surprised by my naïveté.

"Did you think they were all saints in the camps, then?"

I heard his hoarse laughter for the first time.

"Oh no, right from the start there were people of various shades of opinion there," he went on. "Anyone who had German connections at all could be arrested and, what with the panic in London when the invasion was expected daily, they weren't taking too much trouble about who shared quarters with whom."

I looked at him and said nothing, while he thought it over, a touch of mischief in his eyes which I hadn't noticed before, not dismissive, not mocking, but knowing, so to speak, as if suggesting that it was only to be expected.

"Well, no point in rehashing all those old wives' tales about spies," he finally began again. "They were scare-stories blown up out of all proportion as it turned out, but who was to know that at the time?"

I couldn't help thinking of Max, who would certainly have been amused by my strong feelings, when I said that it must have been very humiliating for the refugees to be suddenly regarded as enemies.

"They surely can't have been shut up with the swine who would have been baying for their blood at home."

"You've no idea," Mr Stewart replied. "As far as I know nobody drew any distinction, and it was only later they began separating one lot from the others."

"You mean they were treated just the same?"

"Probably worse if anything," he said. "It seems that many of them weren't too popular with the guards."

This was the first I had heard of it; neither Margaret nor Catherine had said anything about the existence of different categories of internees, and I still wonder why Hirschfelder's diary gives not the slightest indication of it, as little as it does – of course – of any murder, not the faintest suggestion that there was constant quarrelling among them. Here and there he mentions ordinary misunderstandings, minor matters, disputes arising from boredom, or because one man had taken something from another or failed to give it back, and it was only months later that I heard of the Brown House, ridiculous as the term sounded to me, like some trite invention, in fact I didn't know about it until I was back in Vienna and found that Madeleine was at last prepared to meet me. She spoke of it in matter-of-fact tones, and gave me some idea of the interrogation for which it was obviously the reason, before the card game and the departure of the ships taking deportees to Canada or Australia, since he had not written a word about it at the time. In fact there are some very strange gaps in his own account, for he never once mentions Harrasser, the fourth man, he does not speak of him anywhere at all and, if I were going on this alone, I would have assumed that he had never shared the room with anyone but Lomnitz and Ossovsky, whom he discusses at length, the pale man and the man with the scar, as he calls them, but despite their regular appearance they remain indistinct figures.

It is the omissions, the balance between what he says and what he leaves unsaid, that make Hirschfelder's diary so interesting, and

I remember clearly how surprised I was, when I first looked through it, to find nothing at all about Clara. From all Catherine had told me he must have been thinking of her day and night, and I thought that he might perhaps have destroyed the passages about her later, he might have found it uncomfortable to read of his longing for her in the years that followed. There was no other way of accounting for her complete absence which made any sense, nor could I understand how he often enumerates the tiniest insignificant details, but in all that time he never seems to have remembered the judge's house, and I could make even less sense of it because I was increasingly inclined to idealise my own idea of the situation and turn his love for her into a grand passion.

Catherine herself, however, does appear; he refers several times to his getting to know her, and then notes, usually very briefly, whether there was a letter from her in the mail, or more often says, in tones of surprise rather than complaint, how long it has been since he heard from her, and he mentions the parcel she sent him, adding that she "seems to think I'm at the front", with no further explanation, although I imagine he is referring to its contents. But there are no heartfelt outpourings, on the contrary, the passages about her sound quite down to earth, as if he were not particularly interested in her, he does not seem to have been worried about her and, if I am not to take him for a monster, I have to keep reminding myself that back in London she told me he had written her letters every other week throughout that period. All the more surprising, in view of his distinct lack of attachment to her, is his long account of the first reunion between the women from the camp in the south of the island and their husbands in Douglas. It obviously took place some time after the first few weeks of internment, at the Derby Castle, the old Palais de Danse at the northern end of the bay: a showy building of which nothing now is left. Also remarkable is the way he dwells on subsequent meetings in following months, return visits, trips to Port Erin by a few specially selected prisoners, sent out first, with a few guards in attendance, to pick flowers in the countryside, then making in military formation for the coaches waiting outside the gate and, when I try to imagine him standing there, watching them go, and the men left behind shouting goodbyes, his picture blurs before my eyes yet again.

These meetings, obviously part of the accepted legend of life behind barbed wire and thrown out as a sop to satisfy the curious, were also the favourite subject of Leo, a former internee with whom Mr Stewart had put me in touch. He was from Mecklenburg and, like Clara, he had stayed on the island after the war. I met him, at his own suggestion, in the Sefton Hotel, which together with Castle Mona was the most elegant building still standing on the promenade. He was already sitting in the bay of one of the first-floor windows when I arrived, the sea shining in the sun behind him, and I felt a curious effect of reversal: paradoxically, the fact that he was the first person I had met to have experienced life in one of the camps at first hand made him seem unreal to me. Without realising it, I must have been expecting someone different, not this rather awkward, shrunken old man on whom his black suit looked like a pair of pyjamas and who was staring past me, but, judging by what I had been told, a more sociable character, for he was said to be so keen to meet fellow countrymen that he would positively lie in wait for holidaymakers in summer just to exchange a few words of German with them and, in the motorcycle racing season, he would often drive his platform truck down to the town from his hill farm every day and drink himself half insensible if he found some good-humoured visitor to whom he could pour out his sentimental reminiscences.

He probably meant to be gallant, but I scarcely knew where to look when, as soon as we had exchanged greetings, he began paying me the kind of compliments I would have thought more typical of a nineteenth-century Viennese dancing master.

"I can't get my head around your interest in the camps," he said, when he had to some extent calmed down again. "No subject for a lady like you, if you ask me."

He leaned forward in his chair, his tie hanging almost down to the floor between his legs, and I saw his naked skull through his hair, which was combed over it in damp strands. Glass in hand, he stared at me, one eye fixed and the other apparently out of control – a man like that, I thought, would probably have worn a monocle in the past – and when his smile grew even broader I suddenly forgot exactly what I had wanted to ask him. But he went on talking anyway, and I sank as far back as possible into the upholstery of my chair to keep him from coming any closer to me, and watched him, amused by the efforts he made not to gesticulate as he told me about the first time the women arrived.

I don't know why, but his opening remark has stuck in my mind like a story in itself, needing no sequel, although he immediately added one.

"It was a wonderful summer's day, and we stood behind the barbed wire watching as they were led down the promenade," he said. "From a distance they might have been just apparitions, and anyone could see at first glance that they didn't belong here."

He looked out of the window, and of course he closed his eyes as if to visualise them hurrying past outside, a whole procession of them accompanied only by two guards with fixed bayonets, watching to make sure no one broke rank and, when he had turned to me again, I was prepared for something extravagant, and felt sorry I hadn't interrupted him.

"In all these years I have never forgotten that picture," he went on. "I can see it as if it were only yesterday."

That was just the start, but in the course of our conversation he kept returning to it, and if I thought he would perhaps try to give me an idea of the loneliness and boredom of camp life from his own point of view, of the desolation concealed behind the ecstasies into which he fell, would say he had been afraid, then I was wrong, for he inevitably came back to the subject, regaling me with anecdotes sometimes of a melancholy and sometimes of an unintentionally salacious nature, about the women who later quite often came over from the mainland too, taking rooms in one of the nearby boarding houses which had not been requisitioned, and he told amazing tales about men who, it was said, had risked life and limb by climbing over the barbed wire to spend a night with them.

And from time to time he repeated the same remark, apparently intending a witticism that was all the more certain to fail.

"Oh, I could tell you a thing or two."

Then he looked at me and, hoping to stem the flow, I kept asking him to do so, but he would smile and lapse into his former vein.

"The women, ah, the women," he said. "Why, if I were to tell you all I know you'd scarcely believe me."

I wondered why, after all his elaborate compliments, he was now speaking to me as if I were his boon companion, and only later did I realise that there was nothing behind it but a desire to stick to some kind of authorised version of events. To ensure that he did not have to say anything that might touch upon himself, he seemed to have prepared an account of a few recurrent episodes until in the end he believed they were all there was to it and, by way of comparison, I could think only of those callow youths who remember their military service as one long succession of drinking bouts.

Internment as he described it had the character of a weekend at a country boarding school, so of course there was an element of the forbidden about it, and the allegedly forbidden was what he was offering me.

This in fact matched the picture I had built up from accounts of the time, from the newspaper cuttings I ordered next day in the museum library, and indeed confirmed the idea that Catherine had given me of her friends' prejudices when Hirschfelder came back to London. Some of the reports in the Press were not far short of witch-hunting, and I read articles commenting on the luxury in which the internees lived, while England had been suffering heavy bombardment for months, saying they ought to be grateful to be safe in one of the loveliest parts of the country away from all danger, away from the crowds gathering outside the air-raid shelters. Once again the women featured prominently, probably because the reporters were allowed to seek them out and because, unlike the men, they were staying with local people and lived – though behind barbed wire – in other respects almost as if it were peacetime, and when there was talk of well-nourished, healthy females making themselves at home on the island with their bathing suits and tennis rackets, some of them even swimming naked in the sea until autumn came, when it was said that they wore trousers like men and spent their money freely, buying up the stocks of the shops in Port Erin and Port St Mary, I could imagine the attitudes behind such stories.

It may well be that Leo had read such accounts himself, for by the time they appeared newspapers were allowed in all the camps, and he seems to have been echoing them when I remember his saying that locked up or not, he wanted for nothing at the time, and in some ways they were the happiest months of his life. After that he carried on in full flow for some time, uttering clichés about camaraderie among the internees of a kind he had never known since, and I recollect his coming out, rather hesitantly, with the information that it was at harvest-time on the farm he now owned that he had met his future wife. He seemed to feel uncomfortable talking about it, he turned the palms of his hands up as if in apology, and I am sure he was relieved when I looked out of the window in silence, as if I had seen something outside to attract my attention.

I did not ask Leo about Hirschfelder, although after the camp on the Central Promenade was closed they must have spent more than two months at the same detention centre in Hutchinson Square, the only one in Douglas not on the waterfront. I probably wouldn't have believed him even if he had said he did know him, and I don't regret my reserve. In fact I would have thought it odd if he had remembered him, so what he said when I asked him about the disputes Mr Stewart had mentioned to me was the sole useful outcome of my meeting with him.

It was the term "Nazi sympathisers" on which he fastened, as if this was the first time he had heard it, and I knew I couldn't believe him when he denied their existence, saying there had been no one in the camp whom that description really fitted.

"No, the problem was the Communists getting mixed up in everything, same as ever," he said. "Almost every NCO was a Party member."

We had stepped out of doors, and suddenly he really did begin gesticulating, and spoke in a changed voice when he told me about secret meetings in the laundry room of one of the buildings, to which only a handful of initiates were admitted.

"Of course everyone knew about it, but as long as Uncle Joe was still on the wrong side they had to mind they didn't show what they were too openly."

I had repeated it before I understood who he meant, and next moment I couldn't help laughing.

"Uncle Joe?"

"Well, you wouldn't call him Little Father, would you?"

"Uncle Joe?"

Suddenly he snorted with laughter himself.

"At least he gave his followers something to do," he said sarcastically. "Tricky even for the most committed, it was, having to defend his goings-on – that was until the attack on Russia made him a knight in shining armour, of course."

Then he stopped talking as suddenly as he had begun, and I avoided his gaze as he tried to see how I had taken it. I did not know exactly what his own experiences had been during his time on the island, nor did I ask him, and Mr Stewart had never told me either, saying only that he had been there so long no one bothered about it any more, no one had for a long time now, and I was expecting some account of it from him, but he did not seem to have noticed how far he had gone ahead of the subject. Only now did I see that he must be almost half a head shorter than me, for he had turned away, and I took my opportunity of observing him as he looked up and down the promenade and then, to bridge the silence between us, began the usual kind of lament, bewailing the fact that so much of the old splendour of the place was gone. Although the sun was still high above the build-ings, he was obviously cold, his suit flapping round his legs in the wind, and he had already said goodbye to me for the third time and was holding my hand firmly, not moving from the spot, when I finally freed myself and left.

All this would have been enough to make him the villain in one of those novels Max used to spend hours tearing to shreds for their way of depicting everything in black and white, giving the readers an enjoyable shudder, and when I saw him again that very evening, the place couldn't have been better chosen by the most assiduous of authors. I had merely followed the music I heard coming from one of the streets behind my boarding house and, when I located the building, I climbed the steps to a bar on the first floor where he was sitting, and even the pictures on the walls of this gloomy place, photographs of warships and various military decorations, suggested the stage props introduced into melodramatic tales to make a striking impression. Apart from him there were three other old men there, each at his own table and, while I saw them staring at the roughly made wooden platform in front of them on which a woman was singing, cradling a microphone in both hands as if it were an injured bird, I wondered whether to speak to him but then decided not too, and went away with the same curious impression of unreality that I had felt at our first meeting.

It seemed like a natural consequence that next day, when I looked out at the rain, I could have sworn I saw the shadowy outline of the hotel which had stood there during the war on the rising ground at the northern end of the bay, although in reality there was almost nothing left of it but parts of the foundations. Its counterpart on the other side was still standing, and at the time had been bristling with antennae up to and over the skylights; I was told it had been a radar training centre, closed long ago, and the boarded-up windows looked out on the gentle slope leading down to the lighthouse, once a playground for summer holidaymakers who strolled over its wide surface, gentlemen in three-piece suits and ladies with corseted waists and pale complexions, holding parasols like gigantic mushrooms over their heads as they walked. A Norwegian ship lay at anchor in the harbour all day; it had arrived overnight with a cargo of gas and, when it put out to sea again late in the afternoon, the sky was creamy and heavy, casting strange patches of light in which I could see its yellow hull shining even when it was far away.

Mr Stewart had finally installed the long-promised heater in my room, and I took this opportunity to ask him about the release of internees from the camps, since I had come upon the subject in looking through Hirschfelder's diary again, but I could not really make much of it. Judging by what he said it must have been an absurd situation: after the severity shown by the authorities in May and June of that year the arrests stopped in mid-July, and by the end of the month a White Paper was published, apparently containing 18 categories, into only one of which you had to fall to be freed again. The first prisoners left the island at the beginning of August, he told me, and as I might have expected he had a little story on the tip of his tongue to provide some local colour, in this case about the keeper at London Zoo whose qualifications made him one of the first to get out, because the elephants were refusing their food in his absence.

"It's as if they were shoving people about all over the place at random, with no regard for their feelings at all," he said. "When they were suddenly going to be released, quite a few of them weren't sure whether it might not be better to stay put."

I had sat down on the bed while he stood in the doorway, glancing out from time to time into the corridor whence his wife might summon him at any moment, and where she was no doubt already making signals to him to stop talking and join her.

"Most food was rationed in London, you see, and they'd been able to get everything here quite easily until late in the autumn," he added. "Of course, that wasn't the real reason, but if you don't want to admit you're scared, well, no explanation seems too odd."

It was true that in between Hirschfelder's expressed hope of being out again soon, as he wrote directly after his arrival on the island, and the entry late that summer saying that he could imagine getting used to life in the camp, I had found nothing in his diary to explain his change of mind, except for a reference to Lomnitz and Ossovsky who told him he must be a fool if he wanted to leave, although he did not say why.

The most obvious reason is not given, but I have no idea why he never once mentions the air raids on targets in England at the time, and when Mr Stewart spoke of the situation I had to let him instruct me.

"On an island, you see, you were literally out of the firing line," he said in a tone suggesting that this was regrettable. "You couldn't have been much safer anywhere than here."

Nonetheless, it is remarkable that in his entry for 1 July, the date when the ship with his room-mate on board put out from Liverpool, also the day when an airfield near that city was bombed, as I learned from Madeleine, Hirschfelder's diary merely says that he was wondering how to shake off the pale man and the man with the scar, who had apparently been sticking close to him all day, while he appears to have seen and heard nothing else, or at least he did not note it down. This is all the more surprising because later, particularly in the week before Christmas, he writes at length about the burning docks in the distance, the firelight reflected in the sky and visible from the camp, the muted noise of the explosions, and once, although I very much doubt whether I can believe him here, he even claims to have felt the ground vibrate beneath his feet as the bombs fell, but the distance across the sea must be a good 120 kilometres. He also several times mentions the squadrons of planes flying over the island on their way to Belfast, and if anything about that surprises me it is simply his indifference towards them, as if he were not afraid, his coolness when they appeared on moonlit nights eating their way through the darkness like monstrous steel insects, and their growling and humming suddenly came from all directions at once.

The same can be said of his sober diary entries when the major raids on London began in September, for they are confined to the enumeration of whole rows of streets without further commentary, and the factual mentions of bombed cities which he adds one by one over the subsequent months, listing them in a way that reminds me of a hesitant pupil in a geography lesson asked to give the major centres of a country with the number of their inhabitants, but producing only a confused stammer, or of recommendations in an unorthodox travel guide to go to such-and-such a place if possible, or more likely to avoid it at all costs. These litanies of destruction were reduced by him to a few names, and I have never been able to read them without imagining a group of officers standing in front of a gigantic ordnance survey map, one of them stepping forward and pointing a small baton at the gaps still left between the coloured heads of the drawing pins. He was obviously unable to describe such events appropriately and, in fact, there is no term in German that really corresponds to the English use of *Blitz*, which I heard for the first time in Mr Stewart's mouth when he spoke of blitzed areas, a concept that evoked images of buildings going up in flames in the glaring light of a hit, their material coarse-grained and porous, and maintaining their original shape for a moment without anything to hold them together before their soundless collapse.

We were still talking in my room, and I remember just how he relished the word, as if he were proudly cleaning up some borrowed item and returning it in nicely polished condition, and he used it several times in succession when he reverted to the subject of the island and how it had been spared the worst.

"There can't have been more than a handful of bombs dropped here in all," he said before leaving. "The danger wasn't so much from a direct raid as when a pilot lost his way or was being pursued, and had to get rid of his load."

That evening he was sitting in the room with the bay window next to the front door of the house, and beckoned me in as I was about to go out. The TV was on and, although I had sat down beside him, he waited a moment before rising to switch it off. He hovered, uncertain, in the middle of the room, as if trying to remember why he had intercepted me, and offered me a drink as if to gain time.

I must have looked at him as if I were afraid he was going to pay me unwelcome attentions, or at least I can't think why else he didn't move from the spot as he told me that his wife was out of the house, and wouldn't be back for an hour.

This was the first time he had not called her Mrs Stewart, and he laughed at himself rather too ostentatiously for my liking, but then finally walked stiffly over to the little table by his armchair and filled two whisky glasses, one of which he handed me, while he held the other up to the light and inspected it before swallowing its contents in a single gulp.

"I suppose there's still something in particular you're after," he said. "Forgive the play on words, but if it's not a corpse then it must at least be a skeleton in the cupboard, although I'm afraid I can't even offer you that."

I looked out of the window at a waiting taxi with its door open whose driver had placed a newspaper over the steering wheel and was glancing at it, while Mr Stewart took an involuntary step back.

"There was no mistreatment, no torture, no nothing," he continued, with a cynicism I wouldn't have expected of him. "The prisoners' main problem was killing time."

This was the man who had told me about the Nazi sympathisers in the camps, and I wished I could have contradicted him more calmly instead of coming out with a confused jumble of words, talking about loss of dignity like a schoolgirl, and making it easy for him to give me a pitying smile.

"I mean, how would you like to share a bed with your own executioner?"

Instead of reacting to this he sat down, crossed his legs, and examined his foot swinging up and down as if it did not belong to him, while picking invisible fluff off his jacket.

"Those are only words," he said at last. "In the end what matters is having food to eat, a roof over your head, and perhaps enough money for cigarettes."

With this he refilled his glass and, before he even began to speak, I knew what was coming next, I'd heard it so often, the usual truism that is meant to explain the inexplicable, the ultimate justification for every inconsistency, something to silence all doubts.

"There was a war on, you know."

Then he raised his glass to me, and I emptied mine, and a little later I found myself out on the promenade feeling as if a bucket of cold water had just been tipped over me. Despite my cautious attitude to his friendliness, I had not expected him to reprove me in such tones, and what made it worse was that otherwise I would actually have been inclined to agree with him. For in fact I still had only a vague idea of everyday life in the camps, I didn't know what really lay behind the basic timetable, there were hours in between the landmarks of the day, hours between getting up, roll-call and meals when they all had to fend for themselves, so he was probably right to say that ultimately everything turned not on an exceptional situation, not on a few emotive remarks, whether that suited me or not, but on the way the internees adjusted to living together, not on air-raid warnings but on waiting for them, on waiting in general, and this was the prime factor if you wanted

215

to understand anything about life on the island at that time.

It is true that Hirschfelder's diary contains hardly any complaints to that effect, but the ease with which he could become worked up seems to me to show that he was not coping quite as well as he would have liked to persuade himself. The few remarks about his state of health are deceptive in view of his constant moaning, my impression is that almost anything could set it off, any interruption to routine seemed able to knock him off balance, the walks he had enjoyed at first were an abomination to him later, so was being checked by the guards, or the random inspection of his belongings, on which he made sarcastic comments and, in October, when an orchestra of prisoners was to give a Grand Concert open to the public at the Derby Castle, and it was cancelled because of fears that anger at the continuing air raids on London might lead to trouble, he applauded the decision unreservedly. In fact it seems to me that the more he was reminded at all of life outside the camp, the more angrily he reacted, and when he writes of being dogged by the presence of Lomnitz and Ossovsky, who never left him alone and carried on as if they had been bosom friends in the past, he may have been expressing himself in clichés, but he conveys his wish for privacy in the fact that he would sometimes report sick in the morning, merely appearing at the window of the room they shared for roll-call, and then often making no effort to leave his bed until evening.

And from the first all the internees who were trying to get released were the butt of his mockery, as if he were not so sure of his own decision never even to try, as he kept claiming at the time. Often enough he made fun of the way a man would adjust his past history to fit one or other of the categories, claiming to be older or younger than he really was, suddenly making himself out the victim of some disease, or trying to show that with his qualifications he could make a good contribution to the so-called war effort in the armaments industry, or perhaps saying he had been just about to emigrate overseas but happened to have lost his papers. From autumn onwards groups of prisoners could be seen daily being taken out under guard for interrogations conducted at the local magistrates' court by a Metropolitan Police inspector from London and, when they came back in the afternoon, he would sit on the steps outside his building and watch as some of them handed over their luggage for inspection and told everyone this was their last night in the camp, while the others withdrew without a word. He recorded the names of those who had been freed if he knew them, along with the reason why and, on days when his doubts surfaced, he would be the one always asking his two room-mates the same question – what did they miss most? – and if one of them said a good meal, something better than the mush served up here, pancake soup to start with, then boiled beef with horseradish and finally cherry dumplings, and the other one couldn't make up his mind but finally began a list that sounded like the programme for a tourist weekend in Vienna, he seemed satisfied, and would be reconciled to them at least temporarily.

I still haven't entirely understood about the Pioneer Corps, or at least it is not yet clear to me why he volunteered months after his first mention of it, particularly as there are often gaps in the later part of his diary for this period. It seems to me especially surprising that he ended up there, because at first he didn't have a good word to say about the officer who seems to have set up in business in the street in front of the camp buildings on fine days late that summer, recruiting men who would like to join the unit as a way of getting out. He spoke disparagingly of a set of old women, saying that was no place for a real man, if you were going to do war work you ought to be on active service, not standing guard outside a munitions store, clearing bomb damage or acting as a tiny link in the supply chain, or so he wrote that autumn, only, as I have to admit, to change tack without a murmur of protest the next year.

It is possible to overlook his denigration of all the activities in the camp for a while, and indeed I did, but in the end you get annoyed by the way he runs everything down, in particular the lectures given by fellow prisoners, commenting pityingly on them and staying in his room when crowds of other men took chairs out on the promenade and sat in the sun listening to some professor telling them about his specialist subject, as if the worst they had to fear was an occasional period of boredom in the middle of the war. These are the passages in his diary which, when I read them, always made me dislike him for the contempt they express. He still seems to have thought that the only appropriate way to survive his internment was to submit to fate, any effort to do anything active about it one way or another was a betrayal and, when he cannot refrain from sniping at the attempt to publish a camp journal, and even the few hectographed sheets containing articles by his companions in misfortune and distributed once or twice set him off on an angry outburst, it is far from clear to me what is the object of his recriminations, if not himself. I find something repellent in his dismissal of their poems as pitiful, in his ridicule of any idea that the war might last for years, his denunciation of men who, he claims, were currying favour with the camp administrators by praising the magnanimity of Britain in articles accusing themselves, as it were, of exactly what was so often held against them – the fact that London was going through hell while they were safe and sound – and he surpasses himself in carping when he criticises their English in his own stiff German, calling their use of the language opportunistic, and then describing it as a kind of gibberish which only non-Britons would take for a language at all, while native speakers would surely consider it an offence against propriety.

On the other hand the sections in which he describes how he did finally join one of the working parties who left the camp in the morning and came back in the evening do not seem to me to fit this pattern. At least, I doubt if anyone could explain to me how, after all this fault-finding, he can suddenly wax enthusiastic about draining marshy land somewhere in the hills, picking stones from the most unpromising hills, hedging, cutting back gorse, or simply digging peat and helping with the harvest. These passages might have been written by someone else, particularly when he makes a positive idyll of them, describing the farmers or more often their wives who apparently drove down to the camp gates with trucks to collect the prisoners assigned to them, and I could swear he had fallen for his own wishful thinking when finally he loses himself in sentimental exaggeration of the friendship between the internees and the guards escorting them. His trumpeting of the fact that they took turns carrying the rifles and, so he says, would act as look-outs themselves so that their companions could take a mid-day nap, or perhaps enjoy a lovers' tryst, without fear of being caught in the act seems to me, whether accurate or not, typical of a certain kind of attitude.

It reminded me, in fact, of Leo's idealisation of his time in the camp, the presentation in cliché-ridden terms of the war as merely the background against which true friendships could really flourish and, if all this, together with the platitudes proffered by Mr Stewart as eternal truths that evening in his bay-windowed front room, were to be the sole result of my investigations then of course I was sure to be disappointed. Whether or not I admitted it to myself, I had still thought I was on the trail of some mystery, but after his reprimand it was difficult for me to go on pretending to myself. He had shown up my illusions, and now the accounts in the diary inevitably seemed to me like props being moved about on stage, just before a theatrical director with Hirschfelder's features would come out in front of the curtain and announce that the performance was cancelled.

Mr Stewart did not speak to me at breakfast next morning. He ceremoniously switched on the light at my table before I could do it myself, and swept the floor. In the middle of this activity he disappeared into the kitchen for a few minutes and, as the swing doors rocked back and forth, I heard him talking to his wife, although I could not make out what they were saying. Then they fell silent, and I was about to leave the dining room when he appeared again and finally embarked upon another conversation with me.

"Listen, I'm sorry if I offended you," he began carefully. "It's none of my business what you're trying to find out, but I wouldn't like you to get obsessed with it."

"Oh, there's no danger of that now."

My own firm answer surprised me, and I gestured as if sweeping aside everything we had discussed over the last few days with a single wave of my hand.

He laughed at that, and then gave me what was probably the advice he had given thousands of women tourists when he was tired of their company.

"You ought to take a look at the west of the island."

Next moment he explained further.

"Go and watch the sun setting over the sea," he went on. "That'll take your mind off things."

Sure enough, there really was nothing more for me to do in Douglas and, when I had read the paper, I spent the rest of the morning wandering about. I walked to the lighthouse, visited the museum once more – there is a special display in the Tourism section which can only be called "dinky", dealing with the internment period and depicting the prisoners as some unusual kind of visitors, rather like extra-terrestrials – and in the afternoon I went to nearby Laxey to follow the tracks of the electric railway up to the highest point on the island. As I climbed an empty train overtook me and came back down again, still empty, and I did not meet a soul on my walk, which took an hour and a half, until just before reaching my destination I crossed a road and was surprised to see a whole column of cars, which from further away lay as if motionless in the sun like a glittering ribbon.

The peak is called Snaefell, and at the top the wind, which seemed to be blowing from all directions at once, carried away the sound of the motor engines, leaving me with nothing but its singing and piping in my ears as it caught the antenna masts which seemed to sway in their enclosure against the turbulent sky, and I am afraid that the letter I wrote Max on the viewing platform of the hotel terrace was correspondingly emotive. No waiter appeared and, as I sat there and looked down at the slope up which I had just climbed, dropping away steeply to the sea, I did not wonder whether he would even be interested to hear from me after all these years, but gave him the facts I had learnt about Hirschfelder's life, feeling annoyed with myself because I could not refrain from reminding him of his enthusiasm, which had always seemed, at the same time, as an absurd vaunting of his own liking for isolation. Perhaps it was something to do with the view when I turned round and looked at the hills ranged one behind another, lost in the distant haze like mirages, but I remembered again how he had said more than once that the greatest happiness was to be somewhere as far away from home as possible, so that no one knew where you were or could locate you, as if you no longer existed and, ridiculous as this seemed to me in view of the isolation to which the prisoners in the camps had been exposed, I do recollect that I had to guard against being re-infected by his attitude, which was merely a flirtation with something he, being at liberty, could not really understand at all.

The postcards I sent Hirschfelder's three wives when I got back to my boarding house that evening, however, could best be described as light in tone, although even there I could not be sure I had struck the right note. The fact was that Margaret and Catherine had never been to the island, as they themselves had told me, nor most probably had Madeleine, to whom I initially hesitated to write again, and I told myself they might easily get the impression that I was trying to come between them and their memories. In any case, I had chosen the same picture for all of them: a beach scene with bathing machines on big wheels being pulled into the water by donkeys or possibly mules, a photograph taken before the turn of the century when not all of the hotels and boarding houses later to be part of the camp had yet been built on the Central Promenade in the background, and I hoped they would understand the allusion, would trust what I said, implying that there was nothing here I could take away from them, and would not see me as pompous or interfering.

My last day on the island was reserved for Clara. The ferry would be leaving next morning and, on a sudden impulse, I had looked at the telephone book to find the hotel in Port St Mary mentioned by Catherine, but discovered that she did not live there any more. However, I had also been given an address where I could reach her and, half an hour later, I was on my way to Castletown on the bus, sitting at the front of the top deck, which tilted far over as it went round curves, in a state of some excitement but restraining my hopes of learning more about Hirschfelder from her than from his three wives. She was obviously in a private nursing home and, when I had called at once and been asked whether I was a relation of hers, I was told, before I could reply, to get out at the second stop after the airport and then just ask the way.

The house – to which a woman finally gave me a lift in her car after I had asked at about half a dozen farms – lay among the hills and had no view of the sea. No one answered when I rang the bell at the gate, but as I walked down the gravel path I could not shake off the impression of being watched. There were awnings over the windows, the front door was open, and I looked down the dark corridor where a broad staircase curved up to the first floor and was lost from sight in a dusty shimmering haze. Although it was sunny outside the surroundings seemed to be bathed in pale green light, and I imagined the view of the outside world from any of the rooms here must be like looking through bull's-eye panes, showing a rain-washed landscape in which all outlines blurred.

Suddenly a nurse appeared and asked me to wait and, even before she had brought the wheelchair to a halt beside me on the veranda, I knew that the woman in it would be unable to answer any of my questions. She did not seem to notice me at all and, when I saw her eyes, it was clear to me she must have given up talking some time ago. Only a few strands of grey hair emerged under the straw hat she was wearing, and she had slumped slightly to one side against the straps holding her in place, her vacant gaze directed to the distance where a triangle of sky stood vertical as a wall, framed by the hills and crossed by the vapour trail of an aircraft.

This was Clara, whom I had never thought of as anything but a girl making her way delicately, like a sleepwalker, around a house in Smithfield in war-time London, and not knowing how to act I took her hand, but then immediately let it go again.

"Do please talk to her," said the nurse, who was still standing nearby and watching me, without concealing her curiosity. "She won't understand you, but try anyway."

223

I looked at her, then turned back to the woman in the wheelchair, and suddenly it did not seem appropriate for me to be there at all, but I talked away, always coming back to the remark which, for no good reason, I kept repeating as I leaned down to her.

"Can you hear me, Clara?"

Then I spoke very quietly, as if to get closer to her,

"I've come from Gabriel."

I had noticed the gingerbread-heart locket round her neck at once, a tasteless thing that one might pick up at a fun-fair, but it was only when I read the inscription on it that I had something of a shock. It said *Ben my chree*, and I had come upon those same three words in Hirschfelder's diary, where they had a whole page to themselves. They were among the few oddities over which I had not puzzled any further, and I knew it was ridiculous, but suddenly I had to fight back my tears, so moved was I by the coincidence.

I stared at the pink sugar-icing lettering of the inscription and when, on the off chance, I asked the nurse what the words meant, she gave me an answer of which Max, in one of his critical moods, might well have said that such a thing was possible only in real life, because if you put it in a novel it would be the purest kitsch.

"The ferry company in Douglas always used to give one of their ships that name," she said. "As far as I know it's Gaelic and it means *girl of my heart*."

I prevented myself from repeating it parrot-fashion, and took care that she didn't see my eyes, for I was beginning to feel the weight of them.

"It's a present from her daughter," the nurse went on, realising that I was waiting for an explanation. "She lives in Manchester and comes to visit once a month."

It was on the tip of my tongue to put further questions, but then I asked her no more after all, and simply changed the subject before I had really embarked on it, pretending to be interested in daily life in the residential home, and listened to her account without actually hearing it.

To me, at this point, the woman in the wheelchair represented the end of my quest, and it would have made no difference to know more about her life on the island, or even to toy with the possibility that Hirschfelder might have been the father of her child, as I had already wondered about Catherine's daughter, and when I put his book, which I had brought with me, on her lap, and saw it fall to the ground from her powerless hands, I just left it there and said goodbye.

I spent the evening in my room, and I was already setting off for the ferry the next day when Mr Stewart told me that after the war five or six of the prisoners had ended up in Ballamona psychiatric hospital.

I did not ask him about them, and was surprised to find him broaching the subject just before I left, as if he wanted to give me something to take away with me, a saying for the road.

"Ah, well, you're either in love or off your head," he said, as if the two emotions were identical. "No other reason to come here to the back of beyond."

I tried to produce a dutiful laugh, but could only hear my gasping breath as it was torn away by the wind, leaving a roaring silence behind.

"What about you, then?"

"Oh, I'm an old man," he replied. "You mustn't ask me questions – but still, mind it doesn't get to you."

7

SS *ARANDORA STAR*
NORTH ATLANTIC
2 JULY 1940

from quite close, now from further away, the lighter voice belonging to the man who had spent hours telling anyone who would listen how he was arrested at work in his Fitzrovia restaurant exactly three weeks ago, and the deep, soothing voice of the other who kept interrupting him. It was as a concession to you that they spoke English and, despite your alarm at the sight of the grey weather outside, the slanting lines of the rain where the monsters of your childhood dreams lay in wait, except that this time they couldn't be dismissed when it grew light, you were as relieved as you had been in those days, when the sound of grown-ups in the room next door was enough to soothe you, and you thought that it was getting to be quite usual for you to be in the company of strangers, as if this was your war, to lie quiet somewhere while the world came to an end all around. Eyes half-closed, you watched them turning this way and that in front of the mirror, as if shipboard etiquette still demanded an immaculate appearance, you observed them carefully going over their cheeks where the translucent shaving soap formed bubbles, wiping the razor blades on their towels, and you wondered where the brewery rep sharing the cabin with you and the Italians might be, was he already standing in line for bread outside the kitchen, or had he gone out to throw up again, ready to assure everyone on his return that no, he hadn't drunk too much, he was just seasick, as if this distinction might at least save his soul?

It was exactly three days ago that the newcomer had finally turned up his ace, and you had stepped forward in his place at roll-call without a murmur, and by now it seemed to you perfectly natural that no one else had made any fuss either, no one had noticed or wanted to notice the substitution, it was like a fitting punishment for your stupidity in playing at all, it seemed only to be expected that the doctor had scarcely given you a glance during his final medical examination, not to mention the guards, and then you were on the ferry taking you away from the island with the rest of the little group, you had leaned on the rail, overcome by the same weariness that afflicted you now, holding a card with your thumbprint, a stamp and the commandant's illegible scribble on it by way of your discharge papers, and you hadn't looked at the others, you had merely registered that besides the merchant seamen they included the brewery rep and the professor, and you had kept yourself to yourself throughout the crossing. You had been taken to the transit camp on the outskirts of Liverpool overnight, and straight back to the harbour next morning, and there was the ship lying ready, you could still hardly believe it, but it was the very same ship you had so often admired outside the Regent Street offices of the Blue Star Line on your walks through the West End of London, where they had a model of it on display, no doubt about it at all, the name in block lettering could be read on the bows, the ship which the company boasted was the most exclusive in the world, all the cabins first-class. They had been advertising a Christmas sunshine cruise last summer, as if the war were not imminent, and you still had the names of the places to be visited in your head, the Caribbean, the Mediterranean and the Atlantic coast of North Africa, ports where it must indeed have put in during better times, improbable as they might now sound to your ears. All that was over, of course, and you remembered how it had seemed like a hallucination when your group was lined up in pairs at the quayside, its funnels, once red with the blue star in the white circle, now over-painted with grey, the portholes and windows blacked out, wooden hoardings along the sides of the promenade deck, and barbed wire barriers, and a gun both fore and aft, their barrels pointing hesitantly rather than threateningly at the sky. The whole quay had been swarming with prisoners waiting to go on board, and you saw them in your mind's eye once more, suitcases at their feet, and he explained to you, very much the man of the world who was sure of his way around, mentioning the places he knew dismissively, as if he'd seen them once and that was quite enough,

–It's in the Bay of Biscay, last port we put in at before landing in Liverpool to pick you lot up,

and in half an hour it was midnight, but not quite dark yet, he had pulled down the grille over his sales hatch, and you were sitting opposite him in the entrance lobby which gave access to the former dining room down a broad staircase and up to the promenade deck lounge, you sat there and watched the first men stretching on mattresses on the floor in front of you, while he told you about his ship's peregrinations over the last month.

–Going back down the French coast south things were more and more chaotic, he said, if it hadn't been for the Spanish border we'd probably have fetched up in Gibraltar, and you looked at him as if you weren't sure what he was talking about. It was like falling downstairs and hitting your head on every step, he continued, laughing, first they ordered us to Brest, then Quiberon, then Bayonne, then that wretched hole at last, and there's nowhere beyond that, not for a civilised human being – and here he paused as if waiting for you to contradict him. We had enemy bombers over the harbour twice, he went on again at once, undeterred by your silence, we only just got away, and then there was barely time to go back to Falmouth and disembark. You could hardly credit it when he told you that the crew looking after the evacuees on board, the soldiers and refugees they had taken off and who would have been happy enough with conditions on the worst coffin-ship afloat, were the very same men who, last year, had still been anticipating the slightest wish of the easily bored cruise passengers, to keep them from noticing the alarm signals which were not not just on the horizon now, you listened to him in some bewilderment and told

233

yourself these stories couldn't be true, the incidents he claimed to have seen as a bar-tender in the smoking-room during the weeks just before the outbreak of war, his experiences with the ladies and gentlemen who resorted there, the conversations he said he had heard, the gossip, the frivolities, the ridiculous scandals of a few privileged people apparently determined to amuse themselves up to the very last moment.

–It makes my blood run cold now to think our two last ports of call a few days before the invasion of Poland should have been Danzig and the North Sea–Baltic canal, he said in a voice from which all the colour had drained, we were scheduled to be back in Southampton at the end of August, but of course they'd ordered us home already and we were on the way to New York with a few hundred Americans when the declaration of war reached us.

Outside, the first stars had risen over the choppy sea, you must have rounded the most northerly point of the Irish coast, and to give yourself courage you said,

–Seems it's going to be a quiet night,

and he looked at you incredulously,

–I wouldn't be so sure. This is a busy route, and there's usually more traffic than you'd like, this close to the coast. I'm not making any prophecies before we reach open sea,

and you shivered at the idea of the distance that was opening up, the many kilometres of heaving water that lay ahead.

It was the end of a long day, for after the tedious waiting on board your group had to leave Liverpool at the first light of dawn, some time after midnight, and as long as there was land in sight you had felt safe, as long as the Welsh coast accompanied you until morning, and then you could see the Isle of Man to starboard and later on Ireland to port, sometimes so close that you could make out the separate houses of the villages, and you thought of the sea-plane which had approached from the mainland around mid-day, exchanging signals with flashing lights, and it was rather hesitantly that you demurred.

–I'm not too happy myself that the captain didn't order any life-saving drill, he immediately went on, if anything goes wrong we'll have panic,

and you looked at the figures lying so close together on the floor in front of you that there was only a small pathway left free between to the stairs, while the door to the doctor's surgery was blocked, and you said,

–Too late to worry about that,

to which, unimpressed, he replied,

–I've no idea how many people there are on board, but I'm pretty well sure those 14 lifeboats won't be nearly enough,

and he was back on his favourite subject, with which he had been driving everyone crazy all afternoon,

–I can't think why they didn't at least send an escort with us, even the most ridiculous transport of old junk gets a whole convoy to go with it.

Then he spoke of the tests with torpedo nets which the ship had obviously undergone three months after the beginning of the war, complaining that in the end it wasn't equipped with them after all, and you looked out into the darkness and tried to make out the coast as you listened to him talking on and on in his monotonous voice, which at irregular intervals threatened to fail him, suddenly becoming louder and then dropping again.

–Right, so that was in Portsmouth, and we went out into the Channel day after day with those things on our flanks and back again in the evening, he said, sounding as if he were describing some children's game, and as far as I know they got good results, but all the same the project was called off, no explanation given, and

235

no doubt you'll see what I mean when I tell you I sometimes think the worst saboteurs are in our own ranks.

The two Italians had finished shaving, and you didn't need to look to know they were washing their armpits in the icy water. There was still no sound from the promenade deck, however hard you listened for the sentry's footsteps, the brewery rep had not yet put in an appearance, and the bursts of merriment from the pair at the wash-basin, their chattering and laughter as they splashed each other, reminded you of yesterday evening's muted exuberance when, to everyone's surprise, the uniformed stewards served you beer and sticky pink gins as if you were paying passengers, and someone had dug out a gramophone and a couple of records and was playing the same hits over and over again in the former ballroom. You lay there, you heard them laughing, you thought how your tension had gradually ebbed away, and you had stopped staring out to sea every minute or so in case you saw something suspect there after all, then making sure that the look-out man was at his post, you thought of the prisoners who had fallen emotionally into one another's arms, and you wondered what had been going through the canteen manager's head as he kept a suspicious eye on such conduct, and suddenly you had your father's voice in your ears, calling out to you.

You heard the two Italians walking up and down between the mattresses in the cabin, already dressed, judging by the rustling sound, you heard them searching their luggage and you knew, before they said anything at all, what the order of the day would be. You weren't surprised to hear them complain of their fate, for after all they had come to Britain of their own free will, and suddenly had as few civil rights as can possibly be imagined, as few as those refugees with whom, only a few weeks ago, it would never have occurred to them to compare themselves in any way whatsoever. They had told you their story as if they expected that you, of all people, could clear them of suspicion, they had told you they came from near Parma and had left home ten years ago, they conjured up their native land in the most flowery terms, at the same time insisting that they had been English for a very long time, and when you thought how they spoke of their countrymen, as if the mere sound of their names would convince you, their companions in misfortune who were also on board, enumerating them one by one without even introducing themselves first – Zangiacomi and Maggi from the Ritz, Zavatoni from the Savoy, Borgo from the Café Anglais, all of them apparently chefs and waiters with the reputation of demi-gods, no less – well, when they went into raptures like this you thought it quite natural for them to object to what they saw as inappropriate treatment.

–They can do what they like to me in London, just so long as they don't call me a Fascist again, one of them began, and there was much hectic activity as if he were brushing dust from his shoulders with both hands, you mark my words, I'm not taking that from those fish-and-chip eaters,

to which the other said,

–Oh, drop the tough man act,

and the first replied,

–No, really, that self-righteous bunch ought to have seen just which of their own people came to the Charing Cross Road club, all sweetness and light with the embassy folk and drinking to the Duce,

and the other groaned,

–Look, you're on board ship now, no one's interested in your fantasies, not even if you can prove the whole Cabinet was there,

and you saw the brewery rep before you again, lying in his own vomit at ten in the evening outside what had once been the dark-room, he had managed to drink himself insensible very quickly

237

indeed, on his own ration and the dregs he could cadge from other people, you saw him lying there snuffling away like a large, sad dog, mumbling something incomprehensible about his children, and finally beginning to weep when you and a steward managed to haul him into your cabin.

Your father stood by the rail in a white suit, a glass in his hand, waving to you, calling to you again, and the ship lay in a tiny palm-fringed bay, you saw him in the glittering sun, and all the air seemed full of light although it was still morning, the sky was cloudless, pale blue and translucent at the edges, concealing nothing, nothing at all and, when you went over to him, he put his arm round your shoulders and just said,

–It's good to have you here, Gabriel,

and you knew you had been right not to join the party off for a picnic on the beach, now half-way there in the boats that had come out from land, and you tried to sound as casual as possible,

–You said you wanted to speak to me,

and he hesitated in his familiar way,

–Well, no hurry, but there are a few things we ought to discuss some time, if that's all right,

and indeed he had been saying so since the first day of your voyage, and ever since he had kept drawing you aside but then finding some excuse to change the subject, asking if you liked this trip away from home or were you homesick – this when your party had only just embarked – and he always ended up talking about nothing much, telling you Vienna was like one of those women who treat a man badly but you can't break with them, or some other commonplace, or he might simply act as if he had lost the drift of his remarks.

–You must keep an eye on your mother, Gabriel, he said, as if this were not what he had been meaning to say all the time, I'm worried about her, and you looked at the boats and tried to make out her figure and her husband's in the broad sloops with their sun awnings rocking surprisingly gently on the waves, you saw the gleaming, naked black backs of the oarsmen, rising from their benches, seating themselves again, pulling on the oars once more only when the last movement had died down, patches of darkness between the pale splotches and the dappled light of the water, and you knew she must be there somewhere too, somewhere among the ladies all in white and the gentlemen in khaki suits, every one of whom had appeared that morning with his topee as if by previous arrangement, she must be sitting there in her big sun hat even as he spoke to you. She's been looking so pale recently, he persisted, I expect she takes things too much to heart, and you thought of the delight with which, just before the voyage began, she had watched the traders who rowed out to the ship, offering their wares on long poles held aloft from their rafts, and you wanted to ask him what things, Father, what things does she take to heart, you could have told him he should treat her better himself and not avoid her on account of his secretary, as he had been doing ever since you all embarked, and you stared in silence at the palms fringing the distant shore, the air hazy with heat above them in spite of the early hour. She was always very temperamental, but that runs in the family, he went on, please make sure she calms down, and suddenly you feared she might be in danger, might go ashore and never come back, and you were scarcely listening as he put his telescope to his eye and immediately began talking about Clara, who hadn't appeared yet, since you were spending so much time with her you must introduce her to him some day, he said, while the ship's band on the lido deck, which had been playing a waltz at his request, had just come to the end of it, was packing up its instruments, and a couple of its members stood by the swimming

239

pool as if only waiting for the order to dive in head first.

You let a few moments pass by, listening to the groaning sound that suddenly ran through the ship, and only then did you venture on an approach of your own,

–I still don't know why you invited us all on this cruise instead of going alone with your secretary,

and he let himself be persuaded into a remark which he obviously thought suited the part of the generous elderly man he was playing,

–Oh, well, I thought a change of air would do you all good, and it never hurt anyone to see a bit of the world,

but you knew that wasn't the reason, you knew he was hiding something from you, and you tried to break down his reserve,

–I'm sure it's something to do with home,

and he lowered his telescope abruptly, looking you up and down as you instinctively avoided his gaze.

–You're so restless, Gabriel, said Clara, and it was the middle of the night, she was standing on the look-out deck with you and took your hand, it's as if you were afraid of something,

and you stared at the figures stretched out below, lying side by side on the planks, men on one side, women on the other, having fled their cabins yet again, cabins that for days had been full of a dead and stifling air which made breathing almost impossible and felt like heat in the lungs, although the captain had tried again and again to steer into the wind, you looked at the white sheets beneath which the bodies tossed and turned as if in feverish dreams in the blue light of the stars, none of which seemed to be in its right place, and you fought against the trembling that always overcame you at the sight of them, you thought of home, and how on the very first evening at sea it had occurred to you that while you were gone everything might have dissolved into a void and be lost for ever if you stayed away too long.

−That's nonsense, Gabriel, said your father, we'll be back soon and you won't have missed out on anything,

but you insisted,

−There's something you're not telling me,

and he turned sarcastic,

−You're just like your mother, she can get so excited over some tiny detail she starts imagining things,

and as if you had just been waiting for this cue you searched the bay from end to end with your eyes, disregarding the sweat that broke out on your forehead, staring as intently as if a horde of savages might break out of the thickets any moment, shooting arrows at the approaching boats.

You felt Clara pressing close to you and returned the pressure of her body as she began yet again,

−Tell me what the matter is,

and you said,

−Nothing,

but she replied, even more firmly,

−I know it must be something,

and you were afraid she might persist with her probing, and would not let her go on, but laid a finger on her lips as if she were a child,

−Believe me, it's nothing,

and her breathing, which you felt beneath your hand, was the only sound for a while, until you heard her calling in your ears again, saying something you couldn't make out, and next moment there came the voice of the girl to whom you must have spoken in a street somewhere in Mayfair, that summer before the war, uttering a few words that had stuck in your head, in an English that sounded as harsh and clipped as your own in your first few weeks in that country.

241

–Ten shillings, dear, said the girl, puffing out air like cigarette smoke, doesn't come any cheaper unless you do it to yourself,

and there was Clara's,

–Can you hear me, Gabriel?

and the girl began again,

–Ten shillings,

and she already had a hand between your legs and was moving it slowly up and down, and she laughed, she laughed as she looked at you, but she hardly showed her teeth,

–What do we have here for ten shillings?

and Clara said,

–Can you hear me, Gabriel?

and the girl suddenly spoke in German,

–What do we have here for the Führer?

and Clara said,

–Gabriel, what is it?

and the girl asked,

–A countryman of mine, are you?

and you gave her the money you had got from the old lady in Mile End Road so that you could take your girlfriend out, fastened your fingers in her hair and closed your eyes,

–Get on with it and keep quiet.

Your father stood there in silence, the boats had just reached the beach, and you took the telescope from his hand to watch the oarsmen getting out and making their way through the shallow water to the bows, leaning back on their heels and then hauling as if the boats were refractory beasts of burden, until they ploughed their way into the sand and, with one last movement, their keels tipped lazily over to one side. It was only a few minutes before you saw the black figures hurrying back and forth in the sea spray, escorting the passengers to dry land, saw them working in pairs,

242

making a chair of their arms for the women, who embraced their necks and let themselves be carried away as if not of their own free will, dolls, any one of which could be your mother, so much did they resemble one another at this distance, you saw them taking the men up piggyback and marching off with small steps, and you thought how he had been mocking your companions all through the voyage, the foolishness of which they were capable, the lengths to which they went to organise various parlour games which they would have despised on land. There was nothing to be heard but the slap of the swell against the ship's side, and suddenly you missed his complaining and wished he would speak, would break the silence, so that you could finally shake off this sense of menace, you wished he would start going on again about yesterday evening's pyjama party, or the ridiculous suggestion for married couples to swap partners at the next port, would become so heated that the sound-lessness would have no power over you, the frozen sense that you were watching only a magic lantern show, a beach scene with shapes now standing about inactive, pictures from a photograph album, the idea that you were witnessing something from the distant past which had vanished, like the light of the stars which reaches us long after they have been extinguished.

It was scarcely less dark in the cabin when the ship's bell sounded again, and the flat look of the light made objects seem porous, the wardrobe and the little mahogany dressing table, the crystal chandelier on the ceiling, the couple of basket chairs placed together near the wash-basin, and the two Italians were sitting on their mattresses looking at you when you opened your eyes. The sound of the engines came from deep within the hull, as if mighty weights were being pushed around down below, and as they listened intently, their hair combed smooth and still wet, neatly parted, they looked to you, in their white shirts, like children who have been promised a surprise although they gave up believing in such things long ago and are only pretending for the grown-ups' sake, waiting for the curtain to rise at last. It had stopped raining outside, and all of a sudden the sentry could be heard again whistling as he marched up and down, his footsteps on the planks, and from somewhere or other, incomprehensible, came the shouting of a sailor, and you were glad they didn't speak to you yet, for you would have liked to go on dozing, face to the wall, forgetting what the canteen manager had been telling you the evening before, as if to show you, on your very first day aboard, that there was nowhere left to hide.

For having told you what the ship had been doing in the war up till now, he could not refrain from repeating, several times, that comment you couldn't stand any more, the eternal "They're coming, they're coming", obviously essential to every conversation, and you heard him say again,

–Don't think I have anything against you personally, but I couldn't stand that lot even in peacetime,

adding, as if not only in answer to your question when you asked him why, but also as an explanation for the topsy-turvy state of the whole world,

–If there was ever anyone on board who ate more than his share or was too mean to stand a round in the bar, you could bet your bottom dollar it'd be a German,

and you remembered how he then sat with you in silence for a while, and kept looking sideways at you, as if expecting you to refute his accusations by handing him a tip with a grand gesture.

Directly after that you had gone out again, making your way against the wind to a place by the rail where there was a gap in the wooden hoarding. The stars had left the sky, so you could no longer guess at the shapes of the hills which must be somewhere over to port, the ship was beginning to roll, and spray washed over the bows as they dipped into the waves and emerged again. Obviously the look-out post by the foremast had been reinforced, and you also saw a man in oilskins standing on the bridge, smoking a cigarette without troubling to cover the glowing end with his hands, and you stayed out there until one of the guards on his rounds sent you off, you stood on the boat deck watching, as if nothing could happen to any of them provided you didn't leave the spot.

The movement of the ship working its way on through the darkness still seemed strange to you, not a light to be seen and none on board, only the sickly phosphorescence of the bow wave, the water foaming along the ship's sides and a faint gurgling at the stern. The world had never been so dark since the discovery of fire, you told yourself. It was hundreds and thousands of kilometres in every direction to the first gleam of light betraying the presence of human life, and even now, in retrospect, you were overcome not only by fear but by an inexplicable sense of expectation, acquiescence such as you had sometimes felt in the judge's house when you stood by the window with Clara looking out at the night, where the barrage balloons floating above the rooftops seemed to be the only creatures alive. Although it was still cold, the air of the cabin smelled musty, and suddenly you longed to be back on the island, longed for the regularity of the days you had hated for so long, for the routine that would begin with reveille in a few minutes' time, and you pictured the pale man and the man with the scar getting out of bed to see what the weather was like, stretching and then shaking the other man awake, the man who should really have been you, the man who had taken your place, and who perhaps no longer even spared a thought for the situation in which he had put you.

The sentry must be right outside your window now, but you could not see if he was peering in or had merely leaned against it and was looking the other way, his whistling was more penetrating, you heard his sudden coughing, heard him clear his throat, and then several minutes went by in which there was nothing but the sound of the engines and the slapping of the water outside. The two Italians preserved their silence as if they were both listening to something, while steps approached outside the cabin, and you hoped the brewery rep, who must have had some reason to be absent so long, was back at last, but they died away down the corridor, and once again there was only that regular humming, which had something both threatening and soothing about it. Soon the ship's bell would ring, and you strained your ears to discover whether the sound had really grown louder since the last turn, as you thought, listening intently to the growling of the engine from the bowels which seemed to infect everything, setting off a slight, a barely perceptible trembling that was increasingly trans-ferred to you as well.

The explosion came without warning, shaking the whole cabin and, in the first shock, you stayed lying where you were, listening for any further detonation, or for water coming in, as if you could have heard it so high up there on the promenade deck. For a few moments the humming engines were still audible, but then there was silence, and suddenly the monotonous singing of the wind, as if it had only just risen, was the only sound, the ship had stopped moving, and you could have counted the seconds sluggishly passing, one by one, before the two Italians leaped to their feet, talking excitedly in loud voices, the banging of doors and agitated cries came from the corridor, and time resumed its normal course. Then an acrid smell spread, a smell like singed metal, like a fire of wet timber refusing to burn properly, and finally all you could smell was the oil that must be leaking somewhere, its unmistakable odour rising to your nostrils.

Just as you were, clad only in your pyjamas, you followed the two Italians out into the passage, where there was already frantic pushing and shoving. The emergency light was not on, so that at first you could hardly see anything, but more men came out of the other cabins, some making their way to the doors opening into the passages to the promenade area and moving on towards the afterdeck, while others tried to get to the lounge amidships, and it was these you joined, without stopping to think. The noise immediately submerged you, they were all shouting so hard, and it was almost impossible to make progress, you had to push your way through with your elbows and fists, taking blows from all sides yourself, until finally you were simply carried along by the crowd.

More and more people were thronging together the closer you came to the way out on to the boat deck, rushing out of the former ballroom, the smoking-room, making their way up from the entrance lobby, many of them half dressed like you, others carrying luggage. You saw one elderly man with a tie and gold-rimmed glasses in the midst of the maelstrom, looking as if it would swallow him up, his head thrown back at a grotesque angle, fighting for breath, and the calls of the guards were drowned by the shouting, but meanwhile you had reached the first steps of the stairway, and now you suddenly noticed the angle of the ship. The floor was slanting, at every step you took your foot almost imperceptibly sought empty air before you set it down into the abyss opening before you, a difference of only a few millimetres, but in your head they immediately became the very depths of the sea.

The ship had been hit by a torpedo and, once in the open air, you could at last make out separate words as a steward handed you a life-jacket, constantly repeating his mantra,

–Keep calm,

247

and you saw him looking round as he spoke, as if he would drop everything at the first opportunity and get himself to safety, you saw men with more space to move out on the open deck running aimlessly up and down between the boats, which were guarded by soldiers, and heard their voices again and again, emerging from the confusion,

–Let me by,

and after a pause,

–I've got a wife and children at home,

and then again,

–Let me by,

and his constant repetition, like an echo,

–Keep calm, gentlemen, please keep calm, wait for your turn.

–Looks as if your visit to foreign parts is called off, but I suppose you're a good swimmer, said the canteen manager ironically, approaching you from a few steps away, at least, if not I don't know what you're waiting for,

and you saw a boat just being lowered amid the loud shouting of orders to the level of the promenade deck, where men were already clambering into it through a gap torn in the wooden hoarding, and you could think of nothing better to say to him than,

–Women and children first,

whereupon he stopped short in surprise, pointed to the figures sitting shoulder to shoulder hovering over the water, suspended from the cables of the crane, and tried, unsuccessfully, to summon up a laugh,

–Don't be such a fool. Look at that lot and stop playing the man of honour. None of them are wondering if you're a lady or not,

and at that moment you saw the brewery rep sitting in the bows, clutching the sides with both hands, his glance, frozen with horror, looking up at you, and you immediately lost any desire to make light of it.

Standing at the rail you could see the boat rising with a wave as soon as it touched the water, and then seeming to stand still as the oars dipped before it moved away from the side of the ship with apparent ease. Right beside it planks of wood were drifting on the spreading film of oil, with a table among them and a couple of chairs, and the sight of the rafts which had been flung overboard, empty, and were moving away at a ridiculously slow rocking pace made you think for a moment that perhaps it was not so serious after all, or surely they would have been occupied by now. There were only a few swimmers in the water, their heads looking tiny from above, and in spite of the constant screaming you thought you could hear the silence prevailing deep below, the roaring of the sea that extinguished all sounds, working with the suction power of a gigantic vacuum.

In the explosion one of the boats had been blown apart, and a couple of sailors were trying in vain to get another afloat, while you saw that the water in the stern was now almost up to the portholes of the lowest deck, and the canteen manager was telling you the extent of the damage as if reporting to his superior officer. The torpedo had obviously hit the rear engine room on your side of the ship and, if what he said was right, the turbines had been destroyed, the main and auxiliary generators were out of action, and contact with the bridge was lost, hence the absence of orders. He judged the distance from the Irish coast to be at least 100 miles, and he didn't have to say any more, it was clear to you what that meant, he didn't need to utter the name of the place, Bloody Foreland in County Donegal, which was bound to seem like a bad omen, as if you needed one, when finally he couldn't refrain from speaking the words.

−All we can do is hope someone's picked up our SOS, he said, if they have it'd be very bad luck if we weren't fished out in a few hours' time at the latest,

and you looked at him,

−You can't be serious,

and when he did not reply, but merely avoided your gaze with a curiously abstracted smile, you had to make a great effort not to scream,

−We don't have that long,

and he nervously fingered his collar and told you for God's sake to get into the life-jacket you were still holding, he tugged and pulled at it and finally, shivering, helped you to put it on.

−Go on, he told you, fasten it as firmly as possible so you don't break your neck hitting the water when you jump in,

and again you heard the same soothing remarks, now sounding grotesque, the ridiculous repetitions,

−Keep calm, please keep calm,

and he placed a hand on your shoulder,

−If you can't reach one of the boats try to get on a raft as quick as you can, or a few minutes in the cold water will finish you off,

and just as he was saying he could really do with a cigarette if he only had one, the shouting all around became so loud that his voice was drowned out, and you tried in vain to read his lips.

There was no time to ask any questions, although you wondered why he should bother about you at all, why he didn't make sure of getting into one of the last boats himself. The disaster had taken him by surprise in the crew's quarters deep within the ship, and only now did you notice that he was covered with oil, which made his face look even paler, and the wire-framed glasses he wore, which you hadn't noticed before, were propped crooked on his nose, giving his expression a look of mingled ingenuousness and horror.

Perhaps he was in shock, you couldn't explain his erratic behaviour any other way, his initial calm and then his agitation, and suddenly he was calm again, looking at the men still scurrying back and forth in panic as if he were not one of them and he was simply watching in amazement as they did something that made not the faintest sense.

You had long ago lost sight of the two Italians, and you looked around for anyone else you knew, for one of the fellow prisoners who had come with you from the Isle of Man. None of them could be seen, not the professor, who only the day before had been complaining to you in his usual way of having only a mattress to sleep on, nor any of the merchant seamen who, separated from their captain, had taken up residence in the ballroom, and by now the brewery rep was a long way off, in one of the boats visibly making good progress, most of them crammed full. A number of those left behind were now running about on deck as if looking for some way out, a few steps forward and then immediately back again, and many of the men dangling from ropes over the ship's side and letting themselves drop when they were a few metres above the water were soldiers and crew members, while the rope ladders hanging from the promenade deck swung indolently back and forth under the weight placed on them, and among those clinging to the ropes like flies, unable to bring themselves to let go, you saw a few who still had their suitcases and were hitting out with them, warding off the more determined, who were actually scrambling past them down the inside of the ladders.

Suddenly all was still, and you saw a boat hanging, keel upwards, from the cables of the crane, separate images of it reaching you as it rocked back and forth with its full complement of passengers, as it tilted over and tipped its occupants out like toys. It was a few moments – moments in which you hardly dared look – before their heads emerged in the water below and, as if they had seen enough, the sailors who had been operating the boat crane scattered and disappeared in the crowd. A jolt passed through the ship, the stern dipped even further in and then righted itself in part, but it had fallen perceptibly to one side, there was shouting on the bridge, and when you turned you could see the captain and two of his officers looking down at the tumult as if it were all routine to them, as if they had the situation in hand, although in fact they were only waiting for the vessel to take them down with it into the depths.

For a moment you had not been paying attention, and the canteen manager was already overboard when you heard him shout,

–Jump,

and then there was nothing for quite a while, until the sudden cry came, an order to the guards, clear and distinct as it broke the silence,

–Every man for himself,

and it was passed on,

–Every man for himself,

while the deck was still crowded,

–Jump,

and you jumped, you jumped over the rail with your eyes closed, you jumped into the depths without once looking round.

The impact was hard, and something must have struck you on the head, for a burning pain went through you on your first contact with the water. It was not silence that assailed your ears as you came up again but the screaming of the swimmers, the cries for help uttered by men desperately fighting for their lives among the flotsam, while the pool of oil around them grew larger and larger, and you saw that some of them were already dead, caught in their life-jackets like monstrous children wearing outsize bibs, drifting on their backs and staring up at the clouds above the sea with empty eyes. The ship loomed above them like a huge wall that might fall and bury them at any moment, people were still jumping off, and now you were swimming, swimming towards the horizon that bobbed up and down, sometimes near, sometimes far away, having gathered all the light into it, a bright and gleaming gap between earth and sky.

The next thing you knew you were on a raft, without being aware how you had got there. Not much time could have passed, the ship was not 200 metres away, listing even more steeply with its bows right in the air by now, and you lay there feeling the water flow off you, feeling the oil sticky in your eyes and nose, the thud of your heart in your throat, hearing your breathing, which sounded as if it belonged to someone else, the breathing of a man who must be somewhere close to you, and then how difficult the first movements were when you put out your arms and felt the wooden planks, the rough fibres of the boards, how painful when you began exploring the extent of the place where you were lying with the initially hesitant and then increasingly urgent movements of a man abandoned who had woken in the night to find himself alone. You were on something not much larger than a bed, and your fingers felt first electrified and then numb when you touched it anywhere at the edges, so you immediately withdrew them.

. It must have been an illusion that you had heard the canteen manager calling you when you were already in the water, for he didn't even know your name, and you gave up looking for anyone else. A dull pain, a half-dazed feeling was now spreading through your head, which you had not really felt properly yet, but your hands were already covered with blood, and it was with blurred vision that you saw all those still on the boat deck turning towards the bows and beginning to clamber up the slope, saw the first of them losing their grip, stumbling and getting caught on the rail, or dropping overboard in free fall. Vapour still seemed to be rising from the funnels, but you were not sure of that, and suddenly there was an explosion, steam poured out of the portholes near the surface of the water, there was a hail of tiny splinters, and a huge plank which must have worked loose somewhere high above swept away the last lingerers still hanging from the ropes and rope ladders, apparently without a sound. The ship was now standing almost on end, a great lurch shook the entire hull, and it looked to you as if it were first rising almost imperceptibly and then sinking in a single and unstoppable gliding movement, while the sky behind grew wider over the spot now marked only by the pool of oil, the flotsam, the swimmers among it, and a steadily spreading wave that had lost much of its force by the time it reached you and then, further out, died down as if nothing had ever happened.

No more screaming came to your ears, only a curious sing-song chant from the dying, a chant like birds perishing, if they do indeed sing in death, and the boats that had maintained some distance from the ship to avoid the suction and were not already over-full cruised back and forth among the heads, taking in swimmers until there was no more room and they had to leave the last to fend for themselves. The sound gradually died down, and soon you could hear only the splash of oars dipping into the water, a few scraps of words, and the cries of the sailors communicating with each other seemed to come from far away, without aim or direction, echoing too long before they died down as if in the thickest of fog. Otherwise it was still, a muffled stillness like that of mornings on the island, when the gulls were just beginning to cry, and every small sound, such as the lapping of the water against your raft, emphasised that silence, a silence indistinguishable from the weariness that came over you, and you lay there listening as wave after wave approached and lifted you up, until at last one came big enough to drown you.

The water was warmer than expected, almost lukewarm at first, and in different circumstances it might have been quite pleasant to feel it wash over you, bringing a momentary alarm every time, which then ebbed away, while your wound throbbed. It did not feel cold until it had been in contact with your body for some while, when it began to dry on your face, and the thin crust of salt was suddenly icy cold, all the warmth gone now, and the next wave couldn't come soon enough for you. Then your arms were even heavier to move, and your legs, after what seemed to have been a brief thaw, were already becoming fixed in their present position, and instead of motion there was just a splintering sound, barely audible, a quiet tinkling, like thin glass breaking and showering down to right and left of you.

You just managed to raise yourself slightly on your elbows, and saw the scattered boats, ten at the first count, twelve at the second, and about as many occupied rafts. Most of them had lowered their oars into the sea, but no one was taking much trouble to row any more, for those still in the water must be dead by now, but you had only to close your eyes for a moment and they would change places, as if in a gigantic mobile, moving on as though obeying a set of firmly established rules, although they rocked lazily and apparently motionless on the waves. In fact they seemed to be turning around you, the cries they exchanged were fewer now, only names and sometimes an answer, or more often silence, and then you could hear a wail, a sound of lamentation immediately dying down, when someone recognised a friend among the figures drifting motionlessly away, but their faces all looked the same to you. You saw their yellowish skin, already bloated, and one man could just as well have been another, the engineer who turned in a circle for a while in front of you, very slowly, could equally have been one of the merchant seamen who had come with you from the Isle of Man, or the professor, or one of the two Italians, until at last you did not even notice when a head knocked against the raft on which you lay.

It was becoming perceptibly more difficult for you to keep your eyes open, so groggy did you feel. And soon you could not raise yourself on your elbows any more, your arms were failing you, but in the small area that you could still see, without having to move, boats appeared, now more, now fewer. Time passed and, however long it was before you looked again, the sky was still there, and so was the sea, and another day was moving inexorably towards noon and evening, even though its mechanism was clearly out of joint.

The water was no longer warm when it washed over you. Its chill overcame you instantly, taking your breath away, and next moment you lay fighting for air and feeling the wave running off your arms and legs, felt its rivulets like veins down the outside of your skin, with the blood freezing in them. You could still raise your head just a little, though, and you looked down past your chest at your legs, saw your pyjamas, which did not move, their material clinging to you in stiff folds although there was a light breeze, saw your bare toes gleaming greenish blue.

Almost automatically your glance went to the gradually lifting layer of cloud. Then it lingered on the surface of the water, and there were the boats again, and you wished they would finally disappear, go away and dissolve in that hazy light on the horizon, so that you could stop wondering, whenever one of them chanced to come close and you could hear the voices of its occupants, whether it might approach you. Their presence confused you, but when you could not see any you tried to move your head, millimetre by millimetre, until the bows of one of them came into the grey edge of your field of vision, or a stern, and beyond, where sky and sea met, there was still a blank area, a strip of space belonging to neither one nor the other.

You closed your eyes more and more often now and, but for the sounds that still reached you, there was nothing all around except the sea spilling over all boundaries. Your head had stopped hurting, it was numb, and you felt the cold only as a tickling sensation when the water ran down you, seeming to increase the size of your body every time. It was as if the outside world were moving further and further away, and probably you did not even realise how close the boat really was when one finally did come your way, suddenly rocking up and down right in front of you as if it had been there all the time.

At least, its side was now scraping against your raft, with a groaning sound that seemed to come from deep in the sea, and if you saw the men bending over you in turn at all it was as if through a magnifying glass, or a thick layer of ice, and perhaps you could just hear what they were saying about you. You had not been able to move your head for some time, all sensation had left your limbs, and you stared at them with wide eyes, while their mouths opened and shut like those of fish in an aquarium. They were obviously arguing and, whenever one of them pointed to you, he crooked his finger in front of your eyes and then straightened it at a right angle, but you could not feel whether your pupils were moving, following the gesture.

Then you probably heard only a rushing sound, or at the most fragments or scraps of words and, when someone finally nudged you with an oar, his movement came to a halt far from your body, and there followed a knocking sound echoing as if in a huge space. You did not feel him touch your head, and again the sudden stop, as if he had come up against a shroud of glass surrounding you entirely, and when he felt your chest it sounded like ice being scratched, there would surely be white traces left in the air above your ribcage, a scraping along your legs. Although he tried repeatedly he could not turn you over, and when he had prodded you several more times, always producing a different sound, he obviously turned to the men sitting and standing behind him and signed to them to row away.

Perhaps you could still see the oars going up and down as the boat moved off, perhaps you saw the water dripping from the blades, and then nothing for a long time. The sun came out and began to light up the surface of the sea, but you did not notice. Nor did you realise that the wind had died down and, when a sea-plane appeared among the last scraps of cloud, it must have seemed to you like a hallucination, if you were aware of it at all suddenly looming there in the air above you.

It flew low and circled the scene of the disaster a few times before throwing out packets, and the boats made for them from all directions. At first it looked as if it might come down on the sea, but then it stayed just above the water, tirelessly cruising around, and the chug of its propeller came closer and then moved off at regular intervals. Now and then it pulled away, climbed in the cold sky or described a wide arc above the horizon, returned just before it seemed about to disappear and resumed its circling, so that a ship could see it from afar.

8

MADELEINE

It was Madeleine who told me about the ship wrecked off the Irish coast and who had really been on board, which came as such a surprise that I was in urgent need of her step-by-step account before I could recover from my confusion. Months had passed since my visit to the Isle of Man, I had been in my new job at the Baumgartnerhöhe hospital for some time, and I had almost forgotten my investigations when I came upon her by-line in the newspaper for which she wrote and, on impulse, without expecting anything to come of it, made contact with her again. Her article related to documents only just released to the public in London, on the role of the Channel Islands during the Occupation, and I may have felt encouraged to find it in a publication not usually known for its liberal attitude. It dealt with the only German concentration camp on British soil, opened on Alderney in the summer of 1940, where hundreds if not thousands of slave labourers were murdered, mainly Russians and Ukrainians, but including some French Jews and political prisoners from Germany. She also examined the question of collaboration with the Wehrmacht by the local population of Jersey and Guernsey and, when I phoned to congratulate her on tackling the subject, for from an Austrian viewpoint it was at most a mere footnote to the horrors of the war on the Continent,

I found it easy to move on to my own story. She remembered neither my letter nor the card I had sent her, but this time she was friendly instead of taking me to task, and we arranged to meet that afternoon in the Café Griensteidl on Michaelerplatz, where I found her waiting in the half-empty restaurant, even though I was early myself.

I don't remember the exact course of our conversation, but it wasn't long before she began to talk about the identity switch, and she told me she herself had known only for the last few months that she had been married for years to a man who was pretending to be someone else. If her information was accurate, this was not the sole instance of two internees on the Isle of Man exchanging identities because they either wanted or did not want to be deported to Canada or Australia, and such substitutions were facilitated by the initial state of confusion in the camps, and the fact that the authorities were happy to fill their quotas, in case of doubt asking no questions as long as the numbers added up, but when she told me about the interrogations focusing on the notorious Brown House and the card game that decided who was to go and who could stay, I could only shake my head in astonishment. It upset me to realise, from what she said, that the ideas I had formed of Hirschfelder and his life with the judge's family in London after escaping from Vienna did not after all apply to the writer whom Max admired, and whose three wives I now knew, but to a refugee who had probably died in the shipwreck.

According to Madeleine's information, the original Hirschfelder must have been dead for more than 50 years, and it was the mysterious fourth man, one of his room-mates on the Isle of Man, who had not only taken his name, but also seemed to have adopted his past history.

This was the Hirschfelder of whom his other two wives had

spoken without knowing anything of his double existence, his two half-lives, while Madeleine was under no illusion any longer but knew that she had been taken in by an impostor.

"Everything he told me about his life before the war was more or less stolen," she said, without altering her expression. "Perhaps it sounds odd, but since I hadn't even met him then it doesn't make much difference to me."

There was something defiant about her, something childishly rebellious, that touched me against my will, reinforcing my first impression that she was one of those who have learnt to show courage. The way she blew her hair back from her forehead must have been a habit of long standing, an odd one for a woman of 60, even if she seemed to be in a state of some agitation, and I kept expecting her to do it again. Even as I arrived I'd noticed that she never took her eyes off the door and, throughout the conversation, she was in fact watching everyone who came in as if to reassure herself that they were no threat to her; only then could she devote her attention to me again. Although it was late autumn her face was almost aggressively bronzed, she wore an unusually low neckline for the time of year and, as with Margaret earlier, I could not imagine her beside Hirschfelder, in whom I still saw the fine mind Max had admired, or at least that was one of the attributes he ascribed to him, depending on circumstances.

"I don't suppose I need tell you his real name," she went on. "You probably guessed it long ago."

She was right, but I still wanted to hear it from her, and I pretended to be slow on the uptake, asking more questions, as if to clear away all doubt and, for some reason, I was quite surprised by the speed with which she answered.

"It was Harrasser, if you insist," she said sarcastically. "I don't suppose that will alter the high opinion you obviously have of him."

So what Hirschfelder had told Margaret was a fairy-tale, all his chopping and changing between accusing himself of killing a man of that name and protesting that there was no such person, and she must have been making up that part whenever she spoke of it, unless he really meant that in changing his identity he had put an end to his own life. And what he had told Catherine of his deportation to Canada on the *Duchess of York* lacked any kind of background detail; there might indeed have been a ship of the Canadian Pacific line so called which left Liverpool with refugees on board in the penultimate week of June that year, as Madeleine confirmed, but obviously there could have been no Harrasser on board. In fact he had gone on inventing new stories simply as camouflage, erecting a structure of lies out of a guilty conscience because the man he was pretending to be had died in his place, until only the necessity of concealing the inadequacies of his account forced him at least to remain true to the changeable nature of his fantasies.

"Then every time he spoke his real name it was like conjuring up a ghost," I said. "It looks as if he must have entertained all kinds of different ideas for exorcising it."

Madeleine hesitated for a moment, and glanced at a waiter making haste through the bar, calling someone to the phone, and customers at all the tables he passed pointed to a white-haired old man sitting at the very back of the room with a pile of newspapers in front of him, obviously the only one not to have noticed the waiter's quest.

"Oh, that was very like him, believe me," she replied at last. "If you'd ever met him you'd know that there was always something rather unreal about him."

I asked what she meant, but she only shrugged her shoulders and looked at me as if I had cornered her unnecessarily.

"Some people are less firmly grounded on the earth than others," she continued, like any incurable romantic. "The advantage is that you see through them more and more easily as time goes by."

I couldn't make much of that, but I did recall certain inconsistencies mentioned by Catherine without my thinking anything of them at the time: Hirschfelder's contradictory remarks about his father, his curious reaction to the news that his grandmother had died in Theresienstadt, the fact that, after his release from the Isle of Man, he never felt moved to visit the judge's family. I remembered that she had spoken of his sealing up his memory, saying he had offered her a frozen version of his past and, in view of the substitution, it was not surprising, since all he had told her was pure hearsay. And his claim to be Jewish was obviously invented, an allusion to the other man, an arrogant pretence, and I was painfully moved to recollect her description of that war-time evening when he had gone so far as to make much of his alleged eastern European origins, just because it was the thing at the time, painting a merciless picture of a backwater he didn't even know, but in which he claimed to have had a rabbi among his ancestors, and becoming entangled in the most cliché-ridden notions.

All at once there was nothing surprising about his failure to answer Clara's letter when it finally reached him, years later, sent on from the Isle of Man just before the end of the war, for he hadn't known her at all, had never had anything to do with a housemaid in Smithfield, he was simply passing on what he had heard about her from the other man, which also explained her absence from his diary, as well as the fact that the gaps in it were not really gaps any more. If he did not mention the card game that had spared him deportation, it seemed more than understandable in view of the fact that he was living under a false name and, after the disaster off the coast of Ireland, he can hardly have felt inclined even to mention the refugee ships putting out for overseas destinations. Finally, the Brown House and the Nazi sympathisers in the camp might well have been of no interest to him as a non-Jew and, reluctant as one may be to say so, that in itself was not so very unusual.

Madeleine had heard the story of the identity switch from Lomnitz and Ossovsky, as I guessed even before she began telling me how they had visited her a few months after Hirschfelder's death. They came out with it unasked. Apparently they lived in Mödling, one was a retired senior civil servant and the other, at the age of 75, was still working as the director of an electrical goods company and, although she had not really kept in touch with them over the past few years, she knew they were around, she had a link with them through her former husband, and I thought of their visits to Southend-on-Sea as described by Margaret and his tirades when they left, his angry descriptions of them as bastards, scroungers and Jews, although she assured me they were his only friends. I wondered seriously whether they might have been blackmailing him, whether they were demanding payment for their silence about his real background, hence their sombre visitations, but of course that was nonsense, first he had no money, and second he had obviously done nothing for which he could really have been prosecuted, and I listened in silence as she sang their praises, telling me that after apparently not seeing him for ages they had turned up at his house in sentimental mood with no ulterior motives, now that they were old they were going in search of their youth, under the illusion that they would find it with him, of all people, in recalling their months together in the camp, while he had wanted to forget the whole thing. And it was they, she said, who put the idea of writing his biography into her head and, when she told me she had finished her researches, I asked whether she meant the real story or the one he had concocted for himself, which produced a smile, as if she had just been waiting to tell me about that.

"Both, of course," she said. "What do you think?"

I laughed, because she had talked herself into a state of excitement, and she told me how she intended to tackle the subject, constantly repeating a sentence that I couldn't get out of my head afterwards.

"My point of departure will be the shipwreck."

It was now that I heard the name for the first time and, as soon as she had spoken it, she opened her handbag and almost solemnly handed me a brochure advertising a week's cruise on the *Arandora Star* to the fjords of south-west Norway and Bergen, saying she had found it in an antique dealer's in Greenwich. This might be nothing special in itself, but her sudden excitement was infectious and, as she watched me, I leafed through the pamphlet, which looked like the volumes published by a certain house in Paris, Max always had a small collection of them, although he could hardly read French, and this pamphlet had the same blue lettering on a white background, and the blue star which was the logo of the shipping line as well as the colophon of the French book series. She clearly expected some comment, but I didn't know what I was supposed to say, so fascinated was I, so intently did I immediately start trying to decipher the notes in faded, female handwriting beside the various ports, so significant did I find those brief remarks, noting an hour's stop-over, or the kind of weather that day, or simply mentioning a certain word upon which I came repeatedly, a word that kept recurring, and I found that the ticks relating to it, almost without exception, were sightings of glaciers.

I can't say whether that was the reason, but when Madeleine also mentioned that before the ship was fitted out for cruises it had plied between Europe and South America as a refrigerator ship I thought of Max sounding off about the Snow Queen's palace where the refugees met again, the audacious metaphorical language, apparently designed purely for obfuscation, in which he spoke of it. There is no doubt that I was forcibly reminded of his obsession with the subject, his constant references to ice and snow, connecting Hirschfelder with them, his description of exile as a slow process of freezing and, although he might in fact have been right there, I did not like his relish for the theme and his admiration, indeed glorification of him for that too, which reminded me of what he had once told me was his own recurrent childhood wish, a dream of hovering in a glass cage over a storm-tossed sea alone with his books, far from the rest of humanity. As it happens he was crediting him with the most extravagant ideas, but I cannot shake off the image whenever I try to picture the way the other man died in the shipwreck, I always end up yet again seeing him unable to move, lying outstretched on a raft, gradually freezing to death on what was apparently a very mild day.

I was surprised to find out how many details Madeleine knew about the sequence of events in that disaster, until I discovered she had embarked upon, and was still engaged in, a correspondence with a representative of the Blue Star Line, a lively exchange of letters dealing with her questions about the six hours between the moment when the ship was hit and the time when a Canadian destroyer approached the lifeboats, and there was a certain professional coldness in the way she spoke of it.

"There were almost 1,700 people on board, counting the crew and the guards, and half of them perished," she said. "The real scandal was that most of the survivors were sent on to Australia only a week later."

I had not expected her to show personal emotion, but here she let a few moments pass as if she were listening to the sound of her own words dying away.

"And then there are various lists of people who died in the wreck, although a few of them mentioned there must really have survived after all."

While I didn't believe it, I said what I had to say, and could have bitten my tongue next moment.

"Then the other man might still be alive too."

"I'm afraid everything seems to suggest that he isn't," she replied. "As far as I know his name isn't anywhere."

The bar had filled up by now, and she had kept greeting various people who came in, raising her hand to wave to them without interrupting herself, which disturbed me, although I don't know why, as if her acting in this way would of itself tip her narrative over into the merely anecdotal, and to confirm my fears she turned to subjects that had only a rather distant connection with Hirschfelder's story.

"The ship was torpedoed by one of the most famous of the U-boat commanders," she said, as if this conferred an honour on the drowned men. "His name doesn't matter, but it makes you stop and think when you know that he also sank the *Royal Oak* in Scapa Flow in October the year before."

Suddenly she turned her eyes intently on me, emphasising every word she said, like a teacher used to getting her pupils' attention.

"As a naval support ship it was considered impregnable, so afterwards, of course, the rumours about spies in the country became more insistent, and they didn't die down until internment was introduced."

Then, as the crowning touch, she told me tales of other ships carrying deportees, but I wasn't listening properly any more, she had clearly read everything there was to read on the subject, and mere facts meant nothing to me, until I interrupted her and asked why she thought Hirschfelder had settled in England, why hadn't he gone home, as you might have expected, or at least resumed his old name?

"He doesn't seem to have had anyone left back here," she said. "His father must have been killed in the last months of the war, and how his mother died I don't know, but obviously she didn't survive either."

What came next was a surprise to me.

"Perhaps he was ashamed, and that kept him away."

"But the other man can't have been the reason," I said. "Although he probably felt guilty of his death he can't have played hide-and-seek all his life just because of that."

I noticed her initial hesitation, and when she finally spoke again she did so slowly, pausing after a few words, and then making sure that she added the rest as quickly as possible so that she could fall silent again.

"Well, there was the Jewish girl too."

This was the first I had heard of Rachel, or the fact that Hirschfelder himself did indeed come from the Salzkammergut, and there was no need for me to ask her more questions, not that I could have stopped her anyway.

"He would certainly have had more cause to blame himself on her account," she said. "He let her down disgracefully."

Lomnitz and Ossovsky had given her this information too when they visited her and told her how Hirschfelder had been on the Isle of Man under a false name all the time, letting everyone know about his love for the girl, the three weeks he said he had spent with her, their happiness under threat from the first, and then her sudden arrest by the uniformed men.

"The truth seems to have been far more prosaic," she said with considerable sarcasm. "All the same, he must have stuck to his story until he fell into a maudlin mood one day and let the other two in on the secret."

It was a fact that the girl and her father had turned up at his family's inn the spring before the war, half frozen, wet, and in a pitiful condition generally, it was a fact that the university lecturer and his daughter were in flight and, as regular visitors over many years, found refuge there, but he had not previously told the tale of how he was sent to get money out of them every day, he had never mentioned the conversations downstairs when his parents said they couldn't keep them much longer, the neighbours knew who it was they were hiding and, after much discussion, he had always climbed the stairs, knocked on the door, and there stood the friendly, elderly gentleman in the doorway, holding out a few banknotes which he took without a word. Nor could there be any doubt that he had fallen for the girl, but how often he actually succeeded in seeing her face to face over those three weeks was another question, since he generally waited for her to appear in vain – she scarcely left the room at all except for supper – he listened in the corridor and couldn't even hear voices, only footsteps pacing up and down, interrupted by her constant coughing and gasping for breath. He had made much of their walks together by the lake, but that was certainly an exaggeration: he had persuaded her to go out with him only once, when she was feeling a little better than usual, and he had taken her down to the banks of the water by secret pathways, and then sat in the sun beside her without a word, several times taking a deep breath to say something, but unable to bring out more than a few clumsy civilities, and finally just staring in silence at her blue lips and her blue fingers.

I remember how Madeleine's voice dropped as she told me that the girl was sick, how she stopped looking round and gazed

271

down at her hands, a frozen expression in her eyes.

"She had a hole in the heart."

I repeated it at once, of course, and as I looked her in the eye I was thinking of Clara's gingerbread pendant and its inscription.

"I'm not sure exactly what that means," she added, "I got someone to explain it to me, but I can't really tell you much, only that there was a gap in the septum which ought to have closed when she took her first breath as a baby."

Then she hesitated again, as if to make sure I was not the wrong person to receive this confidence, but she obviously shook off her reservations and smiled at me.

"And then there was her asthma."

There was little left of the strong-minded businesswoman who could resist any opposition as she told me how the girl's condition had deteriorated when her father suddenly had to go to Vienna. All at once she looked less rigidly armoured in her suit, and she could not have spoken of a daughter of her own more tenderly or with greater care and concern, telling me how the decline began when the child stopped coming to the door in answer to a knock, and did not touch the food set before her, and sounds came from the room as if she were fighting for breath. Madeleine called her Rachel as naturally as if she were one of her own family, while she no longer described Hirschfelder as her husband, as she had done once or twice earlier, although she immediately corrected herself, but whenever she mentioned his name now it was coolly, and she accused him of failing to stand up more firmly to his parents, who had insisted that they could do nothing more if they weren't all going to end up behind bars.

This was the kind of story bound to end in the worst possible way, at the latest when the girl's father failed to return as he had planned. It was clear next day that he must have been caught, and

Hirschfelder went to her room to tell her. The discussions with his parents continued, the daily arguments over what was to become of her now that there was no one to pay for her, and meanwhile the idea of her lying in her bed, like a ghost, perhaps even hearing them bargaining over her fate, makes one wish in retrospect to intervene, to take him by the shoulders, shake some sense into him and put an end to it. One can scarcely believe that he did nothing, merely waited, and it would be a mistake to think there was some hope for him because he did go to the doctor after all, but that was only the wretched end of the story, a pitiful episode: he knocked and asked for him late in the evening, but when he came to the door he suddenly took fright again and never said a word about her, just made up something about his mother's sending him to fetch valerian drops or a headache powder, or dodged questions on some other trivial pretext, and then simply made off in mid-sentence.

Three days later the girl was dead, and Hirschfelder had brought his parents to the point where they decided it would be better if he went away somewhere for a while, why not to England where he could forget the whole thing, and I remember Madeleine's resigned laughter as she said that, and then she told me what they had done with the corpse.

"They just took it down to the lake by night and left it there, and they got away with their cold-blooded conduct too," she said. "At least, there doesn't seem to have been any investigation."

Then she searched in her handbag again and, when I think of the picture she produced and the way she presented it to me, her look as she did so, the watchfulness I suddenly saw in her eyes, I still cannot accept the end of it all, it seems so unimaginable in connection with that photograph of Rachel given to her by Lomnitz and Ossovsky. Apparently Hirschfelder himself had left it to them in his will. It was a portrait of a girl with light eyes and blonde hair, so worn that it looked over-exposed, and I remember that I was not surprised when she told me about his quarrel with the two of them over it in the camp, but I wondered whether, unknown to any of them, the actual subject of their disagreement had not, even then, been the true story. He had obviously left it to them as a gesture of gratitude for keeping his secret, and had said they could do what they liked with it after his death, they could have it and tell the story of his real life without regard for his memory, and I remember how she laughed at this expression, saying that otherwise no doubt she would never have known he had a "real life" at all.

It seemed to me improbable that what Hirschfelder had done before she knew him didn't bother her, that it made no difference to her who or what he might once have been, as she had seemed anxious to assure me at the beginning of our conversation. For of course it couldn't be chance that when preparing to write her book she had always avoided visiting the Salzkammergut, saying she hadn't been able to bring herself to go to his old home and dig around in his past, which sounded to me like an excuse for inaction. At first sight it appeared to satisfy her to discover at last, from his two friends, why he left England every summer to visit the place. She seemed content to think that he himself had always been in search of something, a man drawn back to his roots, but I sensed that in reality it made her uneasy not to have learned more about it, and I felt sure that her disparaging remarks on the conventional kind of biography, which she dropped into the conversation now and then, were only an admission of her uncertainty because she hadn't really known him; she attacked the usual presentation of a life in chronological order, as if there was any doubt that it began with birth and ended with death, and in between went straight from one to the other, unless you kept creating an illusion for yourself that deviations from this path were at least possible.

True enough, he apparently had no relations left and the inn had been closed long ago, but still she might have gone to see whether there were any traces of him to be found, whether she might not check the few facts Lomnitz and Ossovsky had given her about his childhood and youth, so that Hirschfelder could assume his true contours in her eyes, at least in retrospect.

Well, I for one would have found that to be the natural course of action had I decided to write about him, but when I suggested it she dismissed the subject, and then said something rather odd, as if it had only just struck her.

"It's strange, but the part of his life I shared with him myself seems to me vaguer than anything else in my researches, and rightly or wrongly, I can't shake off a feeling that I know more about the time when I wasn't with him than the years we spent together."

Then she told me that of course she had also turned to Margaret and Catherine for information to help with her project, although neither of them knew who Hirschfelder really was, and here she had asked straight questions and received straight answers, a process that failed completely when she came to her own memories, or at least did not produce a sequence of events of any use for her purposes.

This struck me as a little too clever, too much of a rhetorical figure ending in an elegant, studied silence, and I immediately demurred.

"Well, the best I could do would be to present him in a certain light," she insisted. "But then he'd be almost invisible, a shadow standing perfectly still."

I thought this affected too, but said no more, and luckily she went straight on to tell me how she had met Hirschfelder, and continued darting glances round the room as she fell into that tone of cool irony familiar to me from many all-female gatherings.

It was to have been one of her first big scoops when she went to

275

Southend-on-Sea in the Fifties to interview him after the publication of his book, but even then it had been difficult for her to form any real idea of him, and she fell back on a description of the town and his study at the Palace Hotel. From the first, any attempt to pin him down to a few specific facts was a failure: he gave evasive answers, she said, laughed at her industrious note-taking, and finally took the reporter's pad from her hands and told her that she didn't need it, she'd be able to strike the right tone without that scribbling, and that was all that mattered. As a result she prolonged her stay, the weekend she had planned became a week and, after that, she had abandoned any hope of being able to write about him – but she didn't go home; instead, she left her boarding house and accepted his suggestion that she move in with him, although Catherine had walked out on him not long before, to occupy the attic room, at first for the summer, and by the end of that summer they were sharing bed and board, living in sin, as she put it in a sweetly old-fashioned way, before they married in due course a few months later.

Hirschfelder was in his mid-thirties then, she in her early twenties, and I tried to work out what lay behind her matter-of-fact statement that she had just stayed on. At that time and at her age it can't have been an easy decision to make, although that was how she presented it now. I asked no questions, I merely pictured a young student venturing out into the world for the first time and falling for the resigned maturity of a man who seemed to be living proof that the war was not yet over and shattered her girlish dreams, obliterating them merely with the weight of his claimed experiences, his mother's alleged suicide, his invented flight from Vienna, his internment. Hearing her call herself naïve, I felt sure he had not made much fuss about it: dinner in a fairly expensive Soho café, a weekend visit to the cinema, a ferry crossing to the

Hook of Holland and then on by train to Amsterdam, all carefully calculated, until in the end he confined himself to walks with her up and down the promenade on the sea front as darkness fell, that is if she didn't object, and found some excuse to go along the pier and look at the lights of the Thames estuary, as he had done with Catherine and would do again years later with Margaret. In other respects as well he had quickly fallen back into his old habits and, after the first excitement when she moved in, had continued to live his own life between the house, the library, and his room in the Palace Hotel, while she began sending unsolicited articles to newspapers at home, hardly any of which found their way into print: impressions of London, tours of the city parks, walks in the West End, visits to museums, little sketches which only betrayed how difficult she was finding it to fill her time.

The rest of it was soon told: her constant efforts to get him to mix with company, invitations from neighbours to gatherings where he barely uttered a word all evening, or if he had drunk too much was inclined to make offensive remarks on any pretext, any little thing that didn't suit him, insisting that the opposite was true and reverting to the subject until everyone could see that he actually welcomed a disagreement; her attempts to surprise him with theatre tickets, when he wanted only to know how much they had cost; her requests that he wouldn't retreat to his study on Sunday but would do something with her instead. There was a certain logic in the way that, as she described it, she might not have set eyes on him all day, but in the evening he was able to resume their conversation exactly where he had interrupted it that morning. She could spend the weekend away with a girlfriend and he wouldn't even notice, and when she began going home to Austria, first for a few days and then, more frequently, for longer periods, he took it as a matter of course, just as he did when she called to say when she would be back or, when it was no longer a question of coming back, told him when she would visit, assuring her he would be glad to see her without asking any questions, even when she had been gone for months, even after the year when she thought she had left him for good, but in the end her resolve failed her. At such times she often felt as if he and not she had been away, so dislocated, from her point of view, were time and space, unbalancing each other when she thought of herself travelling from Southend-on-Sea to London, getting into the Tube at Liverpool Street Station, changing at South Kensington or Gloucester Road to the line for Heathrow, then flying to Vienna, and meanwhile he scarcely moved from the spot where she had left him, was gone and gone for good.

I had the feeling of a great gap opening up in time when she said that she felt she could have called him even years after they finally divorced and she would be able to reach him, even after his death she caught herself thinking she had only to dial his number and he would answer the phone in his room at the Palace Hotel, for it seemed to her unimaginable that he could ever have left.

"It struck me that he was all the more averse to coming home the easier it would have been for him," she said. "Anyway, when we were first together it was totally useless for me to try persuading him at least to give it a go."

It seemed he had even been offered a post in the Austrian National Library after the publication of his book, through her efforts, but he turned it down indignantly, as if it were the utmost insult even to mention it to him, even to think he could settle in Vienna of all places, why for heaven's sake would he want to be regarded as an eminent character there?

"But of course he wasn't a refugee at all," she went on. "At least, no one actually made him go abroad before the war, and how many of the real exiles were invited back afterwards as he was?"

278

I made some naïve answer, and she shook her head, as if she had only gradually become aware of his arrogance in placing himself on a par with those who had been forced to emigrate while they still could, and often received not so much as an apology later, let alone anything else.

"Still, one can't say he stayed away just to be coy, or out of a private urge that he had to come to terms with," she said. "Behind it lies his responsibility for the death of the other man, the one who disappeared off the Irish coast."

In fact his attitude reminded me slightly of Max, his aphorisms, the reasons, immature for all their self-mockery, which he gave for going off to write and leaving me alone, the ridiculous way he would proclaim that he was going into exile – since he could perfectly well come back if he wanted, the word was rather too grand for his excursions – his attempts at flight or whatever they should be called, but anyway there was something disturbing behind it, although he had probably never been really clear what it was himself. He used to get up and go off every few months, as if he had to do penance for some nameless sin, as if he had to earn his right to live with other people, it had always been a case of going away so that he could not just come back but come home, he was intent on sitting it out, enduring a punishment he had imposed on himself. Although he would naturally have denied this explanation, speaking in high-flown terms of inspiration, the great cities he visited, life in general, all those vague terms that he made the excuse to perform his equally vague spiritual exercises without having to justify himself to me. That may sound feeble, but it's a fact that he was only giving his loneliness a new location – and why not? I might even have been impressed by his notorious inability to fit in anywhere, or perhaps it was his unwillingness to fit in, emerging in never-ending monologues about his alleged grievances, if his

279

self-pity had not been involved, I might have liked him for it if he didn't always have an eye open for gaining credit, if he hadn't followed the old, old pattern, a frame of mind which has led others before him astray, in which he indulged in bouts of megalomania to the effect that he was going into the desert, even if he really just meant a week in Paris, setting off for the wilderness or, as he would probably rather have put it, into the icefields, and his return must of course be triumphant, comparable only with the return of an Antarctic explorer at the beginning of the century, assuming he didn't have the dubious good luck of perishing on the way.

I don't know whether it was the same with Hirschfelder, whether he had devised a similar set of delusions to ensure that he would ultimately be remembered as a hero, but if so, it's a chilling thought. It was all very well, and might not mean much, for Madeleine to tell me casually that he seemed to lack any sense of closeness or distance, but what she went on to say about his writing struck me as all too familiar: you noticed, she remarked, you heard in every sentence he wrote that the apparent composure of his style was really just detachment. I'm still wondering why I didn't hit on the parallel for myself. Although I had thought no more of it, his narrative manner was familiar to me even before I had read the first of his stories, the absolute nature of his approach to everything, life and death, constancy and betrayal, his disregard for daily routines and the resultant compelling impression of a sterile construct, and this, ultimately, was what I had detected in Max too, nor was I the only one, and it now seems to me as if it were no coincidence, as if there were more to it than his admiration for the old man, more than his perhaps taking him as his guide – dubious as the expression may be, it was an elective affinity and, although it did not strike me for a long time, it may have been one of the main reasons why I started my own researches in the first place.

I did not get a very forthcoming answer when I asked Madeleine about Hirschfelder's manuscript, the one Max had mentioned containing the presumed masterpiece on which he was supposed to have been working for so long, although not a line of it could now be found.

"That sounds to me like pure fantasy," she said. "Try as I may, I can't imagine him writing anything like that."

I repeated what I'd been told about the four school reunions, the 21 lives on which the book was supposed to turn, but I became entangled in my explanations and, in the end, felt that I had made nothing very clear.

"One wonders what might have become of him in different circumstances," I said, trying again. "I mean, suppose he'd had the courage to do something for Rachel."

I felt her place her hand on my arm and pat it as if I needed soothing, and there was a moment's silence before she broke out laughing.

"Oh, then he wouldn't have been the man he was."

I didn't answer that, but it was clear that her amusement was aimed at me and, when I finally mentioned the title, if only to break the silence, she pounced on it at once.

"*The Living Live and the Dead are Dead.*"

I kept my eyes on her.

"Well, there you are, then," she said with great satisfaction. "Simplistic as it may sound, that sums up his dilemma exactly."

Then she paused and looked at me, as if she couldn't believe I didn't see the explanation as easily as she did.

"If you ask me, I think all that guff about a novel was just a game of concealment, and what we're really talking about is his autobiography."

Or anyway, she said, 30 years ago he kept planning to write the story of his life and, after the publication of his book, he had insisted that this was no time for fiction, and he must sit down and say what he had to say whether anyone wanted to hear it or not.

"I'm almost certain he'd already begun it at the time," she went on. "Which would also make it easier to explain why there isn't more of it in existance, or at least, we can guess at the scruples that might have persuaded him to destroy it before his death."

Then she told me, quite casually, that he had always called it *The English Years* and, more to give a complete picture than because I had thought much of it myself, I mentioned Catherine's suspicion that Margaret might have been careless enough to throw away some of his papers, but she merely shook her head, as if she had contemplated and rejected that idea long ago.

"Why in the world would she do that?"

I didn't know either, but I was surprised to hear her attacking Catherine, accusing her of hypocrisy which made her spread rumours plucked from the air, because I hadn't noticed any of that, while on the contrary her rather hostile attitude to his writing, a certain contempt because she thought it was less something a real man ought to do than a mark of irresponsibility to himself and his chances of making a success his life.

"I suppose that some time she'll reconcile herself to having lived with a perfectly normal human being," she said, the malice in her voice unmistakable. "Until then, she may as well believe there's still more about him to be brought to light."

The way she spoke of her reminded me of the unrelenting manner in which Catherine had spoken of Margaret, and I can't help smiling now to think that there again it was only a question of who had the right idea of Hirschfelder. It seems ironic in the extreme that none of them ever knew the original bearer of the name, only the man who had fooled them all for years, and for that very reason I can't see that his comparative honesty to each of them matters. If he really did work on his autobiography, he would probably have mentioned him, the man he met on the Isle of Man, the man who disappeared and whom none of them had ever encountered, but who occupied my imagination more than he did, the refugee known only to Clara, the woman in the wheelchair who could no longer speak about him or correct the possibly distorted fantasies I had formed of him myself, nor could she probably remember him at all, and the only other two people who knew anything about his life were Lomnitz and Ossovsky, themselves shadowy figures who might just as well have been pure inventions as far as I was concerned.

It was like a multiple disappearance – his death off the Irish coast, his extinction from Clara's memory, and the loss of the supposed autobiography if it had ever existed – with stories proliferating around it and acquiring a more independent life of their own the better known Hirschfelder became. In fact he had to wait for some time after the appearance of his book, which attracted little attention at first. He wasn't forgotten, he hadn't even made it to the point where he qualified for oblivion, and it was only a new edition ten or fifteen years later that made him famous almost overnight, in Austria anyway. For a while, and in certain journalistic circles, it was clearly the done thing to visit him, combining a paid holiday in London with a detour to Southend-on-Sea, and the articles and interviews which then followed each other in rapid succession only covered up the nub of the matter even further, smearing printer's ink and high-gloss lacquer over the gap in the centre where there was a hole, an empty space, the story of a man who disappeared.

I find it difficult to explain why Hirschfelder went along with this, why he was not sensitive enough to recognise the unacceptable aspect of being made into the symbol of something he was not: did he enjoy all the fuss being made of him, even if it wasn't really intended for him personally, did he just let himself drift with the tide, or was it mere cynicism which he didn't acknowledge and therefore did not find repellent? It might have been acceptable to pretend to be someone else for as long as he was not publicly fêted for it, but the fact that he promoted the mystery himself, and had actually begun to do so even during the war, seems to me more than distasteful now that I know something about the dead man. He was fostering exactly the kind of sentimentality against which Max was always fulminating in upholding his image as a lonely champion, and I wonder how he could amuse himself at the expense of the most industrious of his visitors, how he could laugh at them for taking the bait when it was he, with the lie he was living, who had often brought them to call on him in the first place, going to "view the Jewish raree-show" as it seems he put it, coming to his house and reducing everything to the same question as their fathers and grandfathers did, except that they no longer asked it straight, not in the tones of a sergeant-major, and at least now the wrong answer did not mean death but their fulsome enthusiasm, their awe-stricken murmurs, the snot and urine that cost them nothing.

At that time, anyway, he had not yet withdrawn into seclusion, and the gentlemen who appeared in succession were all prepared, had been to the war departments of the London museums in due form to see what there was to be seen, had even, if they were interested in deportation overseas, made a pilgrimage out to Greenwich to look through the shipping registers, and were still shaken by a simulated air raid that had been part of the programme when they came to his door, sometimes arriving like field researchers who really thought they were approaching the subject of their study, an example of a species threatened with extinction which, however, they could hardly wait to impale and dissect according to the rules of their craft. He usually took them round his house or showed them his room at the Palace Hotel, telling his stolen story of his flight from Vienna for the hundredth time, decking it out with more and more new details, and they sat there listening to him like children who hadn't even been born then, or weren't old enough to understand what was going on before their eyes, or else they had in fact understood and were now expiating their guilt, watching him anxiously so as not to put a foot wrong, waiting for a chance to embark on their theme at last. It was something to do with the way they looked at the place, surreptitiously searching the most remote corners for some clue or staring at the blank walls, as if the word they dared not speak stood there in giant letters just as it had stood scrawled in blood red on the shop windows of their native towns 30 or 40 years before, and only when he offered them a glass of wine did they thaw out slightly, some of them even venturing on a benediction, and before long they would be asking their standard question at the least – as a survivor, did he feel guilty? – little knowing how accurately it struck at the very core of his existence, talking about their friends in Israel or regretting that they didn't have any, preferably ending up with the Bible, chosen as an innocuous subject, mentioning the exodus from Egypt and comparing his own story with it, and once, in the twilight, one of them had stepped out on the balcony with a bottle under his arm, made a sweeping gesture up and down the Thames estuary and over the lights sparkling on the water, asking what distinguished this night from all other nights, and next moment answering himself, it's our meeting that distinguishes this night from all other nights, and had fallen on his neck, a fellow stinking of sweat and alcohol with a drooping moustache and soft, spongy hips, something in television by his own account of it, a man who didn't feel foolish planting damp kisses on his cheeks, left and right, and even calling him Gabriel.

Of course they hadn't all been like that, there had been decent people among them whose sole aim was not to pin him down to the accident of birth, but the others were those on whom Hirschfelder always held forth, the sentimental sort unable to do anything but fling themselves on his breast, poor well-meaning idiots, as he himself called them, who didn't know how to behave with him, yet had no scruples about asking him to turn this way or that, to present his profile for a photograph, and he let them do it, did not protest, acted the clown for them, until in the end they all wrote in almost identical terms, praising him as a delightful man. If he could think of no alternative to taking them out on the esplanade and dragging them round the fun-fair, some of them would enthuse about his sense of humour, preserved, as they said, in spite of everything, while others could scarcely conceal their astonishment at seeing someone like him still able to enjoy himself at all and, repelled by this reaction, he would often behave deliberately badly, with the result that they told themselves what a hard life he must have had to turn out like this, and the articles they then concocted read as if they were trying to abase themselves for every unkind thought of him, doing penance themselves for his calling them a bunch of old soaks or paying their women companions the most dubious compliments. Then they inevitably mentioned his attractive appearance and, in case of doubt or if at a loss, always spoke of his eyes, to which every colour of the rainbow had been ascribed over the years, they blew the most wonderful soap bubbles and became obsessed with daring notions to the effect that his were the eyes of a prostitute standing on a street corner in the rain, or the eyes of a soldier in the war just back from the front, or they resorted to sophistries, and never tired of wondering whether, in exile, he had gone into exile all over again, isolated as he was, or they speculated on whether he was better described as a cosmopolitan or a stateless man, meaning the same thing by both terms although they probably did not realise it, meaning a man suspended in space who, for all his unseemly conduct, appealed to them because he could call nowhere his own, not at home in Austria anyway, and was no threat to their own positions, where they made themselves at ease on returning from their little adventure as if from a crusade, and put their maudlin tales about him down on paper.

Madeleine obviously did not like discussing this subject, and she several times stressed that she was only passing on what she had heard from him, looking at me as if to make sure I didn't misunderstand her. By that time they were no longer living together, she just visited him in Southend-on-Sea once or twice a year, so what she knew was what he had told her, and now she seemed to expect me of all people to sit in judgement on him. It obviously wasn't good enough for me to try getting out of it by saying it wasn't him I was interested in so much as the other man, for in a way he had never existed, only the man who was missing, and she kept interrupting me or making an impatient gesture, thereby showing me what she thought of my attitude.

"Yes, I know it sounds rather strained, but all such fantasies are," I said. "Everyone picked and chose from the material available to make him into whatever suited them."

"It's easy for you to talk," she replied. "I spent ten years with him and, believe it or not, he was a flesh-and-blood man, not just a construct of the imagination."

I didn't hesitate to contradict her.

"I'm not so sure about that."

But I couldn't get much more out of her, and I was already out in the street and going along the Ring when the words I had just

287

spoken came back to my mind, and I thought how, after that, she sat there looking as if she felt cold and had to hold herself together. In the café I hadn't noticed that dark had fallen, or that it had been raining and then stopped again, and I was glad to have got away from her, I didn't have to see her glancing around again and not troubling to hide the fact that she wanted to be rid of me. I passed the Volksgarten, seeing the car headlights reflected on the wet tarmac, and I saw her before me, slowly freezing again. Without really being aware of it I had observed her from outside for another few moments as she took a handkerchief from her bag and dabbed her face with it, but when I walked on through the rain, which was just beginning again, through the sparkling drops which seemed to refract the gathering night into a thousand tiny splinters, I had almost forgotten her, I was remembering walking through Hyde Park in weather like this on my return from the Isle of Man, somehow making my way to the tiny streets behind the Brompton Road and thus to Rutland Gate, and finally I had been outside the Austrian Institute once more as if, on my last day in London, I couldn't wait to get home again.

It had been afternoon, but a gloomy afternoon with the rain falling at last after weeks of drought, and for a while I fancied myself in another time when a shower obliterated the view of the buildings in Park Lane, or when, as I turned a corner, I saw nothing but a line of gleaming black cabs coming towards me, so it might also have been a dream when I suddenly found myself standing outside the brightly lit Institute. The flag over the entrance was not moving, the first-floor windows were closed and, as I approached, I thought I could see the shadowy outlines of figures moving behind the curtains, I even thought for a moment that I heard a gramophone, with the voice of a woman singing, but then all was quiet again except for the rustling of the trees and the sound of traffic from the main road nearby. To my surprise the door was open, but the porter's lodge was empty as I went in and climbed the stairs unseen, and there wasn't a soul in sight up in the large room with the piano which I knew already, only the sound of the light fitting humming like a captive insect, and there were the photographs of the exiles still hanging on the walls, seeming to quiver on their long silk cords at the slightest breath of air.

At first I did not notice that the picture of Hirschfelder was gone and, just as the empty space where it must have hung leaped to my eye, the director of the Institute appeared behind me as if out of nowhere, asking what I was looking for. It was obvious that she was not expecting anyone else today and had only glanced into the room by chance before locking up and going home, and I was so taken aback that I couldn't bring out any answer for a couple of moments, I just pointed to the blank space near the sign indicating the lavatories, but she ignored my finger and took shelter behind the comment that I was the first visitor to the exhibition since the beginning of last week, making it sound as if she thought I ought not to be there either. So saying, she looked at the time, and had some difficulty disguising her impatience with me for arriving so late. When I finally told her why I had come she went very much on the defensive, reacting as if I had attacked her and she had to fight back.

"I don't know what makes you think that," she said, her gaze at last following the direction of my finger to the gap where the picture had been. "There was never a photograph there."

I denied this and, for a moment, she seemed to be wondering whether she should simply ask me to go away, but then decided against it.

"What did you say this gentleman's name was?"

Taking no notice of her irony, I repeated it, and she took a slim catalogue out of a desk drawer, laid it on the piano and ostentatiously opened it. Even before she looked at it she was reiterating her claim that what I said was impossible, she was never wrong, and treating the pages so roughly that I feared the leaflet would come to bits in her hands. Then she looked through it in silence for a while – only now did I notice that she was wearing the same dress as on our first meeting – and when at last she turned back to me the patronising tone in her voice which I had noticed before was more marked than ever.

"Well, there does seem to have been something there."

She mentioned a number, and I supplied the name again, but she was not to be thrown off balance by my identification.

"His wife must have withdrawn it," she said, without the least apology for her abrupt manner. "Obviously she came here herself a few days ago and fetched it."

If she knew the reason why, I did not learn it, for at that moment a couple of young women had appeared in the doorway – they reminded me of the two I had seen here before, as if no time at all had passed since then – and she just walked away from me, making haste once again to greet these innocent young creatures, positively angelic in their pallor, as if there were some special power of attraction about girls of good family which stamped any other person who happened to be present an outsider, as if there was some kind of conspiracy between them, and they would discuss nothing but horses and future lovers in riding boots, and I heard her repeatedly calling them by their first names, but addressing them with the respectful *Sie* pronoun, and for their part they called her Frau Magister, like someone in authority, in fact all that was lacking from the scene was for them to hitch up their skirts and make a little curtsey every time they said it, while I stood in front of the empty place on the wall racking my brains to work out why the picture wasn't there. Not that I expected them to go about in sackcloth and ashes, but it was a curious combination; the exhibition no one was bothering to visit and these children: one shouldn't hold it against them but I did, ready as they were to give another nice little recital of flute or guitar music in front of the photographs of the exiles, and it made me involuntarily wonder to whom they owed the chance, whose influence was behind them, whose offspring they were, and I had already walked out into the afternoon where the rain was now steaming as it dried on the asphalt, and thin wisps of mist clung to the trees, before realising that as I passed them they had not turned to look at me.

Nor was the matter of the withdrawn picture really cleared up when I wrote to Margaret a few days later, and she sent it to me, asking me to keep it but saying no more. This is the photograph which now hangs over my desk and, for a long while, it has looked to me as if it had been over-painted a hundred times, as if old layers of paint would come to light if I scratched it, as if not only would the other man's face appear beneath Hirschfelder's, but more and more faces under that. As long as I knew nothing about their identity switch I could look at it with an easy mind, but abstruse as this may seem I always connected it with Vienna, and ever since I had been living there I couldn't look at it without reflecting that the walls of that city positively exude a sense of absence and disappearance. It reminded me of Max, who always said that nowhere else in the world, among so many people who had reached the top, did he feel as if they had achieved their positions unjustly, nowhere else did he think so often that they occupied a space too large for them, independently of whether they were on the right side or the wrong side, it did not belong to them, they were only deputising and consequently must puff themselves up, only to move closer together again next moment until they were touching and had body contact to enable them to endure that emptiness, those huge gaps opening up in front of them, as if the famous charm with which they are credited were nothing but a mixture of outrageous self-assertion and their already half-forgotten awareness of it.

When Max began sounding off along these lines I had always felt he was expressing the provincial's resentment of the capital, but when I went home from my meeting with Madeleine that evening I suddenly knew that I should not feel as if I had finished with Hirschfelder's story until I had spoken to him about it. After all, he had acquainted me with the man, he had given me my first images, and now he should have them back again, I thought to myself, unrecognisable as they had become. Half an hour later I phoned his mother from my apartment, I had also addressed my letter to him from the Isle of Man care of her, she told me he must be in Vienna, and a few minutes later I had fixed a place to meet him next day. He was clearly not surprised to hear from me, he immediately agreed to everything I suggested, and the conversation ended in silence, as if all the time he had been working towards the point when I would ask if he was still there.

At first he didn't answer, and I heard his breathing quite close and then abruptly becoming quieter, as if he had noticed it himself and were trying to suppress it.

"What do you mean, am I still here?"

I repeated my question.

"Of course I am."

I heard the splutter of a match and knew he had lit a cigarette, and there followed a slightly sticky sound as he removed the filter from his lips before blowing out the smoke, while the hum of traffic in the background came to my ears. As if it were his heart-beat, a thumping which had nothing to do with him came on the line, and I began counting the separate pulses, but I hadn't reached ten before they fell silent again. All was quiet for a moment, and it made me feel nervous when I realised that he was listening too, just as I was, although I didn't notice the noises in the building until he had hung up again without another word.

This would be the first time we had seen each other since our divorce five years ago, and I don't know what I expected. We met in a café in the Fourth District, where he lived, and I remember the exaggerated confidence he radiated, as if he were under a compulsion to prove something when he talked about himself, but I tried not to look into his eyes, for their uncertain, enquiring gaze did not suit the rest of his appearance. In a way quite unlike him, he wore trousers with sharp creases in them and a black shirt, and he avoided speaking of the past, interrupting himself or changing the subject abruptly if danger threatened, or else he just left the talking to me as if to avoid putting a foot wrong, and I was relieved to find that he was making it so easy for us. Until he really began to let fly: I had thought this was the one time he would start moaning, when he said à propos of nothing that we never should have gone to Switzerland, where we had lived for two years, and then he came out with his complaints at length, saying it had been just like his days at boarding school when his father was late coming to fetch him on a Saturday afternoon, all the others had gone off for the weekend long ago and he was still waiting, he felt he would be shut up there for ever and lose what little youth still remained to him. I was beginning to fear he was never going to drop the subject, but he pulled himself together and asked why I had called him, and I can't say whether he had expected some other answer, but he became very attentive as I began talking about Hirschfelder, and at the end he expressed his surprise in his own way.

"You could write a novel about that."

I couldn't help myself, and began to laugh as if this were the most ridiculous idea imaginable, and he ought to know I had better things to do than waste my time like that.

"It's the last thing I'd think of doing," I replied. "There are far too many different versions of it already, and I don't see why I should add another."

I hadn't been thinking of his *Hommage à Hirschfelder*, but he immediately wanted to know if that was what I was referring to, and I realised he didn't believe me when I said no and asked him not to be so touchy.

"Oh, I was sick of all that myself, ages ago, but of course if you were to make me a present of your story I might be able to start again," he said. "I feel sure something different would come of it this time."

I was surprised, because he had just been telling me he hadn't written a line since then, and was getting by on occasional work, for instance teaching an annual course in creative writing for holiday-makers on a Greek island. None of his old ambitions showed, and I'd been wondering whether that was doing him good, and now the slightest hint was suddenly enough to make him jump at the idea, scarcely able to restrain his enthusiasm. He had obviously talked himself into a frenzy, and didn't even notice that I never took my eyes off him, he could have been speaking to himself, manoeuvring himself straight back into his old groove in no time at all.

"And I already know how I'll begin."

I saw the excitement in his face.

"'The best of luck with your new novel.'"

I don't remember exactly who had said that to him, but it was the maliciously intended wish he kept repeating after his unfortunate appearance in Vienna, and it made him laugh to be reminded of his monologues at the time. It struck me that his tone had changed, it was back the way it used to be when he embarked on his tirades, a monotonous sing-song, and even before he had really got into his swing I heard that characteristic raising of the voice at the end of a sentence which allowed him to move straight on to the next point, making it impossible for anyone to interrupt. As if he had noticed this himself he seemed to hesitate for a moment, but I knew it was too late and was prepared for the worst.

"I shall write it from your point of view," he said. "Of course, there's a danger that some idiot will feel particularly clever and claim that a woman would look at things quite differently, so I'd have to make myself the narrator."

He cleared his throat.

"I'll need a pseudonym too," he added, without pausing for breath. "Maybe I should call myself Lomnitz or Ossovsky."

I tried hard not to take him seriously.

"Why would you need a pseudonym?"

It was a moment before he reacted, but then he raised his voice and leaned over so close to me that I could see the shadowy stubble beneath his skin.

"I need a pseudonym in order to obliterate myself," he said. "I'm not making things so easy for the Viennese gang this time, setting myself up as a target."

"Oh, Max, that's nonsense."

"No, I'm not handing myself to that lot on a plate again."

I took his arm.

"Forget them, Max."

"They're not about to finish me off."

"Forget them, Max," I tried soothing him again. "Go ahead, write a novel about Hirschfelder if you like, but forget them."

And with these words I left him there and walked away, and perhaps that was really the end which I had felt was still lacking,

295

the missing piece I needed to be rid of it all – telling him that it was his story. At least, that way I had put it into his hands, whether he accepted it or not, whether he told the tale or decided to keep it quiet. It made no difference to the facts, although the idea both reassured me and at the same time, when I thought what an unreliable man he was, left me uneasy.